AN EXCELLENT
THING IN A WOMAN

Also by Allison Montclair

The Sparks & Bainbridge mysteries

THE RIGHT SORT OF MAN
A ROYAL AFFAIR
THE HAUNTING OF THE DESKS
A ROGUE'S COMPANY
THE UNKEPT WOMAN
THE LADY FROM BURMA
MURDER AT THE WHITE PALACE

AN EXCELLENT THING IN A WOMAN

Allison Montclair

SEVERN HOUSE

First world edition published in Great Britain and the USA in 2025
by Severn House, an imprint of Canongate Books Ltd,
14 High Street, Edinburgh EH1 1TE.

severnhouse.com

Copyright © Allison Montclair, 2025

Cover and jacket design by Piers Tilbury

All rights reserved including the right of reproduction in whole or in part in any form. The right of Allison Montclair to be identified as the author of this work has been asserted in accordance with the Copyright, Designs & Patents Act 1988.

British Library Cataloguing-in-Publication Data
A CIP catalogue record for this title is available from the British Library.

ISBN-13: 978-1-4483-1237-5 (cased)
ISBN-13: 978-1-4483-1238-2 (e-book)

This is a work of fiction. Names, characters, places and incidents are either the product of the author's imagination or are used fictitiously. Except where actual historical events and characters are being described for the storyline of this novel, all situations in this publication are fictitious and any resemblance to actual persons, living or dead, business establishments, events or locales is purely coincidental.

Typeset by Palimpsest Book Production Ltd., Falkirk,
Stirlingshire, Scotland.

Praise for the Sparks & Bainbridge mysteries

"Another winning blend of humor and mystery"
Publishers Weekly on *Murder in the White Palace*

"The banter between Iris and Gwen remains brisk and hilarious, and Montclair does a particularly good job throwing readers off the culprit's scent. Series fans will be over the moon"
Publishers Weekly on *Murder in the White Palace*

"A page-turning mystery full of local color and angst-filled romances"
Kirkus Reviews on *Murder at the White Palace*

"Montclair continues to impress in this lively fifth outing for Iris Sparks and Gwendolyn Bainbridge . . . This will delight fans of Dorothy Sayers"
Publishers Weekly on *The Lady from Burma*

"Intriguing characters and two mysteries are intertwined with little-known regulations on mental health in postwar England"
Kirkus Reviews on *The Lady from Burma*

"Montclair portrays 1940s speech and culture well, with many allusions to postwar concerns. This will appeal to mystery readers who enjoy humor, historical fiction, and well-written crime-solving teams"
Library Journal on *The Unkept Woman*

"Montclair's capable, funny, and fully developed leads set a gold standard for the amateur sleuth subgenre. Dorothy Sayers's fans will hope this series has a long run"
Publishers Weekly Starred Review of *The Unkept Woman*

About the author

Allison Montclair is the author of the Sparks & Bainbridge mysteries, beginning with *The Right Sort of Man*, the American Library Association Reading List Council's Best Mystery of 2019. Under her real name, she has written more mystery novels and a damn good werewolf book, as well as short stories in many genres in magazines and anthologies. She is also an award-winning librettist and lyricist with several musicals to her credit that have been performed or workshopped across the USA. She currently lives in New York City where she also practised as a criminal defence attorney.

To Dan Frischman, Rob Paustian,
and Lily Lee, for the many decades of friendship.

'Her voice was ever soft / Gentle and low –
an excellent thing in a woman.'

King Lear, Act V, Scene 3

ONE

Archie was dead, to begin with. He had lasted longer than anyone had expected after the bullet pierced his chest, especially the doctors, and every time he drew breath, as wet and as ragged as it was, it offered some hope to his family and to Iris that he might keep on doing it out of stubbornness. Iris was with him every moment that she could spare from The Right Sort, overlapping shifts by his hospital bed with Lily, his sister. Gwen, Iris's friend and business partner at the marriage bureau they had founded the previous year, would have gladly let Iris take time off, but Iris needed to work, needed to know that she was contributing something positive to a world that she secretly felt didn't deserve her small attempts to restore happiness to it, for why should it when it had taken away her own chance for happiness so suddenly?

She had moved her belongings, all of which could fit into two suitcases plus a carton for her books, into Archie's cottage in Hackney right before the calendar tipped from 1946 to 1947. She did this with Lily's blessing, acting as an informal caretaker for the eventuality, or the possibility, or more accurately the very faint hope that Archie would come home from London Hospital. Iris, who was a small woman, had never before lived by herself in anything larger than a one-bedroom flat, and the large amount of extra space swirling about constantly spooked her. She took to seeing killers hiding in the shadowy corners of the rooms she left unlit, and was always startled by the weekly arrival of the charlady, no matter how cheerfully the latter greeted her. Iris had little need for the charlady, but Archie had paid her in advance through the end of the quarter, so there was no reason not to accept her services.

Iris cooked meagrely for herself, having turned over Archie's coupons to Lily. The cottage was cold, on top of everything else. It had been one of the coldest winters in London in recent memory, and the coal shortages didn't help. She piled every piece of bedding she could find on to the double bed in the master bedroom and huddled under them like a mole in hibernation, but she never could manage to feel warm.

She wanted him huddling in there with her. It was unfair that they had spent so few full nights together, which was her fault. She hadn't wanted to sully her reputation with her previous landlord by not coming back to her flat every night, and Archie had kept his cottage a secret from her for the first few months of their relationship. Then came the presentation of the key, followed by the ring.

Followed by the bullet.

It was mid-March when Lily tearfully broke the news that the estate duties were forcing her to sell the cottage. Even a well-heeled gangster of Archie's stature couldn't stave off the government locusts sent to ravage his wealth once he was no longer alive to hide or defend it. Iris thanked Lily for allowing her the ten weeks' occupancy that she had had, and quietly turned over the thick packages wrapped in wax paper that she had found concealed in the attic. She had never been tempted to open them. The money she suspected was in them was Archie's, and his sister was his sole heir. It would have been different had he lived to fulfil the promise of the ring, but Archie was dead.

His well-stocked wine cellar, on the other hand, Iris regarded as a gift *inter vivos* by that point. She had resolutely avoided raiding it when she first moved in, but after the funeral, with her last shred of hope buried with him in Bow Cemetery, she succumbed to the Sirens' call of the dusty bottles. She held herself to two glasses of Chenin Blanc that first evening, toasting Archie while admiring her self-control, but soon was up to a bottle a night.

When it came time for her to move out, Benny, who had been Archie's driver in the gang and still had access to a small fleet of fast cars of dubious provenance, came to transport her, along with her two suitcases, her carton of books, and the addition of two crates loaded with as many bottles as she could fit. He followed her directions until they arrived at a location by the Regent's Canal.

'Which 'ouse is it?' he asked as they pulled up.

'That one,' she said, pointing.

He looked at it.

'That's not an 'ouse,' he said. 'That's a boat.'

'It's a bit of both,' she said.

She had Benny set the two crates on their sides in the middle of the narrowboat's saloon, with the open ends facing away from each other, forming a makeshift table with easy access to their contents. She gave him a bottle of Bordeaux as a parting gift, and he left, shaking his head.

The narrowboat had the least amount of room she had ever lived in on her own. The tiny space embraced her like a long-absent father, and she welcomed it. She stashed her clothes in all the clever little hidey-holes that the owner, who was on extended absence caring for his elderly parents in Yorkshire, had constructed over years of eccentric isolation. She made sure to have her weapons easily accessible, of course.

She lit the stove, which also provided what heat there was, then ran the taps to make sure the water was clear. She pulled on her thickest jumper, threw her coat over it, then pulled a book from the carton, a bottle from one of the crates, and settled into an overstuffed armchair that had been reclaimed from who knows where or when.

It was then that the heavy drinking began.

'I'm worried about Iris,' said Gwen.

'So am I,' said Sally.

He was driving her home from a late-night date in April after finishing his shift as a stage manager at BBC Television. They had met for drinks, or drinks and a sandwich in his case, as he was ravenous after several hours of shoving flats and furniture in and out of cramped studios for the abridged play that had gone on before the cameras. Sally was a tall man, and there might not have been enough ration coupons printed to sustain his diet adequately, but he survived somehow.

He and Gwen had begun dating in earnest at the start of the New Year, after a tenuous start and stop in 1946. This had been a source of both joy and concern to Iris, who had been Sally's closest friend since their time together at Cambridge in the Thirties. Joy, because her best male friend was now dating her best female friend, and she had been, if not the impetus, at least the nexus for that particular connection. Concern, because her two best friends were now a couple, leaving her on the sidelines, albeit with good seats.

'I've never seen her like this,' said Gwen.

'I have, unfortunately,' said Sally.

'When?'

'When I got back from Italy,' he said. 'She was the first person I came to see. The war had ended and she was full on into her affair with Andrew, measuring herself against the national accomplishments of the previous six years and judging herself wanting. I don't even know how she found so much to drink with the state of supplies available, but she did.'

'Fortunately, she had you to pull her out of it.'

'She did.'

'And now she has Dr Milford. At least she's still seeing him.'

'More importantly, she has you,' said Sally. 'And she has The Right Sort, so there is some purpose to her life now.'

'So we should chalk this up to extended mourning and wait for her to run out of wine?'

'Unless you propose sending her somewhere to dry out. It's a damp country, unfortunately, so that could take some time.'

'I don't like the idea of sending someone away to mourn,' she said quietly.

'Forgive me,' he said hastily. 'That was thoughtless. As I said, she has a job, a psychotherapist, and us. Together, we will help her pull through. And here we are.'

He pulled up in front of her house, a white, Italianate building in a curved row of similar houses in Maida Vale. She had moved in only two months previously, with her son Ronnie; Agnes, his governess; and Millie, whom Gwen had poached from her in-laws and promoted to housekeeper. A cook, Rachel, had been hired as well, and that was the entirety of the staff at the moment.

Sally parked the Hornet, then came around to open her door.

'Could you come in for a spell?' she asked as she got out. 'I have a surprise.'

'I would come in even if there weren't one,' he said.

'Keep your voice down,' she advised him as she unlocked the door. 'Ronnie should have been asleep hours ago, and I told my ladies not to bother waiting up for me.'

She led him into the hallway, and he helped her out of her coat. She unpinned her hat, put both in the hall closet, then held out her hand.

'May I take your coat, Mr Danielli?' she asked.

'Thank you, Mrs Bainbridge,' he said, removing it along with his trilby and handing them to her.

She hung them by hers, then beckoned to him.

'This way,' she whispered.

He followed her into the front parlour, which contained a sofa, a few upholstered armchairs, and, in the corner, a narrow rectangular cabinet of bird's eye maple standing about three and a half feet tall, its front sloping down and away from the vertical. She walked to its side and stood next to it, smiling brightly, both arms pointing to it in her best salesgirl pose.

'Hullo!' exclaimed Sally. 'You've got one of the new Bairds!'

'I have,' she said, lifting the tambour panel concealing the screen. 'I thought since my boyfriend is working in television, I should be keeping an eye on him. Ronnie is very excited about watching you work.'

'My work right now primarily is moving scenery,' said Sally. 'If he actually sees me doing it, someone has made a mistake. Let me get a closer look.'

He squatted in front of it.

'Twelve-inch screen,' he said approvingly. 'Nice.'

'And it has a wireless underneath,' said Gwen. 'I still have to get the aerial installed on the roof. We're having that done later this week, so I'll be taking a half-day off for that. Then we'll have an inaugural viewing to celebrate. I wish you could come.'

'I wish I could, too, but imagine me lurking about somewhere in the wings, right around here,' he said, holding his hand two inches to the left of the set.

'You're not picking up any acting work there?'

'Not lately,' he said. 'I'm trying to ingratiate myself with everyone so they might put my play on. As soon as I've finished rewriting it.'

'The war play?'

'Yes. It would work well on the small screen. There are only two sets involved, unlike *The Margate Affair*. That one's too racy for television, anyway.'

'Even with the limited audience?'

'Especially with them,' he said. 'We don't want to poison the well just yet. We have to lure everyone in first. Well, congratulations on keeping up with the future. I'm finding the whole enterprise fascinating from the inside, and I rarely get to see the finished product. Maybe I could get an evening off to watch it with you.'

'I'd like that, Sally,' she said.

'I suppose I should get going,' he said, standing up. 'It's been—'

'Actually, there's one more thing I'd like to show you,' she said.

'What's that?'

'Come up with me.'

'Upstairs?'

'Yes,' she said, her salesgirl smile gone, replaced by one that somehow seemed both beguiling and determined at the same time. 'But not a sound. I don't want to wake anyone.'

'All right,' he said. 'Luckily, I am a master of stealth.'

He followed her up the stairs to the first floor. She paused for a moment outside Ronnie's door, listening, then nodded to herself. She crooked a finger at Sally, and he followed her down the hall, wondering.

She opened the door to the master bedroom.

Her bedroom.

He had never seen it before. Their romantic intimacies to date had been confined to dancing and kissing, both having progressed to variations more and more prolonged and passionate, leaving them both breathless and tense at the conclusion.

She closed the door, then sat on the four-poster bed, patting the covers by her side.

'This is a very large bed,' he commented as he sat next to her.

'I am a tall woman,' she said. 'And I bought it with an even taller man in mind.'

'That's a relief,' he said. 'I always worry that there might be something vaguely Procrustean involved otherwise.'

She stood suddenly and removed her jacket, then held out her hand. After a moment of confusion, he took off his and handed it to her. She opened her closet and hung them both up, then closed it again and faced him, going still for a long moment.

'Tell me what you're thinking,' he said.

'This is difficult,' she said hesitantly.

'If you're not ready,' he began.

She held her hand up to stop him from continuing.

'I'm ready to make love to you, Sally,' she said. 'But I'm trying to get my nerve up to do something else first.'

She unclasped her necklace and placed it on her dressing table. Next to a framed photograph of her late husband, he noticed, trying not to look at it.

'You know that I was in a sanatorium after my husband was killed,' she said.

'Yes,' he said. 'Although I don't know the details. I never wanted to press you about them.'

'You've been very patient with me,' she said, unbuttoning her blouse. 'What you don't know is that it wasn't merely a breakdown. It was a suicide attempt.'

'Oh, Gwen,' he said, shaking his head sadly.

'And it wasn't a nicely planned deliberate overdose with thoughts of leaving a beautiful, tragic corpse behind for Millie to walk in on,' she continued.

She pulled off her blouse and draped it over a chair.

'What I'm about to show you, only doctors and nurses have seen,' she said. 'You were drawn by my beauty at first. Don't deny it.'

'I don't,' he said. 'Shallow of me in retrospect, but it was like you were lit from within the first time I saw you.'

'Beauty is only skin deep,' she said, reaching behind her back with both hands to unhook her brassiere. 'And skin is soft and penetrable.'

She turned away, removed it and tossed it on to the chair, then turned back to him, keeping her arms across her breasts.

'To this day, I don't remember all the details,' she said. 'I remember screaming. I had run into the kitchen, not able to see clearly for the tears, not able to think clearly at all. All I wanted was to end it so I could be with him again. And there was a knife on the counter.'

She lowered her arms. He willed himself not to wince, but she saw him react nonetheless.

'Not quite the Greek statue that the face promises,' she said. 'These two scars were self-inflicted.' She pointed to each in turn. 'I didn't know what I was doing, fortunately. The first attempt struck bone. The second would have been more successful, but I'm told Percival managed to wrest the knife away from me.'

'Thank you, Percival,' said Sally fervently.

'This one was from the surgery, of course,' she said, pointing to a third scar, a longer one that, unlike the other two, appeared to have been made with skill and purpose. 'They had to open me up to repair the damage. If it had only been an accident, there might have been some follow-up surgery to restore the aesthetics involved, but I was a suicidal crazy lady, and legal wheels had already been set in motion to bundle me into oblivion. The nurses at the sanatorium who gave me sponge baths while I was sedated and strapped down would utter these clucks of sympathy when they saw me. "Pity," they'd say. "She would've been able to land someone else with that body if she hadn't ruined it." When I got out, I could have hid under pretty underclothes and dim lights for the rest of my life, but I wanted you to see me, Sally, as I truly am, with the light full on. I hope it isn't a disappointment.'

He looked at the scars, then up at her face. Then he stood, walked towards her, and bent down to kiss her. First on one scar, then the second. By the time he got to the third, the tension had loosened within her. She wrapped her arms around him, pressing him against her chest and leaning down to rest her forehead on top of his head.

They stayed like that, holding each other awkwardly, rocking slightly. Finally, he straightened up and stepped back.

'Right,' he said, quickly unbuttoning his shirt. 'I'll see your three scars and raise you one.'

He threw the shirt on to the chair over hers, then pulled the undershirt up over his head and stood back.

'Oh, Sally!' she exclaimed.

'German,' he said, pointing to a long jagged weal across his left collarbone. 'German. German. Italian.'

Each was white against his slightly olive-toned skin. Each told a story she was frightened to hear.

'Oh, and I got this one falling off my bike when I was eight,' he added, pointing to an ancient, ragged section of skin on his left elbow. 'I cried for days. But the rest of them – I could be a relief map of northern Italy. I didn't exactly have access to hospitals when they happened. Three of them I stitched up myself as well as I could. This one, however . . .'

He tapped a souvenir from a single thrust of a knife on his right side.

'This one nearly did me in,' he said. 'I had to run, jamming a handkerchief against it the entire way. I was lucky. It rained, so they couldn't follow the trail the blood made. I had been hiding out in a small cave in the hills, more of a burrow, really, not much larger than I am. I made it back there, collapsed, and lay there for days, drifting in and out of fever. It could have been my tomb.'

'What happened to the three Germans and the Italian?' she asked.

'Let's just say they didn't get the opportunity to heal like I did,' he said, grimacing. 'When I got back home, I saw the army surgeon before I was demobbed. He made some crack that I could play Frankenstein's monster without makeup now, and that struck home. If my freakish height hadn't scared the ladies off before . . .'

She stepped forward and embraced him, shivering as her flesh met another's for the first time in years.

'I'm not scared,' she whispered.

She kissed him. He picked her up, carried her to the bed, and lowered her gently on to it. Then he stepped back to contemplate her.

'Probably should have pulled the covers down first,' he observed.

'Probably should have,' she agreed.

She got back up and pulled them down.

'I haven't been with anyone since Ronnie died,' she said as she kicked off her shoes and clambered back on to the bed. 'And the last time I saw him was in '42. So forgive me in advance—'

'It's been a while for me as well,' he said. 'Let's not have any expectations. We don't have to reach the moon the first time. We'll try each other out, then afterwards you can give me notes.'

He was gentle and took his time. When they were done, she began to cry.

'What have I done?' he asked, dismayed. 'That's the last thing I wanted to make you do.'

'No, no, I'm fine,' she said, holding him tight. 'After all I've been through, I wasn't sure I could ever feel anything again. It was wonderful, Sally. Thank you.'

'You're quite welcome.'

'And if it's all right with you, I'd like to try for the moon now.'

She let him out of the front door at one thirty after one last, lingering kiss.

'When can I see you again?' she asked.

'Tomorrow night, and the night after, and the night after that,' he said. 'And I'll throw in all the rest of them. I was thinking – would you and Ronnie like a tour of Ally Pally? There's a new variety programme rehearsing on Saturday afternoon. We would include John, of course.'

'They would be thrilled, I'm sure,' she said. 'We should ask Iris, too. She hasn't seen it, either. She'd feel bad about being left out.'

'Agreed. Good. I'll make the arrangements and get back to you. Good night, Gwen.'

'Good night, Sally.'

She watched as he squeezed himself into the Hornet and roared into the night, then closed the door and locked it.

She slept soundly for the first time in years.

* * *

It was less than ten minutes' walk to the *Cecilia*, Iris's narrowboat. Gwen stepped carefully between the gap in the rails on to the fore well, then rapped on the cabin door.

'Request permission to come aboard, Captain!' she called.

The door opened and Iris stood there, squinting in the early morning sun, her toothbrush dangling from one corner of her mouth.

'Technically, you've already come aboard,' she said. 'Under the Law of the Sea, I have the right to repel you.'

'If you don't finish brushing your teeth, you will,' said Gwen.

'Be right back,' said Iris.

She closed the door. Gwen could hear her brushing vigorously, then the sound of water running in a sink. A minute later, Iris reappeared, an empty wine bottle clutched in one hand.

'Better?' she asked, smiling broadly.

'You could be an advert for Maclean's,' said Gwen.

Her teeth did gleam in the sun. It helped that last night's varietal was a white wine, thought Gwen. She looked puffy around the eyes, though.

'Let's get going,' said Gwen.

Iris locked the cabin door, then followed her on to land.

'Does the Law of the Sea apply to canals?' Gwen asked.

'Probably not,' admitted Iris. 'Just as well. I can avoid "the delicate question" when I have guests and the larder hasn't been adequately replenished. Although with the food shortages being what they are, cannibalism might still be an option.'

They passed by the common bins, and Iris stopped to toss her wine bottle into one, producing a satisfying clink as it collided with other empties.

'Are we walking today?' she asked.

'The weather is fine,' replied Gwen. 'Why not walk?'

'I had a nice date with a Mr Riesling last night,' said Iris. 'A lovely German gentleman. We spoke of happier times.'

'You're hung-over, in other words.'

'I am.'

'More reason to walk, then. You'll get it out of your system, and the noise from the Tube won't give you a headache first thing.'

'You're mean, but you're not wrong,' said Iris. 'Very well, here we go! No singing, though.'

'Alas. I had "Marching to Pretoria" queued up and ready to go.'

They walked down Warwick Avenue, crossed the canal into Paddington, then angled towards Mayfair.

'How was your date with Sally?' asked Iris.

'It was nice,' said Gwen dreamily.

Iris looked up at her sharply. Gwen tried to control her expression, but the blush seeped through. A slow smile spread across Iris's face.

'Well, well, well,' she said. 'It finally happened, didn't it?'

'I have no idea what you're talking about,' said Gwen, blushing more.

'Of course not,' said Iris. 'But welcome back to the land of the living.'

'Please don't tell him you know,' said Gwen.

'I won't,' promised Iris. 'But even though he won't tell me it happened, and I won't tell him that I know, he will know that I know and I will know that he knows that I know because we've known each other too long and too well.'

'You don't mind?' asked Gwen. 'I know the two of you don't keep secrets from each other.'

'We say we don't,' said Iris. 'But there are always secrets.'

'Do you know the stories behind his scars? He told me about one of them.'

'I've never seen them,' said Iris. 'We didn't exactly go on any beach holidays after the war ended. The last time I saw him shirtless was in an informal rugby match at Cambridge in 1938. I don't think he likes to be seen now.'

'Something we have in common,' said Gwen. 'It was refreshing to let go of that finally. It was nice to be desired for something more than my looks. To be liked instead of worshipped.'

'Men who put women on pedestals end up with statues,' said Iris.

'I'm not competing with the Venus de Milo at this point in my life,' said Gwen.

'You're far superior, and you still have both of your arms.'

'They do come in handy.'

'This will be an adjustment for me, you know,' said Iris thoughtfully.

'How so?'

'I'm used to being the one coming into the office fresh from the latest amorous adventure. Now you've taken over that role, and I've become – well, I can't rightfully call myself a widow, can I?'

'It's no different,' said Gwen gently. 'You loved Archie, and now he's gone.'

'I keep thinking this is the longest I've been without a man since I don't know when,' said Iris. 'The first relationship to turn me celibate. That's what keeps me home at night with a bottle ever ready. I'm afraid that if I didn't, I'd go out and let myself get picked up by the first fellow I bump into, and that's a dangerous road to take.'

Gwen didn't respond to that, merely walking in silence.

'You're supposed to be judging me harshly right now,' said Iris.

'I'm in no position to judge a woman on how she reacts to the sudden death of the man she loved,' said Gwen. 'You will work out how to pull yourself out of this when you're ready. Any help you require of me, anything at all, name it, and I will move the nearest mountain to make it happen.'

'No, you won't.'

'How can you say that?'

'The nearest mountain is Muswell Hill,' said Iris. 'Where BBC Television is located. If you move it, Sally's out of a job.'

'The second nearest, then. Wherever it is. I'll have to look it up.'

'Fine,' said Iris. 'Thanks. I'd say don't worry about me, but I actually like it when people worry about me.'

'Done.'

They reached Mayfair and turned off Oxford Street down towards where their offices were located. They paused to assess the construction next door, a four-storey brick building that was nearly complete. A team of glaziers was busy installing the windows on the second storey.

'After all this work, I was hoping for something more architecturally interesting,' commented Gwen. 'They didn't even put any nice little design flourishes in the bricks over the windows. It's a flat-faced monolith of a thing, when all is said and done.'

'Not even the glaziers are worth looking at,' observed Iris.

'Certainly not compared to the bricklayers,' agreed Gwen. 'Although the scaffolders remain my favourites.'

They went inside their building and climbed the four flights of steps to the level containing The Right Sort. Mrs Billington gave them a wave from behind her desk when they poked their heads in.

'No appointments scheduled until this afternoon,' she said. 'I've sorted the post and put it on your desks.'

'Thank you, Saundra,' said Gwen.

They went into their own office, which contained two enormous vintage partnership desks sitting side by side.

Gwen patted hers affectionately, whispering, 'Hello, Cecil', as she sat behind it. Iris smiled at her partner's morning ritual.

'I still haven't named mine,' she said as she sat down and slit open the top envelope from her pile.

'Why not?' asked Gwen.

'I don't believe in naming inanimate objects. That's why I can't remember my first fiancé's name.'

'Ouch. Very well, who shall we work on this morning?'

'Deirdre Currier has rejected our latest attempt,' said Iris, looking at the letter.

'Blast. She's become quite impossible. Sometimes I think we should arrange to have her carried off by pirates and call it a day.'

'Isn't Mr Wheeler a pirate?' asked Iris, reaching for her box containing the index cards of their male clients.

'Merchant Navy,' said Gwen. 'Not quite the same thing. Although he's not a bad idea, come to think of it. Maybe what she needs is someone who won't be around constantly to be annoyed by her.'

'Absence makes the heart . . .' began Iris.

Then she stopped, closing her eyes for a moment.

'Sorry,' she said. 'Mr Wheeler and Miss Currier. Let's talk them out.'

Later that morning, Sally appeared in the doorway, his hands behind his back.

'Good morning, ladies,' he said.

'Hello, Sally,' said Iris. 'What brings you here?'

'Two missions,' he said, coming in. 'First, a tribute.'

He produced a bouquet from behind his back with his left hand and presented it to Gwen.

'Thank you, Sally,' said Gwen, blushing as she accepted it.

'Nothing for me?' protested Iris.

'Patience, small one,' said Sally.

He came over to her desk and brought his right hand forward, holding a single yellow rose.

'Only one?' she complained.

'Proportionality,' he said. 'She's taller than you. Now, as to the second mission. I have a referral for you. There's a chap at Ally Pally who I have convinced to sign up for future bliss. His name is Laurence Haight. He's an engineering type. Tends not to talk much unless it's about the innards of electronic gadgets, so be forewarned.'

'We've been subjected to all manner of topics here,' said Iris. 'We'll try to find him a woman who is interested in things technical.'

'I'm finishing up an hour early tonight,' he said to Gwen. 'Shall we go dancing?'

'Let's,' she replied. 'Pick me up at home.'

'I will fly there on Cupid's wings,' he said. 'Nine fifteen.'

He kissed her hand, then waved to Iris.

'No hand-kiss for me?' she asked.

'Proportionality, Sparks,' he said. 'Have a profitable day, ladies.'

Iris waited until he was safely out of earshot, then turned to Gwen.

'Dancing,' she said. 'Is that what the kids are calling it now?'

'Stop,' said Gwen, blushing again. 'I'm going to put these in water. Throw me your rose and I'll take care of it.'

Iris tossed it to her. Gwen caught it deftly, then retrieved a pair of small vases from inside one of Cecil's lower drawers and went off to the ladies' lav.

Laurence Haight did indeed call, taking the two thirty slot. He arrived at two fifteen and filled out the questionnaire provided to him by Mrs Billington. At two twenty-nine, she led him to her bosses' office, holding the forms and walking with enough ceremony to make one believe she was a votary leading a new celebrant to the inner sanctum of the priestesses. She knocked on the door, then opened it.

'Mr Laurence Haight to see you, ladies,' she announced, coming forward to hand them the questionnaire and its carbon.

'Mr Haight, so good to meet you,' said Mrs Bainbridge, coming around the table to shake his hand as Mrs Billington left them to it. 'I am Mrs Gwendolyn Bainbridge, and this is my partner, Miss Iris Sparks. Welcome to The Right Sort Marriage Bureau. Do sit down and make yourself comfortable.'

'Thanks, ma'am,' he said, sitting in one of the guest chairs in front of the desks.

He glanced at Sparks, and his eyes widened in recognition.

As did hers.

'Mrs Bainbridge,' she said immediately. 'Could I trouble you to step outside for two minutes?'

Mrs Bainbridge glanced at her in surprise, but nodded quickly.

'Of course, Miss Sparks,' she said. 'I'll wait in the other office. Buzz me when you're ready.'

She left, closing the door behind her. Sparks waited until she heard her footsteps recede down the hall, then smiled at their new client.

'So your name is Laurence Haight,' she said.

'And yours is Iris Sparks,' he replied. 'Funny, I thought that was you when I saw your picture in the papers a few months back, but I wasn't certain.'

'Well, it's nice to finally put a name to the face,' said Sparks. 'And don't worry. Your secret is safe with me.'

TWO

Mrs Billington looked at her in surprise as Gwen came in and sat on the sofa.

'Did Miss Sparks kick you out?' she asked.

'She did.'

'That's a first. Usually it's the other way around whenever your voodoo kicks in and you want to get personal with them.'

'It's not voodoo,' said Gwen. 'I'm just good at reading people.'

'It might as well be voodoo. I wonder what Miss Sparks saw.'

'No idea,' said Gwen.

'Maybe he's an ex,' speculated Mrs Billington.

'Not one I've heard about,' said Gwen. 'I guess she'll tell me afterwards if so.'

'Or not,' said Mrs Billington.

'Or not,' said Gwen.

'You were there in '43 for a while,' said Haight. 'At the place in Eynsford. All of you would come in every day on the afternoon train from Victoria Station, take your seats in front of your radios, and have your secret chats with whoever was God-knows-where doing God-knows-what.'

'And you kept the show running pretty much by yourself,' said Sparks. 'I remember the transmitting tower was set up in the middle of a stand of trees, with boughs lashed around it so it wouldn't be visible to any German reconnaissance planes.'

'Yeah, that was a bad idea,' he said, laughing. 'They turned brown pretty quickly. I had to requisition a couple of cans of green paint and go over the whole mess, swinging from a rope. Bloody terrifying.'

'There was no heat,' remembered Sparks. 'It got so cold some nights. We cheered whenever you brought in whatever you were using to make tea.'

'And we never knew anyone's name,' he said. 'More's the pity. There were some real corkers in that group, present company very much included.'

'Thank you. In any case, I wanted to reassure you that anything I saw or heard there is covered by the Official Secrets Act. I don't know how much any of that matters to you—'

'But rules are rules,' he finished. 'Thanks, I appreciate that. Not that I've got anything of vital importance to share. Is Mrs Bainbridge also a signatory?'

'She is not,' said Sparks. 'But she is the most trustworthy person I have ever met, so in the unlikely event that anything slips out from me, she won't let it slip any further. If that is satisfactory to you, I'm going to bring her back in.'

'I'm ready,' said Haight.

The intercom on Mrs Billington's desk buzzed. She picked up her telephone, listened for a moment, then said, 'Very good, Miss Sparks.'

She nodded at Mrs Bainbridge.

'You've got the all-clear,' she said.

'Thank you,' said Mrs Bainbridge.

She walked back to the other office.

'Are we ready to begin?' she asked as she resumed her seat.

'We are,' said Sparks. 'Thanks for waiting.'

'Not at all,' said Mrs Bainbridge. 'It gave me a chance to familiarize myself with Mr Haight's questionnaire. You turned forty recently, I see. A belated happy birthday.'

His age surprised her, she thought. He looked older, his brown hair heavily mixed with grey, and had more than his share of lines around the eyes. He was fit, though. Not a tall man, but at five foot eight, he was wiry and projected strength, his arms evidently well-muscled even when concealed by his jacket sleeves. An acrobat's build.

'Thank you, ma'am,' he said. 'I admit that was part of the reason for me coming, once Danielli put the bee in my bonnet. Settle down, Larry, while there's still a chance someone might take you.'

'You're from Sheerford originally. That's in Kent, I believe?'

'It is. My dad was an engineer in the Royal Navy, stationed at the dockyard there. Quite an exciting place for a young lad to be running about. You could see out to where the Thames emptied out, and ships of every kind.'

'It sounds grand,' said Mrs Bainbridge. 'But you didn't join the Navy.'

'No, ma'am. I was a tinkerer. I liked to take machines apart and put them back together. It was something Dad and I would do in his workshop after I got my schoolwork done. When I was ten, I built my first crystal radio set, and that fixed my path after that.'

'What did you listen to?' asked Mrs Bainbridge. 'There was no BBC then.'

'Whatever people were putting out there,' he said. 'I was fluent in Morse code before I ever mastered Latin. Lots of war chatter, of course. Nothing between the trenches and me but the English Channel, so I'd listen in, especially at night, lying on my bed with my earphones on. I could even pick up some German transmissions. I kept figuring out ways to improve the reception and the range, so naturally when it came time for me to go to university, I applied to Chelmsford College. That's the school that the Marconi Company set up to teach electrical engineering. When I graduated, I walked down the street to Marconi, and I've been an engineer ever since.'

'What sorts of things did you work on?'

'I wasn't quite clever enough to be an inventor, but I was very good at finding ways to make other men's inventions work. I was one of Charlie Franklin's technical assistants when he was running independent research. We had to build a lot of devices from scratch, then test them out. I saw plenty of electrical fires, I can tell you that.'

'How did you wind up at the BBC?'

'One of the last things Franklin did before he left Marconi was the installation of the sound and vision antenna at Ally Pally. I helped out on that. This was when the Great War was happening—'

'Excuse me,' she interrupted. 'The Great War? Surely you were too young for that.'

'Sorry,' he said, laughing. 'That was what we called the battle between Baird and Marconi. There were two competing systems being tried out for television: Baird's mechanical version, and us with the all-electronic one. Poor old Baird. Brilliant, but he backed the wrong horse. There was an upper limit to how far the mechanical system could go, and every stopgap measure he came up with, no matter how ingenious, was just another cumbersome piece of machinery to wedge into a space that could barely hold it. Marconi had teamed up with EMI on the cathode ray tubes, and that's what won out. After we installed the antenna, they more or less installed me there to watch over everything as each new piece of equipment came in. I'm the resident Jack of all trades there now.'

'I just purchased a Baird television,' said Mrs Bainbridge. 'Did I go wrong?'

'Oh, those are fine,' said Haight. 'Baird finally saw the writing on the wall and switched over to the CRTs. I heard he came up with a colour one a few years back, but he passed away last year, poor old sod. I went to the funeral.'

'BBC Television shut down for the war. What did you do then?'

'I joined the Royal Corps of Signals, working on communications. Spent my whole war fixing radios.'

There it is, she thought. Not a big lie, but a concealment. Fairly glib with it, but nevertheless . . .

'And now you're back with the BBC,' she said.

'I am. Television started back up last year, and I started right back with it. Never a dull moment. Everyone's learning on the fly, and there are a lot of mad geniuses dashing about.'

'Yourself included, no doubt,' said Mrs Bainbridge.

He shrugged, but his smile showed he appreciated the compliment.

'Now, what are you looking for in a prospective bride?' she continued.

'Ah, there's the great question,' he said. 'I enjoy my life, but the hours are chaotic, to say the least. I work long shifts, mostly afternoons through midnight, and that's not exactly conducive to meeting ladies.'

'Not even the ones at Ally Pally?' asked Sparks.

'Oh, the ones who work there are out the door the second we sign off each night, usually on the arm of some exec, while we technical lads are still stuck there shutting down the shop. Everything has to be checked out and logged in for the next shift, and by the time we stagger home, London is fast asleep.'

'Then you need someone with similar hours,' said Sparks. 'Theatre people, or maybe nurses working night shifts.'

'I've thought about actresses,' he said. 'Sidled up to a few when they were performing at the studio, but they're always focused on their cues, not the fellow in the back who smells of machine oil.'

'Your dating window of opportunity will be from morning through to early afternoon, then,' said Mrs Bainbridge. 'That does narrow the field down. Other than timing, what are some of the characteristics you might find appealing?'

'This may seem odd,' he said hesitantly.

'Nothing is odd to us,' said Mrs Bainbridge encouragingly. 'Out with it.'

'The other fellows and I have the usual chats when we're closing down the place. Which of the actresses we fancied, who looked better when the makeup came off, that sort of thing. I admit that I'm not immune to the allure of a pretty face, but what I find the most attractive aspect of a woman is her voice.'

'You really are a radio man at heart,' said Sparks.

'I am, I am!' he said. 'There are some women – well, if I could close my eyes and listen to them all day, I could be content. And in the long run looks may fade, but voices last.'

'As does the quality of the conversation, hopefully,' added Mrs Bainbridge. 'Well, that certainly gives us something to work with. I will have to summon up the voices of our female clients, but I have a good memory for that.'

'When we do line up a prospective woman for you, I have a suggestion,' said Sparks.

'What would that be?' he asked.

'Wash off the oil and throw on some cologne,' she said. 'Some women like what they hear, some what they see, but they all have a sense of smell.'

'I will be a veritable flower, Miss Sparks,' he said.

'Then sign your contract, pay us our five-pound fee, and we will see what we can do,' said Sparks, sliding over a pair of contracts separated by a carbon.

He took out his wallet and a pen, then signed the contract and placed a five-pound note on her desk next to it. She and Mrs Bainbridge countersigned, then handed him the copy which he folded neatly and put inside his jacket pocket.

'I have to go to work, now, but I look forward to hearing from you,' he said, rising from his chair.

'Say hello to Mr Danielli from us,' said Sparks.

'Will do.'

* * *

'I like him,' said Gwen after he had left. 'It makes me wonder how many perfectly acceptable people are alone because they work unusual hours.'

'This is why we're here,' said Iris, scribbling down her notes for Mrs Billington to type up.

'He did lie about his war service,' said Gwen. 'I take it he was involved in clandestine transmissions of some kind, given your prior connection.'

'I don't know what you're talking about,' Iris said smoothly.

'And there's my confirmation.'

'Stop.'

'As long as he was on our side, it makes no difference to me,' said Gwen. 'Now, who might be a good fit for him? Miss Greenleigh is an actress.'

'Not a very good one,' said Iris. 'She's more likely to be working as a waitress than treading the boards.'

'Either way, she works evenings,' said Gwen. 'I'm trying to remember what she sounded like.'

'Decent voice,' said Iris. 'Good enough for people to have encouraged her too much to be an actress. But a possibility, I agree. Who's a nurse among our ladies?'

'Claire Williston comes to mind, although I don't know her hours at the hospital. She has a lovely voice, though. Very soothing.'

'"Her voice was ever soft, Gentle and low – an excellent thing in woman".'

'Shakespeare, but I can't place it,' said Gwen.

'Lear, talking about the dead Cordelia,' said Iris. 'Another man realizing the value of a woman when it's too late.'

'Well, there are worse reasons to like a person than their voice, so let's not be harsh. I'll have Mrs Billington ring up Miss Williston to verify her hours, and if they work out, let's give her the first crack at him.'

'Suits me,' said Iris. 'In a way, they're both caretakers, aren't they? She with humans, he with machines.'

'And both used to handling crises,' added Gwen. 'The more I think about them, the more I like the idea of them as a couple. Good.'

Despite Iris's suspicions, Gwen and Sally did go dancing after he finished work, towering over the other couples at a Soho club. They subsequently confirmed her suspicions at his flat afterwards.

'How was work today?' she murmured into his neck during one respite.

'Have we resorted to that for pillow talk already?'

'I find myself wanting to know everything about television,' she whispered. 'I want to imagine you at your job, barking orders at stage hands, putting your shoulder to recalcitrant pieces of scenery, your muscles fully engaged.'

'You're making my job sound far more erotic than it is, which is not at all.'

'Never? Not even when they bring in the dancing girls?'

'The dancing girls arrive on a bus, change out of sight, mill about in a hallway outside the studio chattering, even when the "ON AIR" sign is telling them to be quiet, then prance on for their three minutes of fixed smiles and robotic tapping. It's about as titillating as watching a factory line assemble an electric mixer.'

'You're not saying all this to reassure me, are you?'

'Trust me, there is not a woman in England who can hold a candle to you.'

'What about French girls?' she asked.

'Them, neither.'

'Italian?'

'I extend my comparisons to the whole of Europe. No, too small. To the entire planet, and should some scantily clad Venusian temptress land her spaceship outside my door and beckon to me from atop her gleaming silver gangway, I shall merely shake my head and send her home to her mother. Satisfied?'

'I am,' she said, kissing him. 'So how was work?'

'Back to that, are we?' he said. 'No visits from Venus, although we have a contingent of Parisian performers coming in. Freddie Oakes has been putting together a variety show called *Across the Channel*, and we've been having production meetings.'

'Any cancan girls in the mix?'

'Of course. What is French culture *sans les coups de pied haut*? Freddie's been over and back half a dozen times, scouting nightclubs.'

'And he gets paid for that?'

'It's a tough job, but someone has to do it. He's been at it for two months. He's poaching one act each from half a dozen different places so none of them will be overly disrupted. The leggy chorines are from Casino de Paris, which is undergoing renovations for the next two weeks, so they were available.'

'Goodness! Are the ceilings high enough for all of those feathers?'

'Freddie said he measured, and there's room.'

'Measured the ceiling or the girls?'

'Both, I should imagine. He's very thorough.'

'He does sound like a man who enjoys his research. Who is going to be the host?'

'Maurice Highmore, he of the unctuous eyebrows and the leering moustache.'

'Moustaches don't leer.'

'Not usually, which is why his is so remarkable. It must be how he waxes it. I should ask him.'

'Don't you dare grow a moustache!' she ordered him. 'I like your face as it is. When will this extravaganza be televised?'

'Next Thursday – a week tomorrow,' he said. 'That should give us enough time to figure out the sets. They all have to be specially built for the studios. The only thing we're not constructing on site is the marionette theatre. That's being shipped over.'

'You're having a marionnettiste? Wonderful! Ronnie loves puppet shows. I wonder if it's the same one I saw . . .'

She stopped suddenly.

'Go on,' he said. 'Don't hold back on my account. It's all right to talk about him.'

'On our honeymoon,' she said. 'We stopped in Paris on the way back from Italy. My first time there as an adult. As a married woman. A whole other side of the city had become available to me. We went to all the clubs, drinking champagne like there was no tomorrow. And there wasn't, as it turned out.'

'When was this?'

'Middle of July, 1939.'

'Beastly time to be in Paris.'

'It was hot. We didn't care. Anyhow, one of the clubs, the Café des Loups, had acts with a more satirical bent, and there was this rather louche marionnettiste. Very funny and very risqué presentation, with puppets based on political figures. The Neville Chamberlain was made partly of a balloon and deflated whenever he was confronted with the slightest threat. The Hitler was tinier than the rest, and declaimed in German gibberish. He became so apoplectic with his rhetoric that he burst apart, limbs flying everywhere. It was extraordinary. I wonder what happened to the puppeteer after Paris fell. The Nazis wouldn't have tolerated that act for long.'

'Do you remember his name?'

'Goodness, no. I may have saved a programme. I saved everything I could. It's all packed away in a box somewhere in my new place.'

'Well, he'll be rehearsing when you're bringing the boys in, so maybe you'll recognize his face.'

'I never saw his face.'

'His voice, then. Or one of the puppets.'

'Maybe. I hope so. It would be nice to know that a happy memory survived the war.'

It was well past midnight when he dropped her back home.

'Good thing the neighbours aren't up and about,' he whispered as he walked her to her door.

'Who cares about them?' she said as she pulled out her keys.

'Not I,' he said. 'Good night, Gwen. Again tomorrow?'

'I can't tomorrow. I have my ladies coming over for snooker.'

'I have found my competition. Snooker, then me.'

'You are a close second,' she said, kissing him.

'I'll take it. Go ahead, have your fun. Just don't get jealous of all those French girls swarming around me.'

'I won't,' she promised. 'I trust you. Good night, Sally.'

She went in, then closed and locked the door. She leaned against it, listening as the Hornet's engine faded into the distance.

I do trust you with the French girls, Sally, she thought. I just want to know why you twitched like that when I mentioned Italian girls.

She yawned on the walk to work the next morning.

'Danced to the wee hours, did you?' asked Iris, seizing on it immediately. 'I hope the tempos varied. Sometimes a quickstep is played when a foxtrot is what one desires.'

'Don't tease,' said Gwen. 'I'm having fun – real fun – for the first time in years.'

'I thought you were having fun with that snooker player last December.'

'That never got to this point, and it ended badly. This is fun without anything else barging in to disrupt it.'

'Do you think you'll—'

'Do not complete that sentence,' commanded Gwen. 'We are living in the moment right now. No future to consider.'

'Any intrusions from the past?'

Gwen sighed. 'You'll think me silly,' she said.

'People in love often seem silly,' said Iris. 'Dare to be silly, Gwen Bainbridge.'

'Do you know if there were any women in Italy?' she asked.

'He never spoke of any,' said Iris with a shrug. 'Perhaps there were. Who knows? Who cares if he has a past? So do you. So does anyone who's lived a life worth living.'

'I know,' said Gwen. 'But he hasn't talked about it.'

'Official Secrets Act,' Iris reminded her. 'Maybe he's not allowed to.'

'How do lovers live with secrets?' wondered Gwen.

'A question I've asked Dr Milford more than once.'

'Has he given you an answer?'

'You know what he's like. I have to work it out for myself.'

'Why don't psychiatrists just tell us the answers we seek?' Gwen asked plaintively.

'Because that's authoritarianism, not therapy,' Iris replied. 'Besides, who knows if they're the right answers?'

'I suppose,' said Gwen. 'But you're right. I have no business to ask Sally about that. He'll either tell me in due course, or he won't, and I should respect his decision either way. I only hope that whoever she is, Sally's in the past for her as well. I don't want anyone to show up with a very tall toddler in her arms demanding his return.'

'The war ended nearly two years ago,' said Iris. 'I doubt anything like that will happen now.'

The woman who burst into their office later that morning was in her twenties, pretty, slender, brunette, and tall. And French. Very French, judging by her heavily accented English.

'Are you the ladies who find me husbands?' she cried as she came in.

'Husband, singular, and yes, we are,' said Mrs Bainbridge with a laugh. 'But there is a form to fill out first, then—'

'I have no time for that!' said the woman. 'I must be back soon. But I need to be married.'

'Well, we still have to interview you, but you see, there is—'

'I need to be married as soon as possible!' said the woman. 'By next Sunday.'

'Next Sunday?' exclaimed Sparks. 'You actually think we can find you a husband in nine days?'

'Any husband will do,' said the woman. 'Give me your worst one. The ugliest, the oldest, the one with the worst manners, with the bad breath, I do not care. I will make him happy. But I must get married. Can you do this?'

'I'm sorry, Miss, or should I say Mademoiselle?' said Mrs Bainbridge. 'First, tell us your name.'

'Jeanne-Marie Duplessis,' she said.

'How do you do? I am Mrs Gwendolyn Bainbridge, and this is Miss Iris Sparks.'

'Hello,' said Sparks. 'If you're more comfortable speaking French, we're both fluent.'

'My English is good,' said Miss Duplessis, looking miffed. 'I am in England. I wish the English husband. I will speak the English. Now, I would like to get married. Right away.'

'But that's not how this works,' said Mrs Bainbridge. 'There is a process involved. We have to find someone compatible.'

'Compateebull? What is that?'

'It's the same word in French,' said Mrs Bainbridge. '*Compatible.*'

'Oh, that!' said Duplessis with a wild laugh. 'I am *très compatible. Trop compatible.* That is my problem. This service of yours – it can work quickly, *non?*'

'Even if we took you on as a client, we would have to review our male clientele, choose who we think would be the best match, and contact him by post. He would then write to you—'

'Is the English post very fast?' she asked.

'If you're currently in London—'

'I am.'

'Then you would probably hear from him within two to three days,' finished Mrs Bainbridge.

She chewed on her lip fretfully. Then her eyes lit on the telephone on Sparks's desk.

'Can you not contact him by that?' she asked. 'Ask him to call me? I can meet with him tomorrow. I promise once the man meets with me, he will want to marry me right away. How long does it take to get married in England?'

'May I ask why it's so urgent for you to be married by next Sunday?' asked Sparks.

'Because that's when I have to go back,' she said. 'I cannot go back.'

'Why not?'

'It's . . .' she began. Then she shook her head. 'I cannot say. It is not good for me in Paris.'

'Paris is your home?'

'It is,' she said sadly. 'Or it was. It cannot be any more.'

'Forgive me,' said Mrs Bainbridge. 'The source of your urgency concerns me. You're not by any chance—'

She paused, summoning up the word.

'*Enceinte?*'

'*Mon dieu, non!*' exclaimed Duplessis indignantly. 'What sort of girl do you think I am?'

'We don't know yet,' said Mrs Bainbridge. 'Which is why we are trying to interview you. How did you find out about us?'

'I hear someone talking about it where we are working,' she said. 'I thought, maybe these ladies can help me. Can you?'

'I need to discuss your situation with Miss Sparks,' said Mrs Bainbridge. 'Would you mind waiting in our other office for a minute? And while you're waiting, please fill out one of our questionnaires. It will save us all time.'

'Before you do that, I would like to be sure that you have the fee with you,' said Sparks. 'There would be no point in discussing this any further if you haven't.'

Duplessis reached into her bag and pulled out an impressive wad of currency, peeling a crumpled five-pound note from the top and waving it at them.

'Very good,' said Sparks. 'Our other office is to the left. We will return to you shortly.'

Sparks walked to the door and peered down the hall until she saw Duplessis turn into the next room. Then she closed the door and turned to her partner.

'What do you make of all this?' she asked.

'It's quite mad,' said Gwen. 'But she's not pregnant, at least.'

'So you think she was telling the truth about that,' said Iris. 'I'm relieved. That was the first thought that crossed my mind, I admit. I kept thinking about that woman from last year. I don't want to repeat that particular experience ever again.'

'Neither do I,' said Gwen. 'But to find her a husband in a little over a week! I wouldn't want to see anyone married on that short an acquaintance.'

'It happened during the war,' said Iris.

'Between men who were about to be shipped out and women

who wanted to give them something to live for,' said Gwen. 'Or between people who thought they had no other chance for marriage. I doubt that many of those marriages that survived the war also survived the reunions.'

Iris, remembering her wartime affair with a married man, did not comment.

'She doesn't seem to be very particular,' she observed. 'I wonder who she's running from in Paris.'

'Do you think she's in some sort of legal trouble?' asked Gwen.

'I didn't mean that, exactly,' said Iris. 'It might only be some failed romance that made living there impossible.'

'Still, it could be something more serious.'

'It could be,' agreed Iris. 'So what?'

'So what? How can you say that?'

'Everyone has a past, remember?' Iris reminded her. 'Unless we have something specific to look into, we can't go about giving all of our clients the third degree. We won't get much business if we do.'

'I don't suppose you have any contacts with *la préfecture de police de Paris*, do you?'

'Not currently.'

'But before?'

'Can't talk about it,' said Iris. 'Look, Gwen, every couple we set up will eventually have to ask each other about their pasts. Or not, if they prefer. We're only here to make the introductions. The rest is up to them.'

'Then maybe we should take a chance on her,' said Gwen. 'Even if we don't succeed within the nine days, she might be able to return if we find her someone suitable.'

'Or our eligible bachelors could travel there to meet her,' suggested Iris. 'That would put some extra romantic adventure in it for our gentlemen. Sirs, we have a lovely French girl waiting for you! All you have to do is go to Paris and bring her home!'

'They'll be queuing up if you put it like that,' said Gwen. 'It seems we both are in favour of accepting her.'

'Always up for a challenge,' said Iris. 'And she's right. We could use the telephone to speed things up for once.'

'Oh, this modern age,' said Gwen with a sigh. 'Where are the days of *billets-doux* brought on silver salvers?'

'Is that how you were wooed?' asked Iris. 'I had boys whispering rude invitations directly into my ear as they passed me in school hallways. Much more efficient when you cut out the middle-man. And cheaper without the salver. I am now going to use this ultra-modern telephonic device to have Mrs Billington send her back.'

She pressed the intercom buzzer. Shortly thereafter Mrs Billington knocked on the door, then entered carrying the completed questionnaire.

'She has signed a contract and paid the fee already,' she said. 'She's very eager.'

'That's one way to describe her,' said Iris.

'Are you sure about this one?' asked Mrs Billington. 'She seems flighty.'

'As do all angels,' Gwen said blithely.

'An angel, is she?' scoffed Mrs Billington. 'Then there's a crater somewhere in Paris from when she fell.'

'Thank you, Saundra,' said Iris. 'Give us two minutes, then send her over.'

The two partners glanced at the questionnaire together.

'She's a dancer,' said Iris, pointing to the line for occupation.

'Aha!' said Gwen. 'I thought that might be the case.'

'From her figure?'

'Sally told me there was a group of Parisian performers coming over for a new variety show. I'll bet she's with the Casino de Paris ladies. That would explain the deadline.'

'Maybe she heard Mr Haight talking about us,' Iris speculated. 'When is her performance?'

'Next Thursday.'

'Maybe we could set her up with Mr Haight? No, scratch that. I don't think he could spend a lifetime listening to that voice.'

'Well, we'll have to listen to it now,' said Gwen. 'She's coming back.'

Duplessis came in, slightly more subdued than she had been previously.

'So you are a dancer,' began Mrs Bainbridge.

'Yes,' she said, a defensive tone in her voice. 'I trained with the Paris Opéra Ballet. I joined the corps when I was sixteen, but when the Occupation come, Lifar, he was the man who run the company? He collaborates with the Germans. So I quit. The problem, though, was where to find work as dancer? The solution was wherever I could. And now I am cancan girl at the Casino de Paris, doing the same show three times a night, six nights a week.'

'That sounds exhausting,' said Sparks.

'Ballet was exhausting,' she said. 'Classes all day, then perform. Cancan is easy. Starvation is difficult. I do not starve.'

'Do you intend to keep dancing after you're married?' asked Sparks.

'Of course! Why would I not?'

'There are men who would prefer that you should stay at home and keep house.'

'I do not want these men,' said Duplessis immediately.

'Then you've just eliminated half of our bachelors,' said Sparks.

'At least half,' said Mrs Bainbridge.

'Oh,' said Duplessis. 'I did not think about that.'

'You see now why the interview is so important.'

'Well,' she replied with a shrug. 'There is still the other half. I am sorry, I have to be at rehearsal.'

'But—' started Mrs Bainbridge.

'Pick one,' said Duplessis as she stood up. 'Have him leave a message at my hotel. And I will marry him, you will see.'

Before they could stop her, she walked out through the door. The two partners stared after her, then at each other.

'You wanted a challenge,' said Gwen.

'Not that much of one,' said Iris. 'What have we got ourselves into?'

THREE

'What did you do when she walked out?' asked Dr Milford.

'We sorted through our male candidates,' replied Iris, who was curled up in a chair in front of his desk. 'It was odd, working with so little to go on. We ended up looking at the men with whom we've had the least success in matching. It didn't feel professional using that as the main criterion, even if this is a profession that we are more or less inventing as we go along.'

'Any luck?'

'We settled on one, finally. He's a shy, awkward fellow, which is why he came to us in the first place. But he also speaks French, and we thought that should be a requirement.'

'So he could communicate with her,' said Dr Milford, nodding approvingly.

'That was Gwen's thought.'

'What was yours?'

'That she shouldn't be able to hide anything from him behind a different language.'

'Interesting that you thought that.'

'Because I'm a woman who hides secrets? Is that what you're saying?'

'What do you think?'

'There's that question again,' she said with an exaggerated groan. 'I'm here to talk, not think. That's why they call it the talking cure, isn't it?'

He didn't respond.

'Bit of a laugh, that,' she continued. 'I talked all the time, virtually non-stop, and I didn't cure a damn thing with it. And that was when I was just a piddling little neurotic with mood swings. Now I have some real trauma to play with.'

'You talk to conceal your thoughts,' he pointed out. 'You talk about anything other than what's hurting you the most. Even with me.'

'That's the nice thing about having been a spy, I suppose,' she said. 'You're supposed to keep part of you locked away for life, and once you have that secret vault built in, it becomes very easy to throw other parts of you into it.'

'Who could you talk to about those other parts?'

'You. That's why I'm here.'

'But this is not your quotidian existence. This is another vault in which to store things, only I work in it.'

'Goodness, Doctor!' she exclaimed. 'It sounds like you could use some therapy.'

'I get it. It's a requirement of the profession.'

'I didn't know that,' she said. 'It's good that you have someone to talk to.'

'So who could you talk to?'

'Sally, about the secret things from the war. And Gwen, about the secret things from my love life. But I can't speak to them when they're together, and they're together all the time now.'

'Does that make you jealous?'

'No. Well, maybe.'

'You knew Sally at Cambridge.'

'Yes. He was my best friend there.'

'Anything more than that?'

'No. At least, not for me.'

'How about for him?'

'He had a crush on me,' she said. 'Quite dangerous when a man that size has a crush. It's more like an avalanche.'

'Why wasn't it mutual?'

'I've often wondered about that,' she said. 'When I look back at the woman I was then, I see someone trying too hard to overcome her perceived disadvantages. Being a woman. Being middle-class. I wanted to show the rich party boys that I could outdo them in everything.'

'And Sally?'

'I couldn't outdo Sally because he wasn't a rich party boy,' she said. 'He was middle-class like me. He adopted their tones, actor that he was, became more snooty sounding than any of them, but if you listened closely, you could hear the irony underneath. Or at least I could. We were alike. Too much alike, I think. Maybe I couldn't love someone like me because I didn't like myself. That's interesting! I've never thought of that before.'

'You have had a pattern of loving men you knew you ultimately couldn't have,' he pointed out.

'Except for Mike Kinsey. And that relationship I destroyed myself.'

'You don't make that exception for Archie?'

She didn't respond, but clutched her knees to her chest, as if she was trying to take up as little space in the world as she possibly could.

'I'm not ready to talk about him yet,' she said softly.

'That's all right,' he said. 'What would you like to talk about?'

'I must say that life on a narrowboat is much better now that spring has arrived,' she said, sounding more enthused. 'It's a simple but regular existence. On the first and third week, a man with a lorry comes to fill my water tank. On the second and fourth week, a different man with a different lorry comes to empty my toilet tank. Really, that's all one needs in life: two men with tank lorries.'

She continued until her session was up.

Ted Farrell, the man they had chosen for Mademoiselle Duplessis, rang the next morning.

'She called me!' he said in excitement. 'We actually have our first date tonight. My lord, she's a torrent of words on the telephone.

I almost feel I should wear a mackintosh when I meet her. Anything I should know?'

'She wants to settle in England with an English husband,' said Mrs Bainbridge. 'Quickly. Don't let her overwhelm you. Make sure she knows who you are and what you're about.'

'Honestly, I wouldn't mind being overwhelmed,' he said. 'I've had rather an underwhelming existence so far. Even to be whelmed would be a step up.'

'Well, have a wonderful time, and do ring us up on Monday and let us know how it went.'

'Will do, Mrs Bainbridge. My thanks to you and Miss Sparks.'

She hung up, then looked at her partner.

'Should we line up another suitor for Monday, just in case?' she asked.

'I have no idea with this woman,' said Iris. 'I'm almost prepared to come in to man the telephone over the weekend just for her.'

'Maybe that's a service we could add,' said Gwen. 'An emergency number for urgent courting. Sudden need on a Saturday to bring a date to a wedding? Call The Right Sort, and we'll have one sent right over, complete with boutonnière.'

'I don't think we should cross that line,' said Iris. 'Being a marriage broker is an honourable profession. Procuring is not.'

Gwen left at noon and caught a cab back to Maida Vale. She had to get out short of her house, as a small crowd of servants and residents had gathered by it, Millie, Agnes and Rachel at the front. There was a long ladder resting against the house, going all the way to the roof.

Gwen joined her ladies as they watched two men on her roof hauling up a thin metal post with several cross-pieces jutting from the top forming an H, the overall appearance of the framework resembling a particularly ungainly and unsuccessful box kite. Once the men had it in their hands, they carefully made their way up the roof tiles until they were next to the chimney. They secured the base of the pole to the ridge of the roof, then one negotiated his way to the other side of the chimney. He and his partner passed a thin skein of wire back and forth, wrapping it three times around the chimney, anchoring the pole in place. Then his partner took a coil of cable hanging from his belt, attached one end to one of the cross-pieces, then turned to face the crowd.

'Look out below!' he called, and the crowd hastily withdrew from that side of the street.

He tossed the cable, which rapidly unspooled as it fell across the face of the house, the end landing in an ornamental shrub.

'He wants to drill a hole through the wall,' said Millie grimly as the man started down the ladder. 'A hole! Through our wall!'

'What's the alternative?' asked Gwen.

'They could run it through the window,' said Millie.

'But then the cold air would get in during the winter, and the flies in the summer,' said Gwen. 'We want to watch television in comfort, especially during the winter. A hole could be sealed, I should think.'

'But a hole, Mrs Bainbridge!' protested Millie.

'It's my house,' said Gwen. 'I could drill as many holes in it as I want.'

The man reached the bottom of the ladder, then came over to where they were standing.

'When does the lady of the house get in?' he asked Millie.

'That would be me,' said Gwen. 'I'm Mrs Bainbridge.'

'Ah, how do you do, missus?' he said, removing his cap. 'I'm Terry Barnstable. We spoke on the telephone. That's my nephew Lenny up on the roof.'

He turned and yelled upwards, 'Lenny! Say hello to Mrs Bainbridge!'

'Hello, Mrs Bainbridge!' shouted Lenny, waving his cap.

'Hello, Lenny!' she replied, waving back to him. 'Be careful up there!'

'I will, ma'am.'

'What's the next step?' she asked Barnstable.

'I'm going to connect the cable through the window for the moment,' he replied. 'There is going to be a test programme broadcast from one to two, which is why we had to get the antenna set up now. I'm going to watch for the reception, and Lenny's going to stay on the roof and position the antenna until we get the best picture. Once we have that, we'll fasten the cable to the roof and outside wall with some clips so it won't go flapping about in the wind.'

'Millie said you want to drill a hole through the wall.'

'I would need the owner's permission, but it would be better.'

'How long would that take?'

'Not long. It's wood under the stucco by the window frame, and we have a power drill.'

'Very well,' said Gwen. 'I am the owner and I give you permission.'

'Right, then. Let's get cracking.'

'I must go and fetch Ronnie,' said Agnes reluctantly. 'He'll be disappointed to have missed all this.'

'We'll have a proper inaugural viewing tonight,' said Gwen. 'What time does the evening programme begin?'

'Eight thirty,' said Millie.

'And they're starting with a cookery programme,' Rachel added eagerly. 'Nice of them to have me in mind.'

The earthbound Barnstable went to retrieve the end of the cable from the shrub and fed it through the window. Gwen looked back up at the roof, where the antenna now stood silhouetted against the grey sky, Lenny sitting next to it, taking a breather while awaiting instructions. She was not the first to acquire one of these, she noticed. There was another one down the street.

Harbingers of things to come, she thought. Like we're the first members of a new religion, erecting our peculiar crosses to let the world know we are here.

Barnstable picked up his toolkit and walked into the house, the three women following him. He took the end of the cable, squatted behind the television, and connected it. Then he glanced at his watch.

'One o'clock on the button,' he said. 'Mrs Bainbridge, please do the honours.'

She stepped forward and turned on the power. Barnstable came back from his position, and the four of them watched intently as the screen gradually lit up.

'There it is!' squealed Millie in excitement.

A grainy picture of a circle filled the screen. Inside it was a drawing of a pyramid of three cubes angled towards the camera, their visible faces shaded black, white and grey. On either side of the circle were five black vertical lines. Above it were the letters 'B.B.C.' and below it the word 'Television'.

'Hooray!' cried Rachel.

'We'll make that better in a jiffy,' said Barnstable.

He raised the window, then leaned out and twisted his body so he was facing upwards.

'Lenny! Can you hear me?' he shouted.

A faint 'Yeah!' sounded from above.

'Start with five degrees clockwise,' shouted Barnstable.

He pulled back into the room and watched the picture.

'They chose this design for tuning,' he explained. 'You got your contrasting shades on the cubes, and the vertical lines for sharpness. There! See the difference?'

'It's better now,' said Gwen.

'We're angling it towards the Ally Pally transmitter,' he said. 'Let's try some more.'

He leaned back out through the window.

'Another five degrees, Lenny!'

Gwen watched as the picture improved marginally.

'I feel as if I'm at an eye exam,' she commented.

'Yeah, is it better this way or this way?' said Barnstable as he rejoined her. 'Let's see if we are heading to the right point, or if we've already passed it.' He leaned out the window. 'Lenny! Two degrees this time!'

'Oh, that's made it worse,' said Millie immediately.

'I agree,' said Gwen.

'Good, we're zeroing in on it. Lenny, anticlockwise now. Three degrees.'

'That's made it better,' said Gwen.

'Better than two settings ago?'

'I would say so. Wouldn't you agree, ladies?'

They did.

'One degree now, Lenny!'

'Better still,' said Gwen.

'And one more degree.'

'Maybe slightly worse now,' said Gwen, squinting at it critically.

'Good. Lenny, clockwise one degree again. Mrs Bainbridge, is that the best picture you've seen so far?'

'I would say yes,' said Gwen. 'Millie?'

'Me, too.'

'Rachel?'

'It's the best picture of a circle with cubes in it I've ever seen,' declared Rachel.

'We are unanimous, Mr Barnstable,' said Gwen.

'And who said giving women the vote was a bad idea?' he said with an impish grin. 'We got it, Lenny! Lock it in and start securing it.'

'Righto!' called Lenny.

Mr Barnstable detached the cable and fed it back through the window, then lowered the screen.

'Make sure you're not standing near the wall,' he said. 'The drill bit can break through suddenly sometimes.'

He took a measuring tape from his kit, measured the distance from the base of the windowsill to the top of the baseboard, then nodded.

'I'll be outside,' he said.

Agnes returned with Ronnie just as Barnstable was finishing the drilling. The boy stared at him as he turned off the drill and put it back in its case.

'Did you just make a hole in our house?' Ronnie demanded.

'I did, my lad,' said Barnstable. 'You must be young Master Bainbridge. I'm Terry Barnstable. That's Lenny, my nephew, on the ladder.'

'Hello, young fellow,' called Lenny, waving from by the eaves.

'My name is Ronnie,' said the boy, coming forward to shake Barnstable's hand. 'May I look through it?'

'Certainly,' said Barnstable.

Ronnie came up to it, stood on his tiptoes, and peered through.

'It's right above the floor, isn't it?' he said. 'I feel like I'm a mouse looking out of his hole.'

'Come on in now, Ronnie,' said Agnes. 'Wipe your shoes extra well on the mat. You've been standing in the dirt.'

'May I watch him work when he comes in?' asked Ronnie.

'Ask him properly,' said Agnes.

'May I watch you work, please, Mr Barnstable?'

'Of course, Ronnie,' he said. 'I'll be coming inside in a moment. You mind your nanny, now.'

The test show had ended before Ronnie had come home, so all he was able to see when Barnstable reconnected the antenna cable was static. He sat on the sofa and watched it.

'How does it work?' he asked. 'How do they get the pictures inside?'

'Oh, Lord – that's one for the boffins, not me,' said Barnstable. 'Let's see. Do you know how radio works?'

'No,' said Ronnie.

'Hmm, that would have been helpful. Right, so radio is sound, only they turn it into these invisible beams.'

'Like torch beams?'

'Like them, only you can't see them.'
'Not a very good torch if you can't see them.'
'True enough. So the sounds ride along on these invisible beams, and when they get to the radio, the radio can turn them into sounds we can hear.'
'How?'
'No idea. And television works the same way, only with moving pictures. They send the invisible beams out from Ally Pally on that big metal tower, bounce them off the heavens, then they hit that antenna we just put up on your roof, run down the cable into the back of your set, and get turned back into pictures again.'
'But how do they do that?'
'Once again, I'm not the one to be answering that,' said Barnstable. 'But maybe your mum can find someone who can. I've got to go and plug up the hole around the cable. That is something I do know how to do. Nice to meet you, Ronnie.'
'Nice to meet you, Mr Barnstable.'

When the installation was complete, Gwen came outside with a cheque. She handed it to Mr Barnstable while his nephew collapsed the ladder.
'Thank you for tolerating my son,' she said. 'He's very curious about things.'
'As he should be,' said Mr Barnstable. 'Bright lad. Sorry I couldn't explain it better. I should study up on it for the next bright lad with questions. Good day, Mrs Bainbridge. Call us if you have any complaints or troubles.'
'Will do, gentlemen,' she said.
She walked inside to take another look. Ronnie was there, sitting on the floor in front of the set, staring at the roiling profusion of black, white and grey dots.
'Ronnie, there won't be anything to see until after dinner,' she said. 'Let's turn it off.'
He turned to face her. She was shocked to see tears streaming down his face.
'Ronnie, what is it?' she said, immediately kneeling and putting her hands on his shoulders.
'I was looking for him,' said Ronnie.
'For who?'
'For Daddy.'

'Daddy?' she exclaimed. 'Why?'

'The man said the beams bounce off Heaven and come here. And Daddy's in Heaven. I thought – since he's watching me all the time – I might see him.'

'Oh, Ronnie,' whispered Gwen, pulling him into her. 'Television can't do that. I wish it could, but it can't.'

'But Daddy is watching from Heaven, isn't he?'

'He is, my darling boy,' she said. 'And I'm sure he's very pleased and proud about what a wonderful person you are and how well you are growing up.'

He started crying in earnest. She held him tight and let him, the tears soaking through the shoulder of her blouse.

'I don't remember him,' he said, sobbing. 'I want to remember him.'

'Look in the mirror, then,' she said. 'You are his image. There never was a boy who looked more like his father than you do.'

'Do I?' he asked, looking up at her, sniffling.

'You do,' she said, pulling out her handkerchief and wiping his face. 'Every time I see you, I think of him.'

'Does that make you sad, Mummy?' he asked.

'Never,' she said. 'Looking at you always makes me happy.'

'Even when I'm crying?'

'Oh, when you're sad, then I'm sad, too,' she said. 'But I am happy that I can be here with you to make you feel better. Do you feel better?'

'A little,' he said.

'Well, we'll keep working on that until you're all the way better. And tonight, I'll let you stay up to watch the new television.'

'Will Sally be on it?' he asked.

'Sally works behind the scenes,' she said.

'What does that mean?'

'Remember that panto we saw? Remember how that nice friend of Sally's took us backstage afterwards and showed us all the pieces of scenery folded up and put away in the wings?'

'Yes.'

'It's the same with television. Sally is one of the people in charge of moving all of that on and off the stage. Or the studio, I suppose it's called. In fact, I have a surprise for you.'

'What is it?' he asked eagerly, his tears subsiding.

'Sally has invited us and John to come and see the BBC Television studios at Alexandra Palace. We'll get to see how they do everything. Iris is coming, too. Won't that be fun?'

'Gosh! Will we be on television?'

'No, dear, but we may get to see some of the people who are. Would you like that?'

'Very much!'

'Good. Are you feeling better still?'

'Yes. Mummy, are you going to marry Sally?'

The question caught her completely by surprise.

'Oh, I don't know,' she said, blushing and stammering as she responded. 'We haven't got that far along yet.'

Not how one should present oneself before an all-too-perceptive child, she thought.

'Why not?' he asked.

'It takes some time to decide things like that,' she said.

'How long did it take for you and Daddy to decide?'

'Let me think. I was only seventeen when I met him, and I was twenty-one when we got married. So I was twenty when your daddy asked me to marry him. No, it was before my birthday, so I was nineteen.'

'Did you say yes right away?'

'I did. And then we told his parents and my mother, and they took over all the wedding planning, which is why it took so long after the engagement.'

'If you and Sally get married, will he be my daddy?'

'He would be your stepfather.'

'Why do they call it that?'

'You know, I don't know why they use that word.'

'Maybe it means we're taking the next step,' said Ronnie thoughtfully.

'Maybe it does. We'll have to look it up sometime. Tell me something, Ronnie. Does it bother you that I am going out with Sally?'

'No, Mummy,' he said. 'I like Sally. He's fun. And he can throw me in the air so high!'

'That's fine, as long as he remembers to catch you when you come back down,' said Gwen. 'Now, I'm sure you have some schoolwork to do. Let's get it done before dinner so you can watch with us afterwards.'

'Yes, Mummy.'

She watched him as he ran from the room, then turned back to the television, which was still on. She watched the static for a few seconds, searching for patterns lurking in the chaos. There were none.

She turned it off.

Out of the mouths of babes, she thought. Will I marry Sally? Or is this only an affair for the moment?

She had never been involved in something like this before. She had gone on a few carefully selected dates after she had been presented, then met Ronnie Senior, and that was that for a long time. Sally was only the second man ever to make love to her. She didn't know where it was going, or how to react to it. That was part of the attraction for her, the lack of knowing for once, as opposed to the lovely but all too predictable course she had embarked on with her engagement and marriage to Ronnie. The all too predictable aristocratic course which was upended by the unpredictable incursions of war and death.

Do I want predictability? she thought. Patterns are safe and comforting, but they can be deceiving. Chaos might be a better descriptor of the world she lived in. It demanded more of her, forced her to acknowledge the horrors of daily existence. But once she came to terms with them, she could embrace the unexpected wonders that came with opening herself up to worlds beyond the restrictive circles in which she had been raised. Where people like Sally would never have been permitted.

Will I marry Sally? she asked herself again.

It would upset her family if she married someone like him. Someone middle-class. Someone, let's be honest, Italian. The Bainbridges tolerated Sally for his assistance on matters they would prefer not to have mentioned, just as they did with Iris. Her own family, though, hadn't met him. Didn't even know of his existence. Thurmond, her brother, who came into the family fortune when her father died, had little or nothing to do with her and young Ronnie, which suited her just fine.

Her mother, on the other hand . . .

Alethea Brewster, her mother, had never come to visit her when she was in the sanatorium. Not once. When Gwen was finally released to the custody of her in-laws, she got Percival to put a call through to her as soon as she had settled back in. Her mother started the conversation as if the horrors of the previous months had never happened, calmly asking about Little Ronnie's progress in school.

Finally, when Gwen felt she was about to burst, her mother asked, 'And how are you, dear?'

'Well, considering I was just released after several months in an asylum,' Gwen began.

'Don't be ridiculous,' said her mother, cutting her off. 'There's nothing wrong with you.'

'There was,' said Gwen, starting to cry. 'There still is.'

'Stop that at once,' commanded her mother. 'I won't have it. You're better than this.'

That was how their first and only conversation about her suicide attempt had ended.

Her sessions with Dr Milford frequently invoked that conversation. He brought up her mother's being from an earlier era, where anxieties were expected to be suppressed, and labelled as hysteria when they weren't. Gwen gradually realized that – at some point – she would have to confront her mother, have it out between them.

And then forgive her, which would be the most difficult part of all.

Or she could toss it all, marry Sally, and never see the Brewsters again. That wasn't the ideal solution, but it seemed, nevertheless, to be a solution.

She had brought up her fear of confronting her mother at her recent session. Dr Milford chuckled ruefully. She asked him why.

'What's curious about that,' he said, 'is that you have repeatedly thrown yourself into situations involving murder, violence and personal danger, yet speaking to your mother is what scares you.'

'Murderers are easy. Mothers are hard.'

She lowered the cover on the Baird as she thought about those conversations. She was a mother herself again, now that she had finally regained custody of Ronnie. She needed to be better at it. Having Dr Milford in her life was helping her.

You see, Mum? she thought. I am better than this.

And with that comforting thought, she went off to dinner.

With no outside guests joining them, they dined together, family and staff. It was unusual, but the four women were close in age, Rachel being the oldest, and they all doted on Ronnie, who revelled in the attention. Gwen had been learning how to cook, and with her early arrival had, under Rachel's watchful eye, roasted the cod with shallots grown in their greenhouse. The meal met with approval from all, then Millie and Rachel cleared the table.

When the dishes had been washed, the five of them gathered in the parlour, Ronnie sitting on the floor closest to the screen. Just before the appointed time came, the telephone rang in the hallway.

'Got it,' said Millie, dashing out.

They heard a brief murmuring.

'Must be her boyfriend,' commented Rachel.

But Millie returned, a perturbed expression on her face.

'It's for you, ma'am,' she said. 'A Mr Farrell.'

'Mr Farrell?' exclaimed Gwen. 'Why would he call me at home?'

'Shall I tell him that you're unavailable?'

'No, I had better take the call,' said Gwen. 'Shouldn't be long.'

She went to the telephone which was on a small table outside the kitchen.

'Mr Farrell? It's Mrs Bainbridge,' she said. 'Is everything all right?'

'No, everything is emphatically not all right,' he said. 'I think you sold me a bill of goods, Mrs Bainbridge.'

'What happened? Did Mademoiselle Duplessis not show up for your date?'

'Oh, she showed up,' he said grimly. 'And I was indeed overwhelmed, but not in a nice way at all.'

'Tell me.'

'She was nothing like what she was on the telephone this morning. Oh, she was a looker, certainly, but I thought you said she wanted an English husband as soon as possible, and instead she says first thing that she was no longer on the market.'

'What?'

'She said she was only there because she didn't want to hurt my feelings, but that she had made a serious mistake by coming to you and Miss Sparks, and that she wasn't available any more.'

'How awful!' exclaimed Mrs Bainbridge. 'Did she give you any reason why?'

'She said she had been with someone before who had told her off, and that she signed up with you to make him jealous, and that it worked. She was going to be seeing him tonight.'

'Oh, no! Mr Farrell, I cannot tell you how sorry I am. This is an inexact profession that we practise, but this has gone far more badly than we anticipated. I promise that we'll do better by you the next time.'

'I don't know, Mrs Bainbridge,' he said, sounding less than mollified. 'I don't take very well to being rejected before the soup has even reached the table.'

'No, no, quite understandable,' she said. 'I promise you that Miss Sparks and I will get on this first thing. And that we will speak to Mademoiselle Duplessis about her inappropriate behaviour. On behalf of The Right Sort, I profusely apologize.'

'Well, it's not like I've too much in the way of other prospects,' he said forlornly. 'I'm sorry to call you at home, Mrs Bainbridge, but I thought you should know. Goodbye.'

He hung up.

What have we done? wondered Gwen.

FOUR

The plan was for Nigel, the chauffeur for Gwen's in-laws, to bring them all in the Bentley. Iris managed to get herself out of bed and cleaned up in time, then threw on a cream-coloured linen blazer over a white blouse and a blackout skirt. As she emerged from the cabin and locked her door, she drew an appreciative wave from the man running a hose to her boat from a tank lorry parked on the towpath. It was a water day. She waved back and continued on to Gwen's house.

Gwen herself answered the bell.

'Good morning,' she said. 'Ronnie's almost ready. Agnes is wrestling with his tie. I'm glad you're early. I received a rather upsetting call from Mr Farrell last night.'

'Mr Farrell? He called you here?'

'He did.'

Gwen recounted the conversation to Iris, who was equally mystified when it was over.

'It doesn't sound as if Mr Farrell was rejected for himself,' she said. 'Mademoiselle Duplessis had already made up her mind before she got there. How strange! Why did she even come to us?'

'I don't know,' said Gwen. 'But I think that we should drop her, don't you?'

'We should certainly speak to her about it,' said Iris. 'I don't want to terminate her contract without finding out her side of it.'

'You're being very fair about this,' said Gwen.

'I am.'

'I suspect it's because you don't want to return her fee.'

'There is that,' Iris admitted.

'Hello, Iris!' called Ronnie from the top of the stairs.

'Hello, my handsome young man,' Iris called back. 'Come down and give me a proper greeting.'

He flew down the steps and into her waiting arms. She hugged him, then held him at arms' length to look at him.

'I think you've got smarter since I last saw you,' she said, examining him critically. 'Taller, certainly, but you have an air of acquired knowledge. That school must be doing a good job.'

'I'm learning my times tables,' he said proudly.

'Seven times six,' said Iris.

'Forty-two,' he said immediately.

'Is that correct?' she asked Gwen dubiously. 'You know how terrible I am with maths.'

'Stop teasing,' said Ronnie, giggling. 'You must know that one.'

'I do,' she said. 'But your mother does all the bookkeeping at The Right Sort, so I leave all the difficult calculations to her. Are you excited about seeing Sally at Ally Pally?'

'I am,' he said. 'Would you like to see our new television?'

'I would indeed,' she replied.

He grabbed her hand and pulled her into the parlour.

'We watched it last night,' he informed her. 'I got to stay up until ten o'clock!'

'You are a veritable *bon vivant*,' she said. 'What were the programmes?'

'There was a cooking show, then *Kaleidoscope*, then *Serenade in Sepia*.'

'Did you see anything you particularly enjoyed?'

'The Memory Man. He can remember everything!'

Poor soul, thought Iris. I would pay anything to forget sometimes.

A car horn sounded from the street.

'That's Nigel with the car,' said Gwen. 'Ladies, we're off! Enjoy your day without us.'

'Have a wonderful time, Ronnie,' called Agnes from the upper landing.

'Bye, Agnes,' cried Ronnie.

Nigel tipped his hat as they came out, then opened the rear door of the Bentley.

'I think one of you should be up front with me,' he said. 'It will be more comfortable.'

'Iris, you sit with the boys,' said Gwen. 'They haven't seen you in a while.'

'Delighted,' said Iris as she got in. 'Hello, John!'

'Hello, Miss Sparks,' said John from the back seat.

'Now, John, when there is no other company about, you may stop exhibiting your exquisite good manners and call me Iris,' she instructed him as Nigel closed the door after her.

'Yes, Iris,' he said with a grin.

The boys had both dressed in their school uniforms for the occasion. John was a year older than Ronnie, and had become the brother Ronnie never had in the short time since he had arrived in the Bainbridge house. The biggest wrench for Gwen when she had bought the house in Maida Vale was separating the two boys. At least they were in the same school, thick as thieves during playtime and lunch breaks, and usually together at one house or another after school and on the weekends.

The social circles in which the Bainbridges travelled had yet to learn the family's true relationship to John: That he was the illegitimate son of Lord Harold Bainbridge and a mistress he had kept at his East African holdings. With her death, and after some complications also kept on the q.t., John had come to live with his father, ostensibly as his ward. Only a small, circumspect group knew that he was Harold's son and Ronnie's half-uncle. Fortunately, Ronnie had taken after his own father in appearance, who in turn had resembled his mother's side of the family, so there was little physical similarity between the boys to clue in any outside observer.

To Ronnie, that John was also related to him was just one more wondrous fact in his favour.

The boys and Iris chatted away while Gwen rode in the front, watching the city through the windscreen as it faded into the suburbs while the Bentley made its way to Greater London's highest natural point. There were trains to Alexandra Palace, but the LNER tracks were being renovated and service to the other nearby stations was sporadic on weekends. The Bainbridges, despite maintaining two automobiles, used them infrequently, and could spare the petrol for the occasional adventure. The Bentley seemed to purr contentedly in finding some vindication for its existence.

After half an hour, Nigel turned on to the long, winding road that wended its way up Muswell Hill. There were trees crowding it on both sides, but then there came a break ahead as they neared the top.

'There it is!' cried Ronnie.

Alexandra Palace had been wonderful once. A great, gaudy brick folly that had been built, burnt down, rebuilt, and become a grand destination for expositions and expeditions from the city. A giant central section boasted several arched doorways, although much of it was blocked by scaffolding at the moment. There was a huge round hole over the entrance, with shards of jagged glass jutting out of its perimeter. A man stood on the scaffolding, picking up pieces of glass from several large buckets and holding them against different parts of the hole, then scribbling down notes in a small notebook. The centre was flanked by two-storey colonnades that extended to squared towers at either end.

Standing in front, waving merrily as the Bentley pulled up, was Sally. He came forward to open the rear door as Nigel went around to open the front passenger door for Gwen.

'Welcome, welcome one and all!' said Sally. 'My name is Sally. I will be your host and personal guide today.'

The boys came bounding out, each grabbing an outstretched hand and shaking it vigorously. Sally's body immediately wobbled in response to the handshakes, eliciting giggles from the boys.

'Goodness, I've been attacked by a pair of young earthquakes,' he said, gasping. 'Greetings, Sparks! And to you, my fair Gwendolyn! Nigel, old chap, will you be joining us?'

'With your permission, Mrs Bainbridge, I'm going to stretch my legs in the park, then nip down to the town for a bite,' replied the chauffeur. 'What time would you like me to pick you up later?'

'What time does the show end?' Gwen asked Sally.

'Five past five,' he said.

'Then be back here at a quarter past, Nigel,' she said. 'Enjoy your walk.'

'Thank you, ma'am,' he said.

He got back into the Bentley and drove down to the car park.

'Very good,' said Sally. 'Now, first thing. Look away from this enormous pile of bricks and take in this magnificent view.'

They looked out over the trees and grass, past the clusters of towns and railways, to see the city in the distance.

'There's London, boys,' said Sally reverentially. 'Standing tall and proud despite taking a beating from the skies. You can make out St Paul's dome, and that other tall block is Queen Anne's Mansions. There is no Queen Anne living there, nor has there ever been, which has often puzzled me. Now, turn to your left, and take a good look at one of the few things around here taller than me.'

They turned and gazed at a metal structure soaring from the right tower, supporting a spire at its peak.

'That is the great antenna,' said Sally. 'Not quite as grand as the Eiffel Tower, but impressive, nonetheless. All of British television gets funnelled through there and shot out through the skies into every television set in England.'

'How?' asked Ronnie.

'Excuse me?'

'How does it do that? How do the pictures get from here into our television?'

'That is a very good question,' said Sally. 'So, um, the television camera takes pictures like a normal camera, only lots of them very fast, and not on film, and then it chops them up very quickly into tiny little bits, and then puts them back together in some fancy electronic gizmo – I believe that's the technical term – and then smushes the whole mess into some sort of, not a radio wave, but a beam of light, which gets reassembled again very fast at your end—'

'You don't actually know, do you?' said John.

'Haven't the foggiest,' admitted Sally. 'I know how to write plays, and push scenery around, and far too much about Ancient Greece and Rome which doesn't give me much knowledge about how electronic gizmos and thingies work, although I could give you a very boring explanation of where the word television comes from. But I do know a chap here who can explain it much better than I can, so we'll go and look for him. All right? Excellent. This way, please.'

'You were actually starting to sweat answering that question,' commented Iris as they walked toward the entrance.

'Complete panic,' confessed Sally. 'My technical skills extend to blowing things up and that's about it.'

'And they don't let you do that any more.'

'No, more's the pity. Hello, Ernie! Everyone wave to Ernie.'

This last was to the man on the scaffolding. The party waved to him. He looked down and waved back, then went back to looking at the giant hole.

'Ernie's in charge of fixing the bomb damage,' Sally explained as they went inside. 'That was once a rose window that would have been the envy of most cathedrals. It got blown in when a doodlebug landed outside. They're still picking shards of glass out of the organ.'

'Why did they bomb this place when television was shut down?' asked Gwen.

'Probably got lost and bombed the biggest thing they could see,' he said.

Sparks arched an eyebrow in his direction. He shrugged in his response.

'Probably something hush-hush going on in here then,' he muttered to her. 'But no one's owning up to it.'

'It's good of you to do this,' said Gwen. 'You must be very busy.'

'My shift doesn't start until later,' he said. 'I came in for a production meeting first thing, but I'm free for the interim. I'm grateful for the break, to tell you the truth. The meeting got quite tense.'

'What happened?'

'Oh, nothing one couldn't predict when one imports a group of French entertainers who haven't seen London since before the war. They all went out en masse last night and got plastered, and attendance for this morning's rehearsal was not exactly one hundred per cent. One of the dancers hasn't shown up yet, and they were supposed to be choreographing everything again to fit the studios. Words were exchanged in both languages.'

'Oh, dear. Were there dramatic exits and slammed doors?'

'There were, but fortunately we're too far from the city for any of them to escape. Right, first stop. Follow me!'

He led them down a stairwell into the basement.

'Now, you boys have been to the theatre,' said Sally. 'You know all about sets and props and things. They can be very complex, and have to be built so they can move on and off stage and be folded up and stored away very quickly. And that's just for one play. Here, we put on three or four different plays every week! Plus variety shows, concerts, magazine shows, sporting events – actually, we don't hold the sporting events in the studios because the players need room to run about and kick things, although we had some table tennis demonstrations last month.'

'How was that?' asked Iris.

'Quite enthralling for the first five minutes. Unfortunately, they went on for twenty. Live and learn, that's our motto! Anyhow, since everything needs to be designed for our little studios, we have our own scenery shops. And here they are!'

He opened a door to a large room where a group of men and women were frantically painting flats on wooden frames. One of them, nearly complete, was a backdrop of a bridge over the Seine with Notre-Dame looming behind.

'That's supposed to be Paris, of course,' said Sally. 'See how it's mounted on wheels?'

'Isn't that lovely, boys?' commented Gwen.

They nodded, wide-eyed.

'Maybe I could do that someday,' said Ronnie.

'We could bring you in as a narwhal specialist,' said Sally. 'When your *Adventures of Sir Oswald, the Heroic Narwhal* is adapted for performance. So, on with the tour. Now, you may have noticed that we are on the basement level. The studios, on the other hand, are on the ground level, so when the set pieces are done, we take them here.'

They looked up at an enormous shaft that rose to the upper level. There were hoists and pulleys at the top, with several ropes dangling from them, some ending in large, menacing-looking metal hooks.

Looks like a good place for a hanging, thought Iris.

'Someday, we're going to have a special lift built to take them up,' continued Sally, 'but at the moment, a team of muscular men pulls them up using those winches.'

'Is that what you do?' asked Ronnie.

In response, Sally flexed his arms and grunted.

'See what a Cambridge degree can accomplish, boys?' said Iris.

'I can also grunt in Ancient Greek,' said Sally as they continued down the hallway. 'It sounds very much the same, but it makes me feel like Herakles. Here's where we keep the electronics, and those are the coolers that keep everything from overheating and bursting into flames. And now let's go up and see the studios.'

He led them up another flight of stairs.

'There are two studios built into what once were banquet halls,' he said as they emerged. 'After months of committee discussions, they were cleverly designated as Studios A and B. Almost everything we do here is done in one or the other, or sometimes both if we need multiple sets. That can be quite the exercise for the actors, who have to go dashing from one to the other. We also use the outside terrace occasionally, just to vary things. We're going to go inside Studio A. Boys, I need you to be absolutely quiet. They may be rehearsing.'

The 'On Air' sign next to the door was dark. Sally carefully opened the door, poked his head in, then beckoned to the others to come through.

The room was smaller than they anticipated, maybe thirty feet wide and seventy feet long. There was a trio of bulky Emitron cameras in the centre, a profusion of black cables running from them to a box that was set into the wall underneath a glass window, behind which was the control booth. A small bandstand was against the rear wall, and to the left was a group of several men and two women, standing in front of a miniature theatre, eight feet wide and seven feet high, gaily painted with all manner of fleur-de-lis and grapevines, with a smaller rectangular opening about five feet up, currently covered with a miniature velvet curtain.

A small, bald man with the sleeves of his shirt rolled past his elbows was gesticulating rapidly while speaking to the group in heavily accented English. He wore an odd contraption around his neck, a small wooden yoke holding several differently shaped whistles and a duck call. He glanced over to see Gwen and Iris standing with Sally and the boys. His eyebrows shot up, and he immediately pursed his lips and produced a startlingly loud wolf whistle, then followed with a siren whistle from the yoke, and another that burbled like a nightingale.

'*Bonjour, mes belles!*' he called. '*Et mes enfants!* An audience, *parfait!*'

'We're not babies!' said John indignantly.

'Ah, *excusez moi, pardon! Les jeunes gentilhommes, bien sûr!* And you speak French!'

'I'm learning it at school,' said John.

'So am I,' added Ronnie.

'Then you are the most cultured people I have met since I come to England,' he said, throwing a quick, comical glare at the group around him.

'Sorry, didn't mean to disturb,' said Sally. 'Carry on. I'll make introductions later.'

He turned to the boys.

'That's Marcel Legrenzi,' he whispered. 'He's a marionnettiste. I was hoping we could catch him rehearsing. I hear he's marvellous.'

'Right,' said a man the two women recognized as Mr Haight, their new client. 'You should be able to hear the band with no difficulty. The question is: where do you want the microphone placed?'

'I need two,' said Legrenzi. 'Because I move from side to side. Come, I show you.'

He opened a door on the side of the marionette theatre and disappeared inside. Haight stood by the door and peered in.

'One here and one here,' said Legrenzi, his voice muffled from inside the box. 'You can see where I had them in the club. This one is for the cannon.'

'The cannon?' exclaimed the director. 'You have a cannon in there?'

'Of course,' said Legrenzi, re-emerging.

'But isn't that dangerous?'

'Art is dangerous,' Legrenzi said pretentiously. 'But my cannon is not. It is only powder and noise. Like a politician, *oui?* You there, *mes jeunes hommes cultivés*, how do you make the cannon noise?'

'Boom!' shouted the boys.

'*Exactement!*' said Legrenzi, beaming at them. 'So for the boom, we need a microphone. We call it the boom mike, *oui?*'

There were groans from the crew, and Legrenzi looked offended.

'We can use the mounts you have,' said Haight. 'We'll run the cords out the back and connect them when the theatre is rolled in.'

'Won't the cameras see them?' asked Legrenzi, looking out at the line of cameras.

'Not at all,' said the director. 'We'll be in tight on the puppet stage, so nothing besides that will be visible.'

'Ah, *bon*,' said Legrenzi. 'So. *Musique!*'

He took a sheaf of papers while another man stepped forward holding several pages of piano scores. While they conferred, Haight took a pair of microphones from a case on the floor along with some pliers and two coils of electrical cables and disappeared inside the theatre.

'The timing, it has to be precise,' said Legrenzi.

'Of course,' said the music director. 'We have your fanfare. Then comes "Top Hat", and the break is where?'

'*Ici, la première fois*,' said Legrenzi, pointing to a spot on the score. 'End of the tenth measure.'

'So just after the last beat?' asked the man.

'*Oui*,' said Legrenzi as the other marked it in the score with his pencil. 'And the second time, fourth beat of the second measure.'

'Got it,' said the music director. 'Then comes the 1812 Overture.'

'*Oui*, only the one measure. Then the cannon. It will be one, bompbompbompbompbompbomp bomp bomp bom, stop! And I make the boom on the first beat *suivant*.'

'I love it,' said the music director. 'Then the "Habanera", and finish with the Berlioz.'

'*Exactement, merci*.'

'Once you hear the cancan music, zoom in on them,' said the director to a cameraman. 'Then we'll cut directly to the girls in Studio B. Haight, have you finished connecting everything? We should run it through for balance and timing.'

'Done,' said Haight, emerging from the little theatre. 'All yours, monsieur.'

'*Merci, merci*,' said Legrenzi, disappearing into it.

'Let me move the piano up here for the rehearsal,' said the music director. 'Ah, Danielli, give me a hand with this.'

'Even on my time off,' muttered Sally. 'Larry, join us for a moment.'

Haight came over, smiling broadly when he caught sight of the visitors.

'Miss Sparks, Mrs Bainbridge,' he said. 'I had no idea you were coming. And who are these fine lads?'

'These are my friends Ronnie Bainbridge and John Daile,' said Sally. 'And they have a question that no one can answer better than you. Ask them, boys, while I go use my vast intellect to shove a piano across the room.'

'Hello, boys, I'm Laurence Haight. What's the question?'

'How does television work?' Ronnie asked immediately.

'Well, let's see,' said Haight. 'Do you know how your eyes work?'

'No.'

'Look around you,' said Haight. 'You see everything and everyone in here?'

'Yes.'

'Now, if we turned off the lights, you couldn't see them, but they'd all still be here, wouldn't they?'

'Unless they moved,' said John.

'Let's assume they didn't,' said Haight. 'So the reason your eyes can see things is because light bounces off them and there are special nerves in your eyes that take that light and change it into electrical impulses, and then your brain turns those into what you see.'

'Gosh,' said Ronnie.

'So the television camera basically does the same thing,' he continued, leading the boys to where the cameras stood.

A man watching them made a beeline to Iris and Gwen the moment the boys had separated from them. He was in his late thirties, tall, with brown hair and a pencil-thin moustache, and wore a grey suit with a dark green vest. His eyes travelled across them quickly, taking them in as if he was sizing them up for a fitting.

'Don't tell me, don't tell me,' he said to Gwen. *'Women Aren't Angels.* Am I right?'

'Not as a general statement,' said Gwen. 'No woman is anything all the time.'

'No, no, the Sylvaine play. At the Strand, back in '40 or thereabouts. Weren't you in that?'

'Oh! No, my goodness, no,' said Gwen, laughing. 'I'm not an actress.'

'Are you sure?' he said. 'Then you're a dead ringer for the one I saw. God knows you've got the looks. Well, then how about you, my dear? You have to be one.'

'I haven't trodden the boards since my university days,' said Iris.

'Hmm, clearly opportunities have been missed,' he said. 'I'll have to snatch you both up and get you on stage before someone else finds you. The name's Freddie Oakes, by the way. I'm producing this Parisian extravaganza.'

'Ah, Mr Danielli mentioned you,' said Gwen. 'I'm Mrs Gwendolyn Bainbridge, and this is my partner, Miss Iris Sparks.'

'Partner?' he asked, seizing on the word. 'So you do have an act. Singers, perhaps?'

'Business partners,' said Iris. 'We run The Right Sort Marriage Bureau in Mayfair. Our friend, Mr Danielli, is giving us and the boys a tour.'

'So that's who they are,' he said, glancing over to where Haight was lifting up each boy in turn to peer through the camera's eyepiece. 'Which one belongs to whom?'

'The younger one is my son, Ronnie,' said Gwen. 'John, the other boy, is his friend.'

'Then I must conclude that Miss Sparks is single and unencumbered,' he said, turning to her. 'Perhaps we could discuss your future career as an actress over dinner sometime.'

'I have no future career as an actress,' said Iris. 'So that ends the discussion.'

'We could find other topics,' he said. 'I have a broad range of interests.'

'As do I,' said Iris. 'Sadly, they don't include you at the moment.'

'Fair enough,' he said. 'But if you ever change your mind, I will be at your beck and call.'

'I will add you to the ever-growing queue,' said Iris.

Sally, having placed the piano close to the marionette theatre but just out of camera range, rejoined them.

'Danielli, you've been holding out on us,' said Oakes. 'Where have you been hiding these lovely ladies?'

'Be good, Freddie,' Sally cautioned him. 'You need to be able to go ten minutes without flirting with every woman you see.'

'I can't, you know,' said Oakes. 'And why should I when there are such beauties in the world?'

'Freddie, I think we're set for the run-through,' said the director. 'Come into the booth.'

'Ladies, a pleasure,' said Oakes, touching two fingers to his brow in what he intended to be a jaunty gesture.

'Sorry about that,' said Sally after he left. 'He fancies himself quite the ladies' man.'

'Well, the rake made no progress with us, so no harm done,' said Iris.

Legrenzi poked his head out.

'You! Young men!' he called. 'Come and watch the performance. I need an audience.'

'Stand with us, boys,' said Sally. 'So you won't be in the way.'

'Camera ready,' called the cameraman from behind the central Emitron, as Haight brought the boys back and stood next to Iris.

'Music ready,' called the music director from the piano.

'Sound ready,' came a voice through a speaker.

'Introduction, blah blah blah, cue music,' came the director.

The music director played a fanfare on the piano, and the curtains parted on the puppet stage. In the centre was a tiny man with jet-black hair painted on top of his wooden head, waving merrily, his broad smile revealing pearly white teeth. He was dressed in a white undershirt and brown trousers, with a pair of tiny braces holding up the latter.

"Allo, 'allo!" he said in a high squeaky voice that echoed through speakers on either side of the room. 'I am Marcel! 'Ow do you do? Welcome to Paris, *mesdames et messieurs*. My apologies for my appearance, I was not ready for you. I 'ave special surprise – tonight, we go dancing! But first, I must put on ze right clothes.'

The pianist struck up the intro, and Marcel began to sing, 'Top Hat, White Tie and Tails', bobbing up and down on his strings as he went behind a changing screen. He immediately came out the other side in full formal wear as the boys gasped in surprise.

'Better, *non*?' said the puppet. 'Ze ladies, zey cannot resist Marcel when 'e eez so very 'andsome, *oui?*'

The puppet winked broadly.

'I'd swear that was directed to us,' whispered Gwen.

'Honestly, I'd rather date that puppet than Oakes,' Iris whispered back.

'So, ze night, eet eez young! *Cherchons les femmes!*'

Suddenly, a red devil appeared from stage left.

'Marcel, Marcel!' it cried in a German accent thicker than the French one of Marcel. 'Eet eez I! Ze Devil!'

'Ze Devil? But you sound German,' said Marcel.

'*Natürlich*. What else would ze Devil sound like?'

'Zat makes sense,' conceded Marcel. 'Why are you 'ere?'

'I 'ave come for your soul!'

'*Non*, not tonight!' said Marcel. 'You can 'ave eet tomorrow, but tonight, I go dancing.'

'Dancing?' exclaimed the Devil. '*Wunderbar! Ich komme mit!*'

'*Non, non*, you will get een my way.'

The Devil ignored him, dancing behind the screen. A second later, he emerged, also in evening dress, singing 'Top Hat, White Tie and Tails' in German.

'Stop!' Marcel interrupted him. 'You will not come wiz Marcel.'

'You cannot stop me,' said the Devil.

'But I can,' said Marcel.

The 1812 Overture sounded, and a small cannon rose in front of Marcel. As the piano cut out, the noise of an explosion came through the microphone, and a small puff of smoke blew out of the cannon's mouth.

The Devil promptly separated into several pieces which flew off the tiny stage.

The room was filled with the startled laughter of the few people watching. Iris glanced at the boys, who were howling with delight, then noticed that Haight, alone around their party, was unmoved. He stared at the marionette stage, his brow furrowed in puzzlement, almost shock.

'Now, to ze dance hall!' cried Marcel, and a backdrop of a swanky Parisian club slid down into place behind him.

'Marcel, Marcel!' came a falsetto voice.

'Who calls Marcel?'

'Eet is I, Carmen.'

A marionette woman entered, dressed in black lace. If ever a puppet could be described as seductive, this one was.

'Carmen!' exclaimed Marcel. 'What are you doing een Paris?'

'I 'ave come all ze way from Spain so I can dance ze tango weeth you,' she replied.

The pianist struck up 'Habanera', and Carmen began a series of slinky moves, her white legs kicking up through slits in the skirt as she swirled about. The swirling became more and more frenetic, and within seconds, Carmen found herself wrapped in her own strings as the music slowed to a stop.

'Oh, dear, thees eez embarrassing,' she said with a sigh. 'I must go, Marcel. I would dance weeth you, but unfortunately, I am tied up.'

She hobbled off. Marcel looked out at the camera.

'Ze tango dancer 'as become a tangled dancer,' he said. 'Marcel is alone again. But do not fear. We are in Paris! And eef nothing else, Paris eez full of ze beautiful women. Ladies – *allons-y!*'

He held up one hand and made a gesture, then scampered off as an entire row of cancan dancers dropped from the ceiling, their arms around each other's backs, their legs kicking impossibly high as the pianist launched into the Berlioz. The dancers kept kicking as the cameraman dollied his Emitron forward, the lens nearly crossing the threshold of the small proscenium before the command 'Cut!' echoed through the room.

The pianist stopped, Legrenzi came out and made a deep bow, and the audience applauded.

All except for Haight, Iris noticed, whose hands remained stubbornly at his sides, his fists clenched.

The director came back through the door, consulting a clipboard. Oakes was behind him, clapping loudly.

'Bravo, old chap!' he said. 'They're going to adore you.'

''Ow was the balance?' asked Legrenzi.

'Good, although we'll have to adjust for the full orchestra,' said the director. 'We can do that during sound check for the show.'

'And the timing?'

'I would be happier if we could cut fifteen seconds,' said the director, holding up a stopwatch. 'Are there a couple of lines you could leave off?'

'I will talk faster,' said Legrenzi as he unhooked the whistle yoke from his neck. 'First time is always slow, but now I am getting used to all of you. Young gentlemen, would you like to see inside?'

'May we?' asked John eagerly.

'Only if you answer me a question,' said Legrenzi. 'How did Marcel change his clothes so fast?'

'There are two Marcels,' said Ronnie immediately. 'The first goes behind the screen and the second comes out.'

'And there are two Devils,' added John.

'That is correct,' said Legrenzi. 'Silly me, thinking I am fooling such intelligent people. Come, young gentlemen. I show you.'

'I'd better go with them,' said Gwen to Iris. 'I don't want anyone to disappear.'

They followed Legrenzi around to the side door of the little theatre.

'Now, do not touch a thing,' he warned them. 'I have everything in place.'

They peered in cautiously. The interior was unpainted, and every part surrounding the stage had some marionette or tiny prop suspended from a small peg, including several Marcels in a variety of outfits.

'How did you make the smoke come from the cannon?' asked John.

'Ah, that is not smoke at all,' he said. 'My puppets are very afraid of fire. *Regardez!*'

There were several foot treadles at the base of the box, arranged like pedals for a church organ. He depressed one, causing the tiny cannon to rise to stage level. Next to that pedal was a rubber bulb connected to a long, thin piece of tubing that ran inside the cannon. He stepped on the bulb, and a puff of powder came from the mouth of the cannon as Legrenzi made the noise of the explosion with his mouth.

'Isn't that clever, boys?' said Gwen.

'*Merci, mademoiselle,*' said Legrenzi. 'And now I have to put the Devil back together. Very special puppet, very delicate.'

He retrieved the fragmented parts, which were dangling on thin wires from the cross-pieces. He reassembled them into the Devil in evening clothes, finishing with the tiny top hat, then carefully drew the wires through the top of the framework and looped them around a tiny hook. He turned the completed assembly toward the boys.

'*Guten Tag, meine Herren,*' he growled as the Devil's mouth moved in synchronicity. '*Ich bin gekommen, um eure Seelen zu holen!*'

The boys giggled in delight.

'Don't worry, boys,' said Gwen. 'Your souls are safe.'

'Ah, Madame speaks German,' said Legrenzi, smiling at her.

'I do,' she said. 'And French. In fact, I think I saw your act before the war. Weren't you at the Café des Loups?'

'Me? *Non, madame.*'

'Are you certain? I do remember a Hitler puppet coming apart in pieces like that Devil.'

'*Non*, that was not me,' he replied. 'I knew the marionnettiste you are talking about. He apprenticed with me, in fact. He was a, ah, what is the word in English? *Un voleur.*'

'A thief?'

'*Oui, c'est le mot juste.* I invented this technique, and he stole it when he devised his own act.'

'I'm sorry to hear it,' said Gwen. 'I thought he was very talented.'

'Talent and dishonour are not exclusive,' said Legrenzi. 'Although Fate punished him severely. He lives no more.'

The director came over.

'We're going to need the studio,' he said to Legrenzi. 'Mademoiselle Rivette needs to run through her number for tonight. If you've finished packing up, we'll move your theatre into a rehearsal room where you can practise.'

'Practise?' said Legrenzi huffily. 'But it is already perfection.'

He winked at the boys.

'*Non, messieurs*, one must always practise,' he said. 'Even after achieving perfection, one must maintain it. Like your mother has!'

'Thank Monsieur Legrenzi for showing you his secrets,' said Gwen.

'Thank you, Monsieur Legrenzi,' said Ronnie.

'*Merci*, Monsieur Legrenzi,' said John.

'You are very welcome,' he said, shaking their hands.

'*Merci, monsieur,*' added Gwen.

'*Le plaisir, c'était pour moi, Madame,*' he said, kissing her hand.

Iris, who had been listening to the conversation while waiting for them to rejoin her, felt a tap on her shoulder. She glanced back to see Haight.

'Miss Sparks, may I have a quick word outside?' he asked.

'All right,' she said.

He led her into the hall.

'Yes?' she asked.

'I want to talk to you about something that's bothering me,' he said in a low voice. 'Could you perhaps meet me for a drink after I get off my shift tonight?'

'I don't date any of our clients,' said Iris. 'That's in your contract.'

'Not a date at all,' he said hastily. 'But there is something I need to tell you that may only be discussed by the initiated, if you catch my drift.'

'Ah,' she said. 'In that case, when and where?'

'How about The Hero of Maida, eleven o'clock?' he said.

'Very well. Don't be late. A woman alone in a pub on a Saturday night is considered fair game.'

'Thank you.'

He walked away, passing Oakes who was escorting a beautiful blonde woman in her early thirties. She was chatting away in French, mostly complaining about sharing a dressing room. Oakes made sympathetic little clucks in response, managing to throw a wink at Iris as they passed her. She followed them back inside.

'I have her!' he announced to the room. 'Mademoiselle Claudine Rivette *est ici!* Mademoiselle, let me introduce you to our director.'

Rivette swept past Gwen and the boys without acknowledging them. Legrenzi, who was pushing his theatre toward the door, stopped to let her pass, making a roguish obeisance as she walked by. She ignored him, proceeding to the director who seemed uncertain as to whether he was to bow or kiss her hand, and settled for holding his own hand out which she shook after giving him a mildly condescending smile.

'You have the music?' she asked without any preliminaries.

'Right here, *mademoiselle,*' called the music director from the piano.

'That is not what you will accompany me with,' she said, looking at the upright disdainfully.

'No, no, we'll be bringing in the grand for your number,' the director said hastily. 'This is just for rehearsal.'

'There will be more scenery than this, I hope,' she said, glancing at the bare walls.

'They're putting on the last touches as we speak,' the director assured her.

That must have been the backdrop we saw them working on downstairs, thought Gwen.

'Let's begin,' said Rivette. 'Freddie, *mon cher*, would you be kind enough to bring me a glass of water?'

'*Bien sûr*, my dear,' said Oakes.

As he passed, he whispered to Sally, 'Spectacular, isn't she?'

'*Chacun à son goût*,' replied Sally.

Oakes smirked and went in search of water.

'Let's leave her to rehearse,' said Sally. 'We'll see her in the variety performance later.'

The pianist played an arpeggio into an opening chord as they walked out of the studio, and behind them they could hear Mademoiselle Rivette singing *Que reste-t-il de nos amours?* Sally shut the door behind them.

'One more stop, then we'll swing by the restaurant,' he said. 'I hope Freddie wasn't too obnoxious. He's become quite self-important since they let him produce. He was a lowly stage manager here before the war, same as I am now, but worked his way up quickly.'

'Do you have ambitions to become a producer now that you're here?' asked Iris.

'If I can get my plays done that way, why not?' he said, stopping at a set of doors. 'Here we are. Now, ladies and gentlemen, you must know that Alexandra Palace had a theatre that rivalled any in the West End, and the spectacles they put on drew hordes of Londoners once upon a time.'

He pulled out a set of keys with a flourish and riffled through them until he found the one he wanted.

'Only the most trusted men have this key,' he intoned ominously. 'But you must also say the magic words, boys. The ones used by Ali Baba.'

'Open sesame!' the boys said in unison.

'Actually, I was thinking of when he said, "Enough theatrics, just open the door, will you?"' said Sally, turning the key. 'But those will do. Hold up while I get the lights.'

He disappeared into the dark. A moment later, lights came on.

'My eyes are full of electrical impulses,' whispered John.

'Mine, too,' Ronnie whispered back.

'Come in, and watch your step,' said Sally, reappearing. 'Now, although it would be nice for the BBC to use the theatre as an actual theatre, we're not ready for that yet. But since we put on so many different plays every week, we need ready-made sets built to order. And we end up reusing a lot of them.'

He led them through the left wing on to the stage. It was a broad one, and they could look out into the vast, dark theatre and imagine the crowds of excited day-trippers, waiting expectantly for whatever distraction could be provided.

But the stage itself was crammed with scenery and props: an Edwardian drawing room bumping up against a Victorian boudoir, a cluster of chandeliers, badly in need of dusting, sitting on tables that could have held dinner parties for Louis XIV. Artificial trees stood before flats of forests continuing the arboreal illusion into the distance. A large, stuffed bear drew the boys' attention as it loomed from across the way, its teeth bared fearsomely, its claws extended, its overall terrifying aspect undercut by the pole that kept it mounted on a small, wheeled platform.

'That's from last month's *A Winter's Tale*,' commented Sally as the boys rushed to stare up at it. 'Unfortunately, one of the wheels squeaked badly when the actor was pursued by it. Rather undercut the drama of the moment.'

'I have a question,' called John.

'Yes?'

'If television is in black and white, why are the sets in colour?'

'Now, that is a brilliant question,' said Sally, going over to them. 'Especially since it is one I can actually answer. There are a few reasons. First, the actors feel much happier when there is colour around them, so they perform better. Second, our scenery painters are artists, and they want to keep their skills sharp. And someday, there will be colour television, so we might as well stay ready for it. What's interesting is that not every colour looks good in black and white. Reds look terrible on television, for some reason, and white is too bright – they dip all the men's shirts in some weak coffee to dull them down.'

'That's a waste of coffee,' commented Iris.

'May we look around?' asked Ronnie.

'Of course,' said Sally. 'We'll get a quick bite after this, then I have to get to work. They're starting with the mobile unit out at Wembley for the football match, then I'm needed for the variety show. I hope that flat will be dry in time to place behind Mademoiselle Rivette for her number.'

'She's not with the Parisian show next week?' asked Gwen.

'She very much is,' said Sally. 'She's giving our lucky audience a taste of it this afternoon. I'll get you into the viewing room for all of that. Then we break for dinner, and you can head home while I get things set up for the evening shows.'

'Why isn't there television during dinnertime?' called Ronnie from across the stage.

'What a terrible idea!' said Sally with a shudder. 'Dinner is the centrepiece of English existence. Who would possibly want to sully that glorious hour with the tawdriness of television?'

'Single people,' said Iris, and Sally shot her a sympathetic grimace.

The group descended a set of stairs to where the seats once were, the slanted floor now holding a motley collection of props for every occasion. Suits of armour stood on guard next to Egyptian sarcophagi; giant Chinese urns nestled against Greek statues; behind them was a stand of jungle trees, festooned with realistic-looking vines.

Iris wandered idly among them, wondering if any of them would fit in her current living quarters. There was a group of well-dressed female mannequins nearby, no doubt left over from some department store setting. One of them had fallen over. She went over to take a closer look to see if she should alert Sally.

She stopped short as she came up to it.

No, she thought. That red wouldn't look good at all. Not on television, not anywhere.

'Gwen,' she called to her partner, who was still on the stage. 'Take the boys into the hallway and wait for me there. Sally, come over here, would you?'

Something in the tone of her voice caused Gwen to beckon to the boys immediately, overruling their protests as she looked out at her. Sally came over to where Iris stood, the questions forming. Iris put her finger to her lips and waited for Gwen to herd the boys out into the hallway. Then she pointed at the woman lying on the floor next to the mannequins, the blood on her neck and blouse already drying.

Sally squatted by her and felt her wrist for a pulse, then looked up at Iris.

'Garrotted,' he said. 'I guess that's why she missed rehearsal. It's one of the dancers. I don't know her name.'

'I do,' said Iris. 'It's Jeanne-Marie Duplessis. She was a client of ours.'

FIVE

Sally held the door for Iris, then locked it behind them, testing it to make sure it was secure. Gwen was waiting at the end of the hallway with the boys, who were chattering with each other. Sally beckoned to her.

'Boys, stay right here for a moment,' she said, then she came over.

'What's happened?' she asked softly.

'I found a dead woman in there,' whispered Iris. 'It's Jeanne-Marie Duplessis.'

'Our client?' exclaimed Gwen.

The other two shushed her quickly. They glanced down at the boys, who thankfully were still oblivious to the grown-ups.

'How? How long ago?' demanded Gwen.

'Garrotted, and can't tell,' said Sally.

'The blood had dried,' said Iris. 'I didn't look for any other indications on the body, so it could have been any time since whenever she had that date with Mr Farrell.'

'Oh, God,' said Gwen. 'He was very angry about her when he called. We're going to have to tell the police about him, aren't we?'

'And her,' said Iris.

'What happens now?'

'I'm going to take you and the boys to the restaurant, then call the Wood Green Police Station,' said Sally. 'Sparks, hold the fort until I'm back. Don't let anyone in.'

'Of course,' said Iris.

The boys, sensing the changes in the adults, fell quiet as Sally walked them to the restaurant.

This was an in-house establishment with communal tables for the employees and guest performers. There was a mixture of people there, grabbing a quick meal on whatever small breaks they had in their irregular schedules. Gwen recognized two exhausted-looking artists from the scenery shop, still splattered with paint. At another table, a lively group of young women were happily gabbing away.

They were speaking French, Gwen realized.

'Are those the rest of the dancers from Casino de Paris?' she asked softly.

'Yes,' replied Sally.

'Poor things. They have no idea yet.'

'We'll leave them in ignorance for now,' said Sally. 'I expect they're all in for questioning when the police get here. Ah, there are some seats.'

He led them between tables to a smaller, round one. Madame Rivette was sitting there, by herself, eating a sandwich.

'Excuse us,' said Sally. 'I need to abandon my guests while I attend to something. These seem to be the only available seats. I hope you don't mind sharing.'

Madame Rivette shrugged without saying anything.

'Thanks awfully,' said Sally. He waved to a server, who came over. 'Mrs Bainbridge and the boys are my guests. Anything they want, put it on my bill.'

'Right, Sally,' said the waitress, pulling a pad from her apron pocket. 'Hello, cuties. What can I get you?'

After she took their orders, Gwen turned to Madame Rivette.

'How do you do, madame,' she said. 'I'm Mrs Gwendolyn Bainbridge, and this is my son, Ronnie, and his friend, John. We caught a moment of your rehearsal earlier. We're so looking forward to your performance.'

'You own a television?' asked Rivette.

'We do, but we'll be watching the show from here from a viewing room. It's all quite fascinating, seeing what goes into these productions.'

'Are you performing here?' asked Rivette.

'I? No,' said Gwen. 'My friend, Mr Danielli, works here. He's giving us a tour as a treat for the boys.'

'Ah, a friend,' said Rivette, a raised eyebrow conveying scepticism. 'Does Mr Bainbridge know about this . . . friend?'

'Mr Bainbridge died several years ago,' Gwen replied calmly.

'I am sorry,' said Rivette. 'Then it is good that you have this friend. Where do you perform?'

'I'm not a performer,' said Gwen. 'You're the second person here who thought I was.'

'Because you are so beautiful,' said Rivette. 'What else could you be?'

'I'm a businesswoman,' said Gwen. 'Despite my beauty.'

'Truly? They allow that in England?'

'They don't make it easy, but yes, they do.'

'What form of business?'

'A marriage bureau. We help people find love.'

'Ah,' said Rivette, nodding wisely. 'The English do need help with that.'

'The French do not?'

'I do not have to find love,' said Rivette. 'It follows me wherever I go.'

'Then you are a most fortunate woman.'

'I am not so certain,' said Rivette with a dramatic sigh. 'Love can be a curse as well, *n'est-ce pas?*'

'That's the story of every French love song, isn't it?' commented Gwen.

'Very true,' said Rivette with a quick laugh. 'Young men, this woman is as wise as she is beautiful. You must listen to her.'

'I have to listen to her,' said Ronnie. 'She's my mother.'

'Even better,' said Rivette.

'Where do you perform in Paris?' asked Gwen.

'I am currently at Cabaret au Lapin Agile in Montmartre. Do you know it?'

'I went there once before the war,' said Gwen. 'Boys, Lapin Agile means the agile rabbit. Isn't that a funny name?'

There was a shriek of laughter from the dancers' table. Gwen looked over to see Marcel Legrenzi regaling them with a story, his hands dancing in the air. The ladies shooed him away, and he glanced over to see Gwen and the boys.

'Ah, my new English audience!' he exclaimed as he came up to them. 'And can it be? The Goddess of Paris eating an ordinary English sandwich? How the mighty have fallen.'

'Hush, Monsieur Fantoche,' said Rivette. 'Remember that we are guests.'

'Fantoche?' he cried in mock anger. 'Are you calling the puppeteer a puppet? Remember who holds the strings.'

'I take it you two know each other,' said Gwen.

'*Oui*, she was part of my act once,' he said. 'In 1938.'

'I was the star of your act, not a part,' she said. 'I was the one people came to see.'

'But that was when she was . . . young,' he said impishly. 'Which was a long time ago.'

'Would it be too much for you to leave me alone for the one week we are forced to work together?' she asked sweetly.

'There is nowhere else to sit,' he said, glancing around the room.

She threw her serviette on to her plate and stood.

'Forgive me, madame,' she said. 'I need to prepare. It was enchanting to meet you and your handsome boys. I hope you enjoy my performance.'

'She has already seen your performance,' said Legrenzi. 'Later, she will hear you sing. *Au revoir, ma déesse!*'

She bent down and hissed into his ear, 'You don't hold my strings, Marcel. Not any more!'

Then she straightened up, her face a mask of calm, and walked out.

Legrenzi watched her go, a slight smile on his lips.

'She is always like this when we see each other again,' he said.

'Perhaps you should avoid each other,' said Gwen.

'Perhaps,' he said. 'But where is the fun in that?'

He took her hand and kissed it.

'*Au revoir, madame,*' he said. '*Et vous, mes gentilhommes.*'

Sparks maintained her post by the door, fighting her impulse to pick the lock and go and examine the scene herself. She wondered who was on the rota at Homicide and Serious Crimes Command for this one. Some she had got along with, some she had detested.

And one she had almost married.

After about ten minutes, she heard footsteps from many feet approaching. She instinctively stood to attention. Sally turned the corner, along with an older man in a brown suit and a pair of uniformed police constables.

'I'm told the homicide detectives will be here in half an hour,' said Sally as he came up. 'This is our manager, Avery Conley. And these are Police Constables Higgins and Braverman. This is my friend, Miss Iris Sparks. She found the body.'

'How do you do?' said Sparks.

'Miss Sparks,' said Higgins. 'We'll take it from here, but we'll need you to stay nearby for when the Yard fellows show up.'

'Of course,' said Sparks. 'Do you mind if I rejoin my party in the restaurant? I'm famished.'

'I'll take her,' volunteered Conley. 'But show me what's going on first.'

Sally unlocked the door and led the three men inside. Two minutes later, Conley and PC Higgins emerged, the former looking pale.

'I'll return after I escort Miss Sparks,' Conley told the constable.

'Very good, sir.'

'Miss Sparks?' said Conley, offering her his arm.

She took it, and they walked through the halls.

'I can't believe it,' said Conley. 'So young. So pretty.'

'Yes, she was,' said Sparks.

'I say, you are taking all this with remarkable equanimity,' he observed. 'Not to mention still possessing an appetite after seeing it.'

'Not my first time seeing something like this, unfortunately,' she said.

'So I've heard.'

'Have you? What exactly have you heard about me?'

'You and your partner have not exactly been unknown to the press,' he said.

'Was our little marriage bureau featured on television recently? I'm afraid I don't own a set.'

'I'm referring more to your frequent involvement in crime scenes.'

'Yes, I know you are,' said Sparks. 'If your memory were better, you might have recalled that one of them involved my fiancé being gunned down, so perhaps not the best choice of topic.'

'Forgive me,' he said hastily. 'I should never have brought up the subject.'

'The subject has found us,' she reminded him. 'We will play our parts, then go on. In the meantime, still hungry.'

'Yes, yes, of course,' he said. 'Oh, the police asked me to tell you not to mention what is happening to anyone. And to tell Mrs Bainbridge that.'

'She knows her responsibilities when it comes to police matters,' said Sparks.

Conley guided her to the restaurant. Gwen gave her a tentative wave from across the room. Iris forced a cheerful smile to her lips and joined her and the boys.

'Sorry about the delay, everyone,' she said. 'What's good on the menu?'

'It's mostly sandwiches,' said John. 'We're not sure what the fish is.'

'Then I'll have one with meat,' she said. 'As to what animal it came from, we'll hope for the best.'

Conley returned as they were finishing up.

'Miss Sparks, you're wanted,' he said. 'Mrs Bainbridge, Mr Danielli sends his regrets, and has asked me to bring you and the boys to the viewing room to watch the match.'

'How exciting!' said Gwen with as much enthusiasm as she could muster. 'Let's go and cheer for England, boys!'

'Hooray!' shouted the boys.

'Hooray,' said Iris. 'I'll join you as soon as I am able.'

'I suppose I'll be needed, too,' said Gwen.

'Shouldn't be long for either of us. See you soon.'

Conley pointed her back towards the theatre, then led the rest of the party away. Sparks walked in that direction, then saw Higgins motioning to her from a doorway.

'The detectives have arrived, Miss Sparks,' he said. 'They've commandeered this office. Please come in.'

Spin, Rota of Fortune, spin! she thought as she entered. Let it be someone new.

It was her ex, of course, sitting behind someone else's desk. He looked no happier to see her than she was to see him.

'Detective Sergeant Kinsey, we meet again,' she said.

'Hello, Miss Sparks,' he said. 'It's been a while.'

Not nearly long enough, she sensed him adding.

'Close the door, Constable,' said Kinsey.

Higgins closed the door behind her, and she sat on a folding chair in front of the desk.

He looked more than usually tired, she thought. He had been so energized by joining the unit when she first knew him, but much had happened since, both on the job and in the world. She wondered how many bodies he had seen by now.

She thought back to the last time she had seen him. Another crime scene, another discovered body, only days after Archie had been shot. It was not a good memory.

'I would like you to stay out of police business!' he had shouted

at her. '*I would like you to stay out of my business, whether it's professional or personal. I would like never to see your face again, if you could manage that.*'

Apparently, she couldn't.

'I suppose you're going to tell me this has nothing to do with you, Sparks,' he said.

'I wish I could, Mike,' she replied. 'She was a client.'

'Of The Right Sort?'

'Yes.'

'Good Lord,' he said. 'But she's from Paris. How did she manage that?'

'She walked in two days ago,' said Sparks, and she recounted everything she could remember of the interview. By the time she was done, he was shaking his head in disbelief.

'Strange,' he said. 'Any idea why she was in such a rush to get married?'

'Nothing specific,' said Sparks. 'She mentioned something about Paris, about not being able to continue on there, but we didn't get any more detail than that.'

'She's here with a dance troupe,' said Kinsey. 'Maybe one of them will know. I wish my French was better.'

'Would you like me to translate?'

'No thanks, Sparks,' he said. 'You're a witness.'

'Not a suspect this time?'

'Not yet.'

'I must be losing my touch.'

He grimaced for a moment. Or was it a smile? She didn't know with him any more.

It was almost a year since the last time he had kissed her. A sudden impulse on his part, completely to her surprise, although not entirely unwelcome. So much of her life had changed since then. She spent much of her time with her psychiatrist discussing Mike, trying to rid him from her system, yet here they were again, and the memory of that kiss was pushing its way into the forefront of her thoughts.

She wondered if it was doing the same to him.

'Any thoughts on the body?' he asked.

'Not my area of expertise,' she said.

'Come off it, Sparks.'

'Well, I didn't examine the scene thoroughly. I wanted to get

Gwen and the boys out of the theatre before they saw it. I didn't see any signs of a struggle. Did you find the garrotte?'

'My partner's looking, along with as many locals as we could recruit, but that place is a nightmare. There's a million hiding places. How did you know it was a garrotte?'

The last question was in a sharper tone than the rest.

'It had the looks of one,' she said. 'Sally thought so, too.'

'But how do you know about things like garrottes, Sparks? Ever use one?'

And there was the other side of Mike Kinsey, she thought. The one that would suspect her for the rest of their lives.

'Never used one personally,' she said lightly. 'But I hear good things from my murderer friends.'

'Is Danielli one of them?'

'No, I know him from Cambridge.'

'He's *that* Sally.'

'Yes. Funny, you never met him while you and I were together. I was hoping to introduce the two of you when the war was over, but then we broke things off.'

'Where was he?'

'Something to do with Supplies, I think,' she said, automatically sticking to Sally's cover.

'And how does someone from Supplies know anything about garrottes?'

'You'll have to ask him.'

'I'm planning to,' said Kinsey. 'He's next on my list.'

'Was I the first? I'm honoured.'

'You found the body,' said Kinsey.

'Lucky me. Is there anything else, Mike? I'd like to get back to Gwen and the boys. I don't want them to worry.'

'I'll need your number,' he said.

'No home telephone currently, but you can reach me at The Right Sort. We should get a dedicated line to Homicide and Serious Crimes.'

'Address? You're not at the Marylebone place any more.'

'No. I'm currently living in a narrowboat on the Regent's Canal in Little Venice. The *Cecilia*.'

'A boat? What on earth do you know about boats?'

'Much more than I did two months ago.'

'You're there by yourself?'

'I've been by myself since . . .'

She stopped, then finished the sentence.

'Since January. I've been on the boat since the middle of March.'

He looked down at his notes, gathering his thoughts.

'I should have begun this by telling you I'm sorry about Archie,' he said quietly, almost reluctantly. 'I should have written you a note, or something, but given my role with the Yard and his as . . . as what he was, it was awkward. But I am sorry for your loss, Iris.'

'Thanks,' she said.

There was a moment of silence.

'Superintendent Parham sent me a note,' she said.

'He did?'

'He did. I guess, being your boss, he felt less concern about his position,' she continued. 'Although Detective Florey also sent me one, and you and he are the same rank. aren't you? No, I take it back, Florey's a detective inspector, and you haven't got there yet. And that nice constable from the Essex Police, Hugh Quinton – remember him? He's in training to be a detective out there now. He sent a note. You didn't.'

'None of them were engaged to you,' said Kinsey.

'No, and none of them . . . well, that's water under the bridge, isn't it? How is Beryl doing, speaking of spouses?'

'We're expecting a baby,' said Kinsey. 'In August.'

It felt like an eternity before she managed to force herself to draw breath.

'Congratulations,' she said. 'To both of you, although I doubt she'll want to hear it from me.'

'Thank you. We'll consider it said and leave it there, I think.'

She got up and moved to the door. He didn't stop her. She looked back at him as she opened it.

'I always thought you would be a good father, Mike,' she said.

Then she went out, closing the door behind her.

Kinsey knew that the man coming in next would be tall but, even so, he was caught off guard by how much Danielli towered over him. Danielli, clearly used to both people's reactions or the polite suppression of the same, nodded politely.

'Salvatore Danielli, stage manager,' he said. 'How may I be of assistance?'

'I'm Detective Sergeant Michael Kinsey,' replied the detective. 'Take a seat.'

Danielli sat as the door closed behind him.

'So we meet at last,' said Kinsey. 'The legendary Sally.'

'The infamous Mike,' replied Danielli. 'It will be interesting to find out how much we already know about each other.'

'You're her best friend I never met.'

'And you're the man she didn't marry. Well, that's all of us, isn't it? But you got closer than most.'

'Sparks spoke of you quite a lot when we were together,' said Kinsey.

'Fondly, I hope.'

'Quite. I gather you were off doing clandestine things for King and country back when I was with her.'

'I was with a supply unit. Nothing clandestine about it.'

'Are you sure? Sparks said you were both doing hush-hush work.'

'Sparks was a spy?' exclaimed Danielli. 'Good Lord, I had no idea. Of course, a woman that short would be excellent at hiding behind things, now that I think about it.'

'Fine, I'll move on. Did you know the victim?'

'I met her with her troupe, all of them at once,' said Danielli. 'Didn't know her name, or most of their names. They were the cancan dancers, and I didn't have much to do with them.'

'But you recognized her when you saw her body.'

'Yes. I have a decent memory. One needs that for this job.'

'When's the last time you saw her before this afternoon?'

'I popped in on a rehearsal in Studio B yesterday morning,' said Danielli. 'They had to re-choreograph their numbers to allow for the dimensions of the studio and the placement of the cameras. I was there with the scene designers to work out the logistics for moving things in and out for the show.'

'Anything about her stand out at the time?'

'She was one of a dozen beautiful, leggy ladies in skimpy rehearsal togs. I noticed all of them with momentary admiration, then went back to my job.'

'Anything else about her leap to mind?'

'She didn't show up this morning,' said Danielli. 'That was brought up in the production meeting. Her name wasn't mentioned, but some consternation was expressed.'

'Expressed by whom?'

'Mark Culbert, the choreographer. He brought it up first. Freddie Oakes grumbled something about that's what happens when you turn French girls loose in England, and Barry Postlethwaite looked aggrieved, but he's a director so that's his usual look.'

'Know anything else about her?'

'Not a jot. You'll have better luck talking to her troupe, interrogating one beautiful French girl after another, you poor sod.'

'Believe me, it won't be as much fun as you make it sound,' said Kinsey. 'Are there sign-in sheets that would tell me when she left yesterday?'

'Yes. I can get those for you.'

'And how many people would have been working here then?'

'Over a hundred,' said Danielli. 'Most regulars, some guest artists for last night's programme. I could find those lists as well, or you could just ask Mr Memory to save time.'

'Wonderful,' said Kinsey with a sigh. 'Let's narrow it down. The old theatre is used for scenery and prop storage?'

'Correct.'

'Is it kept locked when not in use?'

'It is.'

'Who has a key?'

'I do,' said Danielli. 'So do the assistant stage managers.'

'How many of them are there?'

'Two. Morton Stansbury and Wally Fenton.'

'Either of them working today?'

'Stansbury is.'

'How about yesterday?'

'Yesterday was Fenton and me.'

'Who else has one? Building manager? Cleaning crew?'

'No. There is a properties manager who works directly for the BBC who has one, but that's it.'

'Seems rather a small number of people to have access.'

'That was the point. They installed the locks back in the Thirties when they took over the building. They didn't want things getting nicked for decorations. Each department runs a tight ship.'

'So how did Duplessis get in there?'

'Either someone was careless, someone was clever, or it was one of the four of us,' said Danielli, looking at him steadily.

'You don't seem overly concerned about making the shortlist,' said Kinsey.

'I like to think innocence is on my side.'

'Is it?'

'I didn't know the poor girl. I had no motive to kill her.'

'We don't know what the motive was, so we don't know who might have had it,' said Kinsey. 'When were you in the theatre last?'

'Yesterday. We were storing the flats and set pieces from last night's programme.'

'And you didn't notice any dead women lying about?'

'We stored everything on the stage,' explained Danielli. 'It's easier to move them from there to the studios. We had the stage lights on, not the house lights, so the area where she was found was dark. And even if it had been lit, she wouldn't have been visible from the stage.'

'So she could have been there.'

'She could have been,' agreed Danielli. 'And she would have remained undiscovered until we needed something from that area, or until . . .'

He stopped, wincing.

'Until what?' prompted Kinsey.

'"But if, indeed, you find him not within this month, you shall nose him as you go up the stairs into the lobby."'

'You and Sparks with the Shakespeare quotes,' said Kinsey, shaking his head. 'Peas in a pod.'

'It would need to be a very big pod to hold me. Is there anything else?'

'It's early yet. There will be further discussions.'

'I will be glad to render whatever assistance I can,' said Danielli, getting to his feet. 'Now, if you have no further need of me, I have a variety show to run.'

'I do have a question,' said Kinsey.

'Yes?'

'How does someone from Supplies know about garrottes?'

'I made a few during my time there,' replied Danielli. 'Some of the lads preferred them to knives for killing quietly. No crying out from the other party.'

'How would you make them?'

'A small length of wire, usually with the ends wrapped around two wooden handles.'

'You ever use wire on the job here?'

'We do.'

'Where do you keep it?'

'The scenery shops have it. So does the electric shop.'

'Also under lock and key, I suppose.'

'Yes, but with many more people going in and out of there. We're supposed to sign for anything we use, what with inventories and rationing and such.'

'Great,' muttered Kinsey. 'Fine. Go run your variety show. Nice to meet you at last.'

'Likewise. Not the best of circumstances, I'm afraid. Oh, one more thought.'

'Yes?'

'We have four pianos on the premises,' said Danielli. 'You might want to see if any of their strings is missing.'

'Thanks,' said Kinsey. 'I think I'll interview those dancers first.'

He walked Danielli to the door, then he and Higgins watched as the tall man disappeared around a corner.

'Tell Harvey I want a man tailing him when he leaves,' said Kinsey.

'Shouldn't be too hard,' said Higgins. 'He does stand out.'

'Don't be too sure,' said Kinsey. 'He's a tricky one.'

'Yes, sir. What now?'

'Bring on the cancan girls, Constable.'

'You want all of them at once?' asked Higgins with a grin.

'One at a time, Constable,' said Kinsey. 'One at a time.'

'Lucky bloody you.'

Gwen and Iris were sitting in the viewing room, the boys cheering for England as the Test match played across a group of different television sets. Some men were comparing the picture and sound quality of each, murmuring to each other and taking notes.

The women started as Sally tapped them on the shoulders. He put his finger to his lips and led them out into the hallway.

'I have to get to work,' he whispered. 'I wanted to say goodbye.'

'How did things go with Mike?' asked Iris.

'I haven't been arrested yet, so that's a decent start.'

'Might you be?' asked Gwen.

'I am devoid of motive but riddled with opportunity,' said Sally. 'It's been knocking on a locked theatre door, and I'm one of the few who possesses the key. I hope Mike figures out someone else done it and clears me.'

'Call me either way,' said Gwen. 'I'll be up worrying until you do.'

'I will,' he promised. 'Say goodbye to the boys for me.'

They watched him hurry off to begin setting up the variety show.

'The police are doing their job,' said Iris.

'We should let them,' said Gwen.

They stood silently for a moment.

'But if it turns out Sally needs us, we're in like a shot,' said Gwen.

'Oh, yes,' said Iris.

SIX

It was hard for the two women to keep their minds on the variety show once it began. The boys, on the other hand, were enraptured from the moment the small, cramped orchestra struck up the opening theme.

'There's the piano player!' whispered John as they saw the man from the rehearsal plinking merrily away, now wearing a black tailcoat over a presumably coffee-dyed dress shirt while flashing a set of gleaming white teeth as the camera passed over him.

The announcer stood in front of a small curtain set to the side of the studio as each act was funnelled in and out. Some of the televisions in the viewing room showed what was happening when the broadcast was focused elsewhere, and the boys cheered whenever Sally appeared with another man to move backdrops in and out.

A team of tumblers engaged the boys' attentions. Gwen fearfully anticipated future attempts at the act being recreated in her back garden when Agnes wasn't looking. Then the camera cut back to the announcer.

'Ladies and gentlemen, next week we will be presenting you a special event,' he intoned. 'A new show called *Across the Channel*, in which we will bring you a sampling of the very best entertainment Paris has to offer. We would like to give you a tiny taste – *un apéritif*, if you will. A woman whose beauty is matched only by her incomparable voice. The BBC proudly presents that ravishing chanteuse, Mademoiselle Claudine Rivette!'

Even in black and white, the gown was stunning, the neckline plunging dangerously low, the fabric sparkling with hundreds of sequins reflecting the studio lights in a hundred directions. Her lipstick glistened as well – whatever camera-ready shade it was projected passion promised, though not yet given. Her shoulders were visibly bare under a sheer silk jacket. She stood in front of a jet-black grand piano, her eyes closed, her expression one of a woman lost in a distant memory, while the pianist, having stepped carefully and familiarly through the tangles of cables on the floor, sat with his hands poised above the keys. Suddenly, she took a deep breath, her bosom heaving, which was the cue to the pianist. With a dramatic gesture, he plunged into the opening chords, and her eyes opened as if she had been startled out of a dream that she both did yet did not want to end.

Her voice, no longer marking the song as she had done in the brief moment of rehearsal they had heard earlier, emerged full-throated, almost a sob at moments, a cry of ecstasy at others. Even through the tinniness of the speakers it filled the room, enveloping everyone in it. The boys sat transfixed, too young to understand fully either the French words or the emotions filling them, yet somehow aware that this was something that could take over their lives some day.

Iris nudged Gwen and nodded towards the technical men, who stood motionless, their hands dangling limply by their sides, their notepads now forgotten and useless, their jaws dropping in wonder and desire.

'They didn't even notice us when we came in,' Iris whispered.

'Shush, I'm listening,' Gwen whispered back.

They didn't know the song. It spoke of love lost, the shreds of memories that remained, as the singer, now alone in an empty house where the autumn winds blew against the door, yearned for the lost spring of her youthful ardour.

When it was over, Mademoiselle Rivette looked directly into the camera, her eyes sending a sad yet defiant message. A challenge, perhaps, to any man who thought he could bring her to that level of passion again. The camera cut to the announcer, who was taken off-guard, as caught up in the performance as anyone. Then he recovered, applauding enthusiastically, and went on to introduce the next act.

Iris glanced up at her partner, then pulled a handkerchief from her bag and handed it over. Gwen accepted it thankfully and wiped the tears from her face.

'Extraordinary how potent cheap music is, to quote Mr Coward,' commented Iris. 'Especially when it's cheap French music.'

'You didn't feel it?' asked Gwen.

'I haven't been feeling much of anything, lately,' said Iris. 'I wonder if she's heard about what happened yet.'

'I doubt it,' said Gwen. 'I don't think anyone could sing like that if she had.'

'She performed in Occupied Paris,' said Iris. 'I'll bet she's sung through far worse news.'

The variety show ended right on schedule, all the performers joining in one place as the announcer thanked them and wished his unseen audience a happy evening's repast. Gwen gathered the boys and joined Iris in the hallway.

'Could we thank Sally?' asked John.

'He is very busy at the moment,' said Gwen. 'But I think he would appreciate a nice note from each of you. Let's take you to the lavatory before we get back into the—'

'Mrs Bainbridge?' called a voice.

She looked in its direction to see Mike Kinsey beckoning to her from down the hall.

'I'll take the boys,' said Iris. 'We'll wait for you out at the front.'

'Very well,' said Gwen.

She walked over to the detective.

'Hello, Mike,' she said. 'My turn to be put through the mill?'

'Not for long, Mrs Bainbridge,' he said. 'Mind coming with me? We've taken over someone's office for the evening.'

'Lead the way.'

Iris found the men's cloakroom and sent the boys inside. While she was waiting, she heard voices nearby arguing. She couldn't quite make out what they were saying, but it was in French.

Curious, she crept noiselessly down the hall and peered around the corner of the hallway.

At the other end, she saw Mademoiselle Rivette storming in her direction. Behind her, his expression impassive, was Legrenzi. They looked at her in surprise.

'Is everything all right?' asked Sparks.

'Is everything all right?' repeated Rivette incredulously. '*Non*, everything is not all right. I managed to survive an entire war, only to walk into this murder palace.'

'You've heard,' said Sparks.

'So have you, apparently,' said Rivette. 'Who are you? Why are you asking me questions? Are you with the press?'

There was something voraciously hopeful in that last question. Beyond her, Legrenzi rolled his eyes in disgust.

'I'm afraid not,' said Sparks. 'I'm a visitor. I heard you sing, by the way. You were very good.'

'*Non*, I am not very good,' said Rivette huffily. 'I am *extraordinaire!*'

'Yes, well, I am English and therefore sparing of superlatives,' said Sparks. 'Very good is at the top of my scale, for whatever that's worth.'

'*Merci*, then,' said Rivette.

She walked past Sparks, then looked back and forth, uncertainty quickly mounting to anger. She turned to face Legrenzi.

'Which way is my dressing room?' she shouted.

He pointed to the right, and the storm continued in that direction. Sparks watched her go, then turned back to say something to the puppeteer. But he had vanished.

She saw the boys come out of the cloakroom, and brought them outside to where the Bentley was waiting.

'Just a few quick questions to clarify the timeline,' said Kinsey as he closed the door. 'Sparks said your Mr Farrell phoned you at home last night?'

'Yes,' said Mrs Bainbridge.

'And that was to complain about his treatment by the deceased?'

She has already been reduced to that word, she thought. And she hasn't even been carried out of the building yet.

'Yes,' she replied.

'What time was that, if you recall?'

'It was right before the television programming came on, so shortly before eight thirty.'

'Thanks. And his full name is Theodore Farrell?'

'He goes by Ted, but I suppose that's his formal name.'

'Know where he lives off the top of your head?'

'Somewhere in Islington. If you like, I could go into the office and get the exact address.'

'No, that should be enough for now. Looks like your bureau is caught up in another murder. I just finished talking to Mr Haight, and he turned out to be another client of yours.'

'Yes. He came to us fairly recently. We were wondering if Mademoiselle Duplessis heard about us from him.'

'He said he never talked to her about you.'

'Any other leads?'

'Dozens,' he said ruefully. 'I will probably follow up with you at some point, but not tonight. You may go. Thanks.'

'Good luck,' she said.

She went outside. Nigel was there, standing outside the Bentley, the others already seated in the back. He opened the front passenger door.

'Thank you, Nigel,' she said, getting in. 'We'll drop Miss Sparks off. Then we'll be dining with Ronnie's grandparents.'

'So I understand, Mrs Bainbridge,' he said as he closed the door and came around to the driver's side. 'Did you have an enjoyable experience?'

'Quite interesting, thank you.'

'Was that part of what made it interesting?' he asked, nodding towards the small group of police cars parked in front of Alexandra Palace.

'Let's not talk about that with the boys in the car,' she said softly.

'Very good, ma'am,' he said, putting the Bentley in gear.

As they pulled away, the women noticed a young woman sitting on the steps at the side entrance, sobbing disconsolately.

There will be ten more like her inside, thought Iris.

Or maybe not like her at all. Find that killer, Mike. The sooner Sally is off the hook, the happier I will be.

Nigel pulled over to let the van from the medical examiner pass by, then took them back down the hill and back to Maida Vale.

It was still light when they pulled up to Iris's narrowboat. John, who hadn't seen it before, looked at it agog.

'You live there?' he asked Iris.

'I do,' she said. 'What do you think?'

'It looks amazing. Could I visit?'

'I would be delighted,' said Iris. 'Tell you what. I will have the two of you and Gwen over for tea some weekend.'

'Could you take us out on the canal?' asked John eagerly.

'Ah, I haven't been properly taught how to pilot a narrowboat,' she confessed. 'I run the engines once a week, following a very neatly written set of instructions, so they'll stay in good working order, but that's the extent of it. But there is a rowing boat that I take out once in a while for the exercise. I could take you out for a small nautical excursion.'

'That would be super,' said John.

'Lovely to see you, boys,' she said, giving each of them a quick kiss and hug.

Nigel got out and opened the rear door for her. Gwen exited the front seat and walked with her to the gangplank.

'Gwen, I'll call by after you get home from church tomorrow in case you hear anything about Sally,' Iris said quietly. 'Unless he pops by your place later, in which case send him down in the morning to tell me himself.'

'He doesn't spend the night,' said Gwen. 'Not with Ronnie not knowing everything.'

'Ronnie will figure it out sooner or later,' said Iris. 'He's smart.'

'Like his father.'

'Like his mother,' said Iris. 'Don't underrate your contributions to that lovely boy of yours. Good night, Gwen.'

'Good night, Iris,' replied her partner as they hugged briefly.

Iris waved as the Bentley drove them off to whatever sumptuous Saturday evening repast awaited them at the Bainbridge house. Then she went inside the narrowboat, lit the stove, and warmed up a can of beans to go with a baked potato she reheated from the night before.

There was something she was supposed to be doing, she thought.

Ah, yes. Meeting Mr Haight at eleven.

At a pub.

She hadn't been inside a pub since after Archie's funeral. At Merle's in Wapping, in the back room where she had first met him, putting on a proper Cockney accent and an improper manner while she was investigating the murder of another client. Little did she know that they would become lovers after that. Or that she would now be living a life only slightly less sequestered than one of those medieval nuns, walled up in their cells for the balance of their existences, believing that's what God wanted.

That last night at Merle's, with Benny and the rest of the Spelling gang, had been one of raucous grief and resignation, knowing that without Archie they were on the verge of being taken over and divided up by gangs from adjoining parts of London. It was one last collective howl at the moon, with Iris howling right along with them, drinking far too much and not caring about anything any more.

And then she had crawled into Archie's bed in Archie's cottage alone, and had been that way every night since then.

She wondered what it would be like being in a pub again.

She wondered what she would be like.

Well, she was going with a singular purpose, and it didn't involve romance.

She promised herself she would stop after one drink.

That was the sort of promise she was good at making to herself.

The driver parked the Wolseley carrying Kinsey and Detective Constable Harvey, his partner, in front of a three-storey brick terraced house on Gerrard Street. The house was only distinguishable from its neighbours by the dull blue paint chosen for its front door. The two detectives emerged from the back of the car and looked up at the house.

'It's Saturday night,' said Harvey. 'Think he's home?'

'He's a client of The Right Sort,' said Kinsey. 'If he could get out on a Saturday night, he wouldn't need them.'

He walked up to the door and rang the bell. A minute later, a light went on, visible through the fanlight.

'Who is it?' called a man from the other side.

'Metropolitan Police,' replied Kinsey. 'We would like to speak with Theodore Farrell.'

There was a pause, then the door opened a crack and a sliver of a face peered through it, one bloodshot eye, one side of a mouth, and a shock of untidy hair visible in a single vertical strip.

'What do you want with me?' asked Farrell.

'May we come in?' asked Kinsey, holding up his identification.

'What's this about? I haven't done it, whatever it is.'

'We don't think you did,' said Kinsey. 'But we'd like to ask you some questions.'

'About what?'

'About a date you had last night with a Jeanne-Marie Duplessis.'

'The police have a Bad Date Unit now?' asked Farrell with a bitter laugh. 'About bloody time. Come in, you've got me curious now.'

He shoved open the door and walked back in without holding it for them. The two detectives looked at each other, shrugged, then followed him.

He was a short man, standing five three in his stocking feet, which he was currently in. He pulled his braces, which had been hanging loose, back up over his undershirt as he led the detectives into the front parlour. He appeared to be in his late thirties. He hadn't shaved, the stubble dotting his face a dark brown.

The parlour was sparsely furnished with a couch, one ancient chair whose cushions sagged alarmingly, and a small folding card table with the remains of a cold supper still on it. An ironing board was set up across from the couch, a stack of pressed shirts on one end, with a pile of clean but rumpled clothes awaiting their turn in a basket next to it. A large radio sat on the mantelpiece over the fireplace, with the Light Programme playing softly.

'You might as well sit there,' said Farrell, ungraciously indicating the sofa.

He leaned against the left jamb of the fireplace, his arms folded across his chest, and waited. Kinsey and Harvey sat.

'You're a client of The Right Sort Marriage Bureau in Mayfair, are you not?' began Kinsey.

'Yeah, I figured they put you on to me,' said Farrell. 'Still don't understand why.'

'It's about your date last night with Miss Duplessis.'

'She make a complaint against me?'

'Did she have reason to?'

'If anything, it's the other way around,' said Farrell. 'Look, you might as well stop dancing. Gents like you don't show up on a man's doorstep unless something bad happened.'

'Miss Duplessis was murdered,' said Kinsey evenly.

Farrell drew in breath sharply, then nodded slowly.

'And now you think I did her in,' he said.

'Did you?' asked Kinsey.

'I didn't,' said Farrell. 'It was a bad date. I've had bad dates before. I don't go murdering the women after.'

'Good to know,' said Kinsey. 'Tell us about this one. Where did you go?'

'I met her at the Sergeant's Arms in Chelsea. They do a decent dinner, not too pricey. She was ten minutes late. The maître d' was looking at me sideways, I can tell you that, and I was wondering if this was going to be the latest in the unhappy series. Then she showed up. Not even a word of apology for being late, just, "Are you Mr Farrell? I am Jeanne-Marie. You are expecting me?"'

'What was she like?'

'Well, I have to tell you she was bloody gorgeous,' said Farrell, closing his eyes at the memory. 'Even for a French girl, she stood out, and there are a lot of lookers over there.'

'You've been in France?'

'I know French. I used to go over every summer before the war, and during it I was the unit translator as we went from village to village. And I can tell you there were a lot of mademoiselles who were very happy to be liberated, even by the likes of me. So I spoke to her in French, and she immediately cut me off and said, "English. We will speak English here."'

'The ladies at The Right Sort said that she seemed quite eager to find an English husband.'

'That's what I was told as well,' said Farrell. 'Guess she had second thoughts after meeting me.'

'When did things start going wrong?' asked Kinsey.

'Right from the start, when I look back at it,' said Farrell. 'It was the way she looked at me when we first met.'

'What kind of look?'

'Women size me up,' said Farrell. 'I'm short. I know I'm short. It matters to some women. A lot of women, to tell you the truth. There's a moment with their eyes, a quick up-and-down flicker, then the lights go out behind them and I know I haven't a shot. That happened with her.'

'But she went through with the dinner?'

'Part of it. It was a free meal for her, wasn't it? Although she didn't eat that much. Guess a dancer's got to watch her shape. The conversation wasn't much. She got by with one-word answers when she could, or a nod or a shake when she could get away with those. She didn't ask me a single thing.'

'Rather rude,' said Kinsey. 'Did you ask her why she was acting that way?'

'After ten minutes of her being like that, I got fed up. I said, "What's the point of you coming to The Right Sort, then not making the slightest effort here?" And it was like she was looking at me for the first time all night. She said, "I am sorry, Monsieur Farrell. I went there because I was angry at a man who disappointed me. But today, we made up again." "Then why didn't you cancel the date?" I asked. "Because I did not want to disappoint you," she said. "We have our dinner, as agreed, but after I am going to see him, and he is all I can think about."'

'How did that make you feel?'

'I was put off, I won't lie,' said Farrell. 'I got angry. I said, "You can't go leading men on like that. It's not right." And she just shrugged, like I didn't matter at all. So I said, "What makes you think it's going to work with this fellow when he's treated you like this? Maybe he's still wrong for you. What's he got that I haven't got?" And she looked across the table with this smile that was full of contempt and said, "You are a small man, Monsieur Farrell, and this one? He is the tallest man I have ever seen."'

'Interesting,' said Kinsey as his partner shot him a glance. 'Did she say where she was meeting him?'

'She said he was working late. She was going to go and surprise him there. I guess he surprised her instead.'

'And where did you go?'

'I came back here. I called Mrs Bainbridge, which I shouldn't have done, but I was pretty hot about it.'

'Is there someone here who could verify that you came back home?'

'My mum's upstairs. She heard me. I could get her down if you like, but she turns in early.'

'I don't think that will be necessary at the moment,' said Kinsey, getting to his feet. 'We'll want you to come down to the Yard tomorrow afternoon to make a formal statement.'

'I'll do that,' said Farrell. 'Poor girl. I didn't like her a bit, but she didn't have that coming.'

'No, she didn't,' agreed Kinsey. 'Better luck with the next date.'

'Doubt it could get worse.'

'Maybe you need to find yourself a short girl,' suggested Kinsey.

'Yeah,' said Farrell. 'Too bad that Miss Sparks won't date her clients. You've seen her, haven't you?'

'I've seen her,' Kinsey said curtly. 'Good night, Mr Farrell.'

Ronnie, coming down from the excitement of the day, was in bed and asleep by nine, despite the temptation of the evening television programmes. Gwen, having had her fill of the new medium, read in the large sitting room across the hall while the sounds of the Saturday night schedule drifted in, the other women of the household exclaiming over it. There must have been a fencing exhibition to close the evening, for she heard the clinking of the foils. When the news came on at ten, she sat up, listening for any mention of the murder, but the story most concerning BBC Television did not get any coverage from their own people.

Bad publicity, she thought. They're hushing it up.

Millie poked her head in as the ladies passed by on their way up to their rooms.

'I've locked up, Mrs Bainbridge,' she said. 'Do you need anything before I turn in?'

'No thank you, Millie,' said Gwen. 'I'm going to read for a while. Goodnight.'

'Goodnight, ma'am.'

Gwen waited until the sounds upstairs subsided, then went to the telephone desk and sat on the small chair next to it. Despite her anticipation, she was startled when the telephone finally rang. She quickly picked up before it could ring again, glancing at her wristwatch. It was ten forty-five.

'Hello,' she said softly.

'It's me,' said Sally.

'What's going on? Where are you?'

'Still at Ally Pally,' he said. 'I think the police are going to be following me in some subtle fashion, so I am not going to be paying you any amorous visits, as much as it kills me to say that. I want to keep you out of this.'

'There's a problem with that,' said Gwen. 'If you're in trouble, then I'm going to be involved. Can you lose the tail?'

'Oh, easily,' he said with a laugh. 'But if I do, it will make me look worse. I will tread my old familiar daily paths, the ones I walked alone before you came along.'

'Now you're being dramatic,' she said. 'What can I do to help?'

'You're helping by talking to me,' he said. 'It soothes my troubled brow.'

'But what can I do that's of substance? Where can I look that the police won't bother looking?'

'We should let the redoubtable Mike Kinsey proceed unobstructed. Do you know, it was the first time he and I ever met? He had become a creature of almost mythological proportions in my imagination until today.'

'I imagine he felt the same way about you.'

'Probably, although I actually am a creature of mythological proportions.'

'Sally, who do you think did this?'

'I know it wasn't me,' he said. 'Which leaves three other people with keys to the theatre. I know all of them.'

'Of the three, who do you think is the most likely?'

'Honestly, none of them strikes me as the murdering type. Maybe Mike will learn otherwise.'

'Could someone else have picked the lock?'

'Possibly, but there were no scratch marks. The fingerprint boys have been all over the place. In any case, my prints are bound to be there, so that won't help me.'

'What can we do, Sally?'

'I'm being as co-operative as possible, but of course that's exactly what a clever murderer would do,' he said with a sigh. 'And we all know that I'm clever. Damn that Cambridge education.'

'Well, get yourself cleared as soon as possible,' said Gwen. 'I want you back now that we've taken the next step.'

'I leave things in the capable hands of Detective Inspector Kinsey,' he said. 'I will call you tomorrow afternoon if I'm still at liberty.'

'If I don't hear from you, I will summon the troops,' said Gwen. 'And by troops, I mean Iris.'

'With both of you on my side, how can I fail? Good night, dearest Gwendolyn.'

'Good night, darling.'

She hung up, then sat in the chair for a moment.

That's the first time I've called him that, she thought.

The theatre was off-limits as the police were still investigating it, although they had finished for the evening, leaving one unlucky constable to stand guard and make sure that no one disturbed it until the morning. Sally and Morton Stansbury finished moving the evening's set pieces into a rehearsal room, placing them against the walls to leave as much space as they possibly could. Legrenzi's puppet theatre stood at one end, its miniature proportions giving the room the illusion of a vast distance separating it from the two men.

'That thing gives me the jitters,' said Stansbury, glancing at it. 'All those little people inside, hanging on hooks, waiting to come to life.'

'They're just wood, cloth and strings,' said Sally.

'Yeah, well, this place is spooky enough without them hanging about. Think that girl's ghost will be wandering around now?'

'I don't believe in ghosts,' said Sally.

'That never stopped them,' said Stansbury. 'Tell me the truth. Do you think it was one of us?'

'It wasn't me,' said Sally. 'I don't believe you or the others killed her.'

'Then I suppose she walked into a locked theatre, strangled herself, then hid the garrotte after she died,' said Stansbury.

'Good luck convincing the Yard on that theory,' said Sally. 'Right, we're done here. I'll lock up. You and Fenton are on tomorrow.'

'Have a good day off,' said Stansbury. 'Let us know if you get nicked.'

'Will do,' said Sally.

He locked the rehearsal room door, then signed out at the night manager's office. He collected his coat and hat from his locker, walked out the front door, then stopped short.

Kinsey and Harvey were standing in front of the building, accompanied by a small squad of constables who looked at the size of the man standing before them with a mixture of apprehension and anticipation.

'Mr Danielli, we would like you to accompany us to Scotland Yard,' said Kinsey. 'We have some more questions.'

Not so subtle after all, thought Sally.

SEVEN

The Hero of Maida was on Edgware Road, just up from Crompton Street. It was one of the older pubs, she knew, named for some British officer who had defeated a portion of Napoleon's army somewhere in Italy and was rewarded with many honours, the one lasting the longest being memorialized as a pub, which had in turn given its name to the entire area.

It was a new one to Sparks. Back in her pub-crawling days, she had favoured the older establishments, delving into the stories of their origins, wondering what the areas surrounding them had looked like when the roads on the outer parts of London passed through farms and private hunting reserves, with just a solitary inn standing as a welcome way station before the final approach to the stink of the metropolis.

Now, with three-storey brick buildings lining the streets on both sides, the pubs still stood as way stations between work and home, refuges of whatever good cheer could be found in the bottom of a pint glass.

She had been living off the dwindling supply of wine from Archie's cellar for so long that she wondered if beer would taste differently now.

A sign depicting John Stuart, the Hero himself, hung in front of the pub, which took up the width of two buildings fronting the street. It couldn't have been the original sign. The red of his military coat was too bright, the white of his wig too clean to have withstood the thick London air for over a century. Nevertheless, she saluted him crisply before opening the door, wondering what reception awaited her.

The smell was right, was her first thought. The exposed wooden rafters dated from when they first cut down trees along Edgware Road to build the place, and their natural scent combined with a century's worth of smoke and beer went straight to the primordial part of her brain that craved alcohol.

The bar was mahogany, stained and pitted, and ran the length of the place. Behind it were shelves of bottles, many of them antique, possibly never opened but standing ever at the ready. The more frequently used casks held the centre, with a few smaller ones waiting hopefully down at the far end.

There was a moment of mutual hesitation when she entered as the regulars turned to size her up. She had dressed down for the occasion, for a change not on a mission to cadge free drinks in exchange for sparkling conversation. She didn't feel much like sparkling. She wore one of her shabbier Utility suits under an old cloth coat that predated the war, a duller and more discouraging shade of lipstick, and had added a pair of horn-rimmed glasses that she didn't need but which imposed one more barrier against those hopelessly hopeful men who thought she might be unattached, or the more predatory ones who thought even if she wasn't, that they could detach her.

Fortunately, she quickly spied Haight raising his hand from the rear of the place. He had secured a corner table, and she smiled in acknowledgment and walked past the regulars who one by one turned back to whatever they were drinking to make up for the week's disappointments. Two had a game of spillikins in progress toward the end of the bar, and a sad clump of men who had nothing better to do were gathered to watch it. She eased her way around them and greeted Haight, who rose to meet her.

'I didn't know if you'd show up,' he said, taking her coat and hanging it on a hook by the table. 'What are you drinking?'

'What's good here?' she asked.

'The stout,' he said. 'Would you like a pint or a half?'

'That depends. Is it a full-pint story or a half-pint story?'

'Full, if you can manage one.'

'I've drunk my weight in stout on a few occasions,' she said. 'Make it a pint.'

He signalled to the barmaid, who came over with a fixed smile that sagged slightly at the edges.

'Larry, you have a friend,' she said, winking at Sparks. 'That's good to see.'

'Bessie, this is Matilda,' said Haight. 'She's from Stepney.'

''Allo,' said Sparks, shifting immediately to Cockney. 'Nice to meetcher. Nice place you got 'ere.'

'We like it,' said Bessie.

'A pint of stout for her,' said Haight, 'and you might as well bring me another.'

'Right,' she said, turning with a practised shake of her hips.

Haight had been sitting sideways to keep an eye on the entrance, but now swung around to face Sparks, which meant that his back was to the rest of the room. The better to avoid being overheard, she thought approvingly.

Bessie returned with the two pints and placed them gently down on the table between them.

'Ta,' said Sparks, picking hers up. 'To absent friends.'

'To absent friends,' echoed Haight, clinking his glass against hers.

She took a sip of the dark brown liquid, which was creamy and somehow sweet and bitter simultaneously. Her palate almost cried out in welcome at the long overdue reunion.

Pace yourself, she reminded herself.

'So,' she said. 'Quite a day.'

'Horrible,' said Haight. 'The worst since the war. That poor girl.'

'Had you met her?'

'Just in a large group,' he said. 'There was a production meeting where everyone was introduced to everyone else. I don't know that I could pick her out of the pack in my memory. But that's not why I asked you here.'

'I know,' said Sparks. 'You wanted to talk about something that came up before we found her.'

'You found her?'

'Unfortunately. Sally was giving us the tour, and when we were exploring the theatre – well, it was me that saw her first. Lucky, in retrospect. I would have hated it to be one of the boys. Gwen hustled them out of there before they knew what was happening.'

'I hope they don't find out,' he said. 'Nice lads. They don't need that particular nightmare. Sorry you have it now.'

'It joins the vast collection,' said Sparks. 'Tell me what's concerning you.'

He took a sip, gathering his thoughts.

'I told you about my affinity for voices,' he began. 'I didn't mention this to you and Mrs Bainbridge when we first met, but I did fall in love once. And all I ever knew about her was her voice.

'I ran that radio post in Eynsford for over three years during the war. I maintained the radios, the transmitters, the tower, the generators, all of it. No one else knew their workings like I did, so I never took a single leave in all the time I was there. I had a workshop in the back where I had a bunk, and a bookcase full of technical manuals and magazines, and I watched as all the women in uniform came through and sent and received their secret messages in French and German.

'I had to listen in to make sure each of them was getting through clearly, going from frequency to frequency, making adjustments, turning dials a fraction of a degree. It was all crucial. Over time, I came to recognize the voices at the other ends. Some of them were our people, gone over to risk their lives. Some were from whatever local underground was operating. Heroes, all of them.'

'They certainly were,' said Sparks.

'There was one in particular. A woman. French, or English passing as French, I never knew, but she had a voice that melted my heart every time I heard it. I admit I lingered over those conversations when I should have been jumping over to others to make sure they were coming through as well. My world became centred on each five-minute segment of the irregular schedule she was on. She was part of a network in Paris that had access to top German officers and bureaucrats. Her handler at our end, I never knew her name, of course, was in her forties, spoke French like a native. I think she and the Parisienne became friends over the airwaves. The handler was all business when she arrived from London, but you could see her face light up when she made contact. It was the same simple exchange of code names each time. "Lisette, this is Albertine.

Are you there?" "Albertine, this is Lisette. It is good to hear your voice. Are you well?" "I am well." And then came the information.'

'I remember that handler,' said Sparks. 'I was at the radio at the next desk. I remember hearing those code names.'

'I know you were, Miss Sparks,' said Haight. 'That's why I asked you here tonight. Do you remember what happened next?'

'I remember what happened in the room,' said Sparks. 'But you must know more about it.'

'I do,' he said grimly. 'I can't forget it. Lisette's last transmission. When her handler asked, "Are you well?", instead of the routine response, Lisette started speaking rapidly. They had been betrayed. The Germans had broken the network, and they were rounding up all the operatives. She had delayed her escape so she could radio in on schedule to inform the Allies, but she had to flee.

'But before she could sign off, I heard the crashing of a door, and she began to scream. Then I heard a man shouting at her in German. Then a pair of gunshots. There was silence, then his voice came over the radio. "*Engländer, bist du da? Hast du dich verabschiedet? Wenn nicht, ist es jetzt zu spät.*"'

Englishman, are you there? Sparks thought. *Did you say goodbye? If not, it's too late.*

'She started to sob,' she remembered. 'The woman next to me. She wouldn't say what happened until the major took her in back. He came out later and asked me to get her back to London since I was finished with my transmission. I never knew what the full story was. That poor woman. And you, Mr Haight. That was the voice of the woman you loved and never met. I'm so sorry.'

'It was a fantasy,' he said. 'I know it. I knew it then. But I was alone in that place for so long, and it was the most intense . . .'

He broke off before completing the sentence and took a long swallow, draining half the glass in one go. Then he set it down and wiped his mouth with a napkin, dabbing a few tears in the process. She tried not to watch.

'Well, one more wartime horror, right?' he continued. 'Never learned her name, never found out who betrayed her or who killed her. No way I could possibly find out, but that German's voice – it's haunted me ever since then, Miss Sparks. I hear it when I close my eyes at night. I can't forget the sound of it, the scorn, the harshness of the tone.'

He looked directly at Sparks.

'And I heard it again today,' he said.

'What? Where?'

'When that devil puppet in the marionette theatre spoke. In German.'

'Legrenzi? The puppeteer? But he's French.'

'Is he, Miss Sparks? What do we know about him? What do we know about how he spent the war? There are plenty of Germans hiding in plain sight who should either be on trial for their crimes or already swinging from the gallows.'

'But you didn't recognize it when you first met?'

'His voice wasn't that voice. I didn't catch it until I heard it coming through the microphone when he ran through his act in rehearsal. The microphone that I set up for him. That was the voice I heard over the radio in Eynsford. I'd be willing to swear to it in court.'

'I don't know if they can convict a man just on a voice,' she said. 'I'm not saying you're wrong—'

'I'm not wrong.'

'But there must be more to it than that. Have you gone to the authorities with this?'

'What authorities would hear me out? I can't take this story to the police without clearance because of the Official Secrets Act, and if I go to my old command, they'll just brush it off. Oh, that's just Haight, who sat alone for too long out in his little outpost in the woods. I was only a technician, and I'm a civilian now. I have no connection with the higher-ups. I thought you might.'

'I don't,' she said. 'Not any more.'

'Isn't there someone you could call in an emergency?'

The Brigadier, she thought. Only he had cut off her only means of contact after that incident with the Polish woman.

There was Andrew, she thought. The operative she had run from her radio in Eynsford, with whom she had a disastrous affair after his return.

No. She had sworn him off for ever, and this wasn't something that she should bring to him.

Maybe . . .

'I have one possibility,' she said. 'I don't know if it will work out, and I can't promise that there will be any interest, but I'll give it a try.'

'I would appreciate it, Miss Sparks,' he said. 'I see you've finished. Another before you go?'

She looked at her empty glass with surprise. She hadn't even been aware that she had downed it so quickly. She looked over at the bar, where Bessie was drawing a pair of pints with practised ease.

One more couldn't hurt, she thought.

Or it could lead to another after that. Then another.

'I'd better quit while I'm ahead,' she said reluctantly.

'Let me get you a cab,' he said, getting to his feet and fetching her coat.

'I live close by,' she said. 'No need.'

'Then let me walk you home.'

'No need for that either,' she said. 'I can take care of myself.'

'No doubt,' he said. 'But it's late, and there's wolves prowling about. I would feel better if you'd let me get you home safe.'

'Well, all right, but only to keep the wolves at bay.'

He helped her on with her coat, paid the bill, then walked her past the envious glances of the other men there.

It was a short walk to the *Cecilia*, and they didn't speak during it. Sparks tried to remember the last time she had simply walked with a man. She had never done that with Archie, she realized with surprise. So much of their time was surreptitious, and even during the brief, wonderful period when they began appearing in public together, the means of travel were strictly automotive, usually with Benny driving. And before him, with Andrew – well, that affair never bothered with outdoor activities. Maybe if she had walked with him once in the daylight, she would have seen him for what he was.

Sally, she thought. They had walked together often after the war, their nearly two feet difference in height making her look like a child beside him. The last time was when . . .

She remembered now, and put it out of her mind.

She wondered when she would ever get to walk with a man without there being a murder involved.

Her mind, against her will, conjured up the memory of Duplessis, lying next to the mannequins, her eyes open and still. Who was she going to meet that night at Ally Pally after leaving Mr Farrell in the lurch? She had been so desperate to find the nearest man in the quickest time, or so she said, yet she had rejected Mr Farrell before even meeting him. So there had to be someone else, a better prospect.

She was surprised in hindsight that Duplessis had even come to The Right Sort. If she had overheard Mr Haight's plans to sign up with them, one would think her opportunistic little mind would have targeted him right away.

Maybe she had, Sparks thought with a sudden pang of apprehension. Was he one of the wolves?

She glanced over at him. He was looking ahead to where the canal was coming into view, the narrowboats bobbing gently in the dark.

'Which one?' he asked.

'That one to the right,' she said. 'The *Cecilia*.'

'You live there by yourself?'

Lie, she thought. Tell this man you barely know that you have roommates waiting up for you. Heavily armed roommates, peering through the windows as we speak. Just in case he's someone who preys upon lonely women.

And he was a man who worked with wire.

Only he had come to her with a story about someone else. Why would he ask for her help if this was an elaborate scheme to get her alone and vulnerable?

And Sparks was anything but vulnerable, she thought, one hand sliding into her bag to rest on the hilt of her knife.

'Yes,' she answered, a split-second after her mind had raced through all of that.

'Interesting,' he said.

'How so?'

'Here you are, in the profession of bringing people together, yet you choose a life of isolation.'

'It's what I need right now,' said Sparks. 'Long story, which I don't know you well enough to tell.'

'That's all right,' he said. 'But speaking as someone who has lived in isolation for so long, don't make a habit of it. It can turn you odd.'

'You're not odd,' she said.

'Nice of you to say, but we both know that's not entirely true,' he said. 'I'll watch you up the gangplank until you make it safe inside.'

'Thank you,' she said, trying to keep the relief she felt from flooding into her voice.

She kept her hand inside her bag, though, until she had crossed on to the fore well, then shifted her hand from the knife to her keys. She unlocked the door, then turned and waved.

'Good night, Mr Haight,' she called.

'Good night, Miss Sparks,' he replied. 'Thank you for taking me seriously.'

He turned and walked away.

I'm getting jumpy in my old age, she thought as she walked inside and locked the door behind her.

She turned on a single lamp, then changed into her night gown and brushed her teeth, all the while thinking back to the night he had talked about. She remembered it well . . .

The woman next to her cried out in anguish, then stared horror-stricken at her radio before slowly reaching out and flicking the switch that ended the transmission. She started to sob as the major hurried toward her as fast as he was able. He was a taciturn man in his thirties with a bad limp caused by a German bullet before his evacuation from Dunkirk, and winced with every step he took despite the cane that he used, but he quickly took the woman out of the room so that the others wouldn't be distracted from their tasks.

Sparks had finished hers, a brief communication with Andrew whose voice back then sent thrills of relief and desire through her every time she heard it. Relief because he had survived another week underground in occupied Poland, desire because of his last night in England with her. She didn't know what had happened with the woman next to her, but she surmised the worst, and couldn't help thinking how she would react if Andrew were to be taken or killed.

After ten minutes, the major came back in, looked around the room, then directly at Sparks.

'You're done?' he asked.

She nodded.

'Get her home,' he said.

He pulled a small tin canister from inside his coat pocket, opened it, and removed a small, white pill, then handed it to Sparks.

'Give her this,' he directed. 'It will help her sleep. Tonight, anyway.'

'Yes, sir,' said Sparks, taking it and wrapping it in a handkerchief.

She grabbed her coat and bag along with the woman's, then went outside.

The woman was leaning against the wall of the outbuilding, shivering violently.

'Please, put this on,' said Sparks, handing the woman her coat.

The woman didn't move, staring into space.

'Here, let me help you,' said Sparks.

She eased her away from the wall and draped the coat over her shoulders.

'It would be better if you put your arms through the sleeves, dear,' said Sparks, coaxing through first one, then the other. 'There, that's better. Let me button you up. I'm to take you home.'

'I don't want to go home,' said the other woman. 'There's nobody else there. I don't want to be alone.'

'I can stay with you,' offered Sparks. 'I don't have anyone else at my place either, so nobody will be the wiser.'

'I don't know you,' said the woman. 'I don't know your name.'

'I'm the woman in the chair next to you doing the same job. If you don't mind breaking a rule, I'll tell you my name, and you can tell me yours.'

'Theresa,' said the other woman. 'Theresa Cosslett.'

'I'm Iris Sparks, Theresa. Where do you live?'

'St Pancras. Near the New Church.'

'Come, then.'

The train from Eynsford took them into Blackfriars in a little over an hour. Cosslett didn't say one word for the entirety of the trip, choosing to stare out the window, crying quietly every now and then. The other passengers noticed with curiosity but looked away. It was wartime, and the sight of a crying woman was no longer cause for comment.

By the time they reached St Pancras, it was past eleven. Cosslett led her past the church to a narrow alley with a series of small shops, closed and shuttered. Above each were two storeys of flats, all dark from the blackout curtains. Cosslett stopped in front of a door by one of the shops, fumbling in her bag for her key. Sparks produced a small torch from her own bag and shone it into the bag, then on to the lock after Cosslett located the key.

They went in, then up one flight. The flat was small: a sitting room, a kitchenette, and a door leading to the bedroom. Cosslett flicked on a light, then collapsed on to a sofa, sobbing again.

Sparks sat next to her and held her until the tears subsided. She glanced around the room. There was a framed photograph of Cosslett with a man, the two of them smiling at each other in some park.

'Is that your husband?' she asked.

'Yes. His name is Tommy,' replied Cosslett. 'He's in the Navy. Somewhere in the Pacific. I haven't seen him for two years.'

'I'm sorry,' said Sparks. 'Could I get you something from the kitchen? We haven't eaten since tea.'

'I can't,' she said. 'I don't know if I can keep anything down right now. I'm too upset.'

Sparks pulled her handkerchief out and unwrapped the pill.

'The major said to give you this,' she said. 'To help you sleep.'

'Will you . . .' began Cosslett, then she hesitated.

'Go on,' urged Sparks.

'Will you stay in my room with me? Just be with me until I'm out. You don't have to spend the night.'

'Of course,' said Sparks. 'And I'll stay the night. Let's get you settled.'

She waited as Cosslett brushed her teeth and changed, then sprinkled some tooth powder on her index finger and scrubbed her own as well as she could. When she came into the bedroom, Cosslett was sitting on the edge of her bed, a glass of water in one hand, the pill in the other.

'If it would help to talk about it, I promise it won't go beyond this room,' said Sparks, sitting next to her.

The woman looked at the pill nestling in her hand, then at Sparks. She started to say something, then shook her head, placed the pill on her tongue, and drank.

'I don't even know what I just took,' she said.

She started to shiver again.

'Here we are,' said Sparks, pulling back the covers.

Cosslett sat there, not moving. Sparks took the other woman's feet and swung them under the covers, then helped her lie back. She removed her own shoes, stockings and dress, then turned off the lamp and slid in next to her. Even with the blankets over them, Cosslett continued to shiver. Sparks turned on her side and drew Cosslett's body to her own, sliding one arm under the woman's head to bring it against her own shoulder.

'I have you,' she whispered.

The shivering was joined by crying, but the pill began to take effect, and Cosslett's breathing deepened and became more regular. Before she drifted off, she raised her head towards Sparks.

'I think I loved her,' she whispered. 'Don't tell anyone.'

'I won't,' Sparks whispered back. She kissed the other woman on the forehead. 'Sleep now.'

Sparks lay in her own bed in the narrowboat, looking up into the darkness. If Theresa Cosslett still lived, if she still resided above that little shop in St Pancras, maybe she could find her again. Maybe she could verify Haight's identification of Legrenzi's voice.

And then what? She didn't know. Alert the appropriate authorities. She didn't know if the death of Lisette was anything anyone cared enough about to prosecute nowadays. Spies were executed during wartime. That was part of the game. It might have been Sparks's own fate had she not flunked parachute training.

But a voice had been stilled, and the man who stilled it should somehow be brought to justice, if there was such a thing left in the world.

And with that thought, her eyes finally closed.

They opened again on Sunday morning. She was not a believer, so the church bells sounding through the air served as no more than a distant alarm clock.

It was a rare Sunday morning without a hangover, one pint of stout being insufficient to do any continuing damage. She wondered how Sally was doing. She knew that Gwen would be off to church and not back until one. She wanted to be there when she returned, to get the latest on Sally.

She got out of bed, washed her face, then donned her exercise togs. She had been remiss with her morning routine, despite Gwen's occasional attempts to rope her into sparring as her partner continued with her self-defence lessons. She had begun again with Gerry Macaulay, Spark's old Army instructor, but the two of them had finally succeeded in finding him a bride, and the happy couple had emigrated to Southern Rhodesia. Gwen now had a private tutor who came to her house once a week.

Sparks, on the other hand, had fallen off. Her occasional half-hearted attempts had only discouraged her when she realized that she wasn't up to her peak self, and the efforts were hampered by her frequent hangovers.

But she wasn't hung-over this morning. Haight's conversation had given her purpose. No doubt it was one she had taken on as a distraction, but it was enough to get her to stop drinking after one pint, and that wasn't insignificant.

There wasn't enough space in the boat's saloon for her to do what she wanted, so she climbed a ladder to the Houdini hatch and pulled herself on to the roof, a towel draped over her shoulders.

The absentee owner had put a number of large planters and smaller flower pots up there, vaguely mumbling about vegetables and herbs when he showed it to her. Some shoots were emerging when she inspected them, but it was too early to tell what they were.

She placed the towel on the rim of a planter, did her stretches, then ran through the basic routine Macaulay had taught them, not wanting to tempt Fate with anything that might pull any muscles unused to the exercise. After about half an hour, she started throwing punches, keeping the force centred and focused on her imaginary opponents, feinting and ducking, making sure her footwork was fluid.

She sweated out whatever alcohol remained in her system by the end of the workout. She turned to grab her towel, then noticed for the first time that Casper, the elderly bearded man from the next boat down, was seated comfortably in a chair on his roof, placidly smoking his pipe while observing her. He saw her looking.

'Good morning,' he said, raising his pipe in salute.

'Good morning,' she said. 'Enjoy the show?'

'I did,' he replied. 'You look like you're going into battle. You know the war's over, don'tcha, luv?'

'I'm getting ready for the next one,' she said.

She climbed back down into the boat, stripped, then ran a wet washcloth over her body, shivering in the cool air. She dressed for walking, then went out to buy the Sunday papers and a hot roll with butter. She nibbled on the latter absently while she returned to the *Cecilia*, scanning the pages for any news of the murder.

Still none. Impressive, she thought. Or maybe Ally Pally was too far off the beaten path for Fleet Street to be bothered with what went on up there.

That bodes poorly for the prospects of television, she thought.

One feature caught her attention: A feature in the *Sunday Pictorial* promoting the upcoming *Across the Channel* show that must have been put together before Duplessis was killed. There was the full kick line from Casino de Paris, right legs extended toward the camera, costumed, smiling, and made up so identically that it took Iris a minute to locate their late client, third from the left.

Her last picture, thought Sparks.

Well, apart from the crime-scene photos.

She sat on a small bench on the fore well and read further.

Opposite the photo of the dancers was one of Freddie Oakes with a spectacularly dressed Claudine Rivette on his arm, a white fox stole draped over her shoulders, her blonde coiffure, somewhat messy but still brilliant, gleaming under the lights. The picture was taken at the Cocoanut Grove, and the underlying story by some 'Special Correspondent', probably dictated by Oakes himself, was effusive:

'Producer and bon vivant Freddie Oakes is a lucky boy indeed, squiring about his latest discovery, the scintillating chanteuse Claudine Rivette, this past Friday night. Although she resisted at first, she soon succumbed to the entreaties of an imploring crowd and sang a ditty or two with the house orchestra, leaving even those who spoke no French quite certain as to her intentions should they ever get close enough to risk getting bitten by that fox guarding the treasures within. It's a wonder that Paris is still standing when a bombshell like that was in its midst.

"'She's a marvel,'" enthused Freddie. "I confess I was smitten the moment I saw her, before she had even sung a single word. I look forward to sharing her talents with the London television audience this Thursday!"

'That's right, Londoners! You have four days to hie thee to ye olde television shoppe and purchase one of these modern miracles. It will be worth it for her alone.

"'She was also a heroine of the Resistance,'" Freddie confided. "I'm not at liberty to reveal more, but someday the story will be told as to all she did to help our cause in the blackest days of the Occupation. But now she is free, and I expect her to take London by storm.'"

Rubbish, thought Sparks. Everyone in France claimed to be a hero of the Resistance now that the war was over. If that were the case, every Nazi occupying the place would have been strangled in their sleep before Dunkirk.

She looked at her watch. It was still early enough that she could travel to St Pancras and see if Theresa Cosslett still lived there.

She decided to walk, not wanting to waste her meagre funds on something this frivolous. Besides, her morning workout had invigorated her.

It was a relatively straight route from Little Venice to St Pancras, mostly along Marylebone Road. She allowed herself a brief shiver as she passed by the spot where Gwen had been waylaid and kidnapped the previous summer, but the street was only a street, so she shook it off and carried on.

When she reached the alley, the shops were closed for Sunday. She looked at them, then closed her eyes, retrieving the memory of that night. It was the middle one, she thought. She went inside the door leading to the flats upstairs and examined the letter-boxes.

'T.&T. Cosslett' read the first one.

Right. Now to see if she was at home instead of church. And Sparks would need a cover story in case Mr Cosslett answered. She dug through her bag and found a flyer for some charity some missionary sort had handed her the other day. That would do.

She held it in her hand as she climbed the steps to the flat, composed herself and put a properly proselytizing expression on, then rang the bell.

She heard footsteps approaching, then the door opened and Theresa Cosslett stood there, staring at Sparks, a look of terror spreading across her face.

'No!' she said. 'I'm not coming back! I told them that.'

'I'm not with them any more, either,' said Sparks, shoving the flyer back into her bag. 'I came to see you about something else. Hello, Theresa. May we talk?'

'You're not with them?' she asked.

'I left two years ago.'

'Then why are you here?'

'Please, Theresa. I can't talk to you out here. Let me come in.'

Reluctantly, Cosslett stood back from the door, allowing Sparks entry.

Not much had changed since that other night so many years before. A small table with the remainder of breakfast was over by the window overlooking the alley. That was new, thought Sparks. And it was set for one.

'Is Mr Cosslett about?' she asked. 'I don't want to disturb him.'

'Is he about?' repeated Cosslett with a wild laugh. 'He's about four hundred miles away. He came home from the Navy after three years at war, then turned around a week later and signed up on a freighter. I see him every few months. This isn't one of them, so your timing is excellent.'

'I'm sorry,' said Sparks.

'I'm not. Seeing him every few months is about as much of him as I can stand.'

'Ah.'

'I never thought I'd see you again,' said Cosslett, sitting at the table. 'Not after that night.'

'That night is why I'm here,' said Sparks, sitting on the sofa. 'You didn't come back to Eynsford after that.'

'No. I was assigned to one operation, and that was . . . well, it was blown,' said Cosslett. 'Wiped out. All of them. And after that – they didn't trust me with anything else.'

'Why not?'

'I had to go in the next day,' she said. 'To be debriefed, they told me. But it wasn't in some office with a stenographer taking down notes. It was down in some dank, cellar room, with two men I didn't know asking me questions, going over every conversation I ever had with Lisette, picking apart each word, looking for any sign of betrayal. Then they asked me about what I did when I went home, if I went out, if I had . . .'

She took a deep breath.

'If I had taken any lovers since my husband had gone off to war,' she continued. 'And I had, you see, but I didn't want to tell them. Only they knew, somehow. And they made me talk about them, over and over. Then they went back to the first questions and repeated them, louder and louder, until they were shouting them in my ears. It was clear that they thought I had betrayed her. As if I ever could betray my beautiful Lisette.'

'How did you know what she looked like?' asked Sparks. 'That she was beautiful, I mean?'

'She had to be,' Cosslett answered. 'Nothing else could have matched that voice. But then that Nazi killed her, and it was as if I saw it happening right in front of me. And when those men interrogated me like I was a traitor in that dark room, I kept seeing her, looking at me as she was gunned down like an animal, and I started to scream, scream obscenities I didn't even know I knew.

'Then finally they stopped and let me go home. But the next day, I came in and it happened all over again.'

'Did you ever learn what happened to her? To Lisette?'

'No,' said Cosslett. 'I don't know if it was ever investigated after Paris was freed. So many terrible wrongs to right, it would only be natural for some to escape their days of reckoning. Who was even left to ask about her? Her network was wiped out, or disappeared. I never even knew her actual name. It didn't matter. She was Lisette. My own Lisette.'

'I'm sorry,' said Sparks.

'You were so kind to me that night,' said Cosslett. 'I never thanked you. I thought we might encounter each other again, but I wasn't allowed back. My security clearances were revoked. I ended up in a typing pool, handling only the most routine matters, and they kept an eye on me for the rest of my service.'

'What about after you got out?'

'I've been here,' she said simply.

'Do you work?'

'I can't any more,' she said haltingly. 'I'm not – I'm not able to keep at anything for long periods of time.'

'So when you say you've been here—' Sparks began.

'I've been in here,' said Cosslett. 'By myself.'

'No one else in your life? No friends or family?'

'No. Not any more. They gave up on me when I . . . look, do you remember giving me that pill that the major gave you that night?'

'Yes.'

'It was the only thing that helped me,' she said. 'The only thing that let me stop hearing her scream when I closed my eyes. After those interrogations, it only got worse. And I didn't even know what it was that I took. So I decided to find out.'

'What did you do?' asked Sparks, dreading the answer.

'I started going to Blackfriars,' she said. 'I went every night, waiting for the trains from Eynsford to come in. I saw the women leave separately like they were supposed to. And finally, I saw the major.'

'He had to have known about your security clearance by that point.'

'He did, but that wasn't what I saw him about. I asked him for another one of those pills. No, I begged him, both for the pill and his supplier. I threatened all manner of consequences if he wouldn't help me. The one that ended up convincing him to help me was that I would throw myself off the bridge right then and there, and that with his limp, there was no way he could stop me. He gave me one on the spot. I slept that night. And that was the beginning of my addiction.'

'You should get help,' said Sparks. 'I can help you.'

'I've tried quitting,' said Cosslett. 'But when I stop taking them, I hear that Nazi's voice, only now he's coming for me.'

'Would you recognize it if you heard it again?'
'What are you talking about?'
'Answer the question.'
'Yes,' said Cosslett. 'Why?'
'Do you remember the man who ran the station at Eynsford?'
'The little fellow who knew everything about radios? Of course.'
'I encountered him recently,' said Sparks, and she summed up what Haight had told her. By the time she was done, Cosslett was shaking.
'He's here,' she whispered. 'In London.'
'If it's him,' said Sparks. 'That's why I came to you.'
'Good,' said Cosslett. 'How are we going to kill him?'

EIGHT

'Kill him?' exclaimed Sparks. 'Who said anything about killing him?'
'Isn't that why you came to me?' asked Cosslett.
'Good Lord, no! I came because I wanted to get another witness to identify his voice.'
'Yes, clearly. But what then? Do you really believe the authorities, whoever they might be, would act based on that?'
'They could investigate further if we can point them in the right direction,' said Sparks.
'They'll do nothing,' said Cosslett, looking at her with a contemptuous smile. 'You don't even believe it yourself. It's been two years since the war ended, more since Lisette was murdered. This isn't a matter for Nuremburg. Everyone's moved on. So, if we have found him, I propose we take matters into our own hands.'
'But murder?'
'Call it an execution. Call it tit for tat. Call it justice.'
'Have you ever killed anyone?' asked Sparks.
'No,' said Cosslett. 'But lots of people have, haven't they? Should be easy enough to manage.'
'Theresa, listen to me,' said Sparks, trying to suppress the desperation that was creeping into her voice. 'You've been living alone and dwelling upon this for too long.'

Oh, dear, she thought. I've just described my own life.

'I know something about that,' she continued. 'Several months ago, the man I loved was shot down in front of me, and all I wanted after that was vengeance. I went looking for the man who shot him.'

'You knew who it was?'

'Not at first,' admitted Sparks, 'but I have a knack for finding out things when I need to. I was cold, furious, and focused like I've never been at any other time in my life. I put myself at risk. Worse, I put my best friend, who I had convinced to help me, at risk as well.'

'Did you find the man?' asked Cosslett.

'I found him. And when I did, I was ready to kill him.'

'But you didn't.'

'No,' said Sparks.

'Why not?'

'My friend stopped me. And I cannot tell you how grateful I am to her for doing it. It would have been murder on my part, and there would have been no coming back from that. I would have destroyed my own life by avenging my lover's. And he wouldn't have wanted that for me.'

'What happened to the killer?'

'He committed suicide rather than face the legal consequences,' said Sparks.

'So you didn't save him, either,' commented Cosslett thoughtfully. 'Well, my dear, that's a lovely little story. I'm beginning to think I've been mistaken about you. Maybe you're actually one of those religious do-gooders, come to pull me away from my sins, waiting for the right moment to produce a flyer from your bag and start waving it about.'

Sparks thought guiltily about the flyer in her bag that she was going to use for her cover.

'I'm an atheist, so that would be hypocritical in the extreme,' she said. 'But I do hold the old-fashioned belief that killing people is wrong.'

'Even when they're Nazis?'

'If they deserve execution, let the authorities be the ones to do it. Not us.'

Cosslett chewed on her lip, thinking it over.

'How do you propose I accomplish this?' she asked. 'Walk up to him outside his hotel and ask him to speak to me in German?'

'That part is going to be tricky,' Sparks admitted. 'We have to get you into Ally Pally at the moment he's doing his routine. It's important that you hear him through a microphone, because that's how you heard him over the radio that night.'

'How are you going to manage that?'

'I'll speak to our radio friend about it,' said Sparks. 'It may take a day or two to arrange. How shall I contact you?'

'I don't have a telephone,' said Cosslett. 'Do you?'

'Here is my number at my office,' said Sparks, writing it down. 'Call me tomorrow afternoon. And please don't go rogue on your own, Theresa. I don't want you to end up with the authorities, either. Will you promise me that?'

Cosslett glanced out the window.

'It will be nice to know that he's no longer out there in the world somewhere,' she said. 'I can wait a few more days for that to happen.'

'Good,' said Sparks.

The house was empty when Gwen returned after leaving Ronnie with his grandparents. Her ladies had the day off, so when she heard her telephone ringing as she unlocked her door, it was all she could do to keep from knocking over every piece of furniture on the way to answering it.

Don't run in the house, Gwen, she admonished herself sternly as she grabbed the handset.

'Bainbridge residence,' she said.

'It's me,' said Sally.

'Oh, thank God. Are you all right?'

'For the moment,' he said wearily. 'They took me in last night, then it was non-stop questioning, a break for tea around three a.m., then more questioning.'

'Oh, Sally. Was it Mike?'

'Himself, and his partner. I suspect our chances of becoming friends after this have been greatly reduced. The more I couldn't tell them, the worse it got. It's amazing how the phrase, "But Detective, I swear I don't know anything about any of this", no matter how heartfelt the delivery, makes one seem as guilty as sin.'

'But they let you go.'

'Around nine thirty this morning. I suspect they still don't think they can charge me for it, but they have me under surveillance and it wouldn't surprise me to learn that my telephone is tapped. Say hello to the police, Gwen.'

'Hello to the police, Gwen,' she replied.

'I don't know what they think they're doing, honestly. They know everything about me that it's possible to know, and suspect the rest, including my wartime adventures. I'm assuming that confidential calls are going up and down the secret corridors. Anyhow, I called an hour ago, but you must have been at church. I checked in with Ally Pally, and received the additional lovely news that I have been suspended from my job until this is all cleared up. I can't blame them. They don't want all our guests rehearsing under the watchful eye of someone suspected of garrotting one of their colleagues.'

'What are you going to do?'

'Until I pick up some day work, I will take advantage of the extra free time by investing in my creative process.'

'Oh, good. I was worried you were going to sit around and mope.'

'That actually is my creative process.'

'I'm waiting for Iris to check in. We'll come over and put our heads together.'

'Mine will only make a resounding, hollow boom at this point.'

'Nevertheless, expect a visit.'

'I don't want you involved in this, Gwen.'

'I choose to override your wishes, then,' she said. 'That's the price you pay for having me as your girlfriend.'

The walk back to Maida Vale seemed longer than the walk from it as Iris wrestled with her thoughts. The biggest problem, as she saw it, was not the plan to get Cosslett into Ally Pally. It was how she was going to manage all of it without telling Gwen.

Gwen knew about some of Iris's clandestine wartime activities as their long-term ramifications came back to intrude on their lives, but the general rule was that Iris would not violate the terms of the Official Secrets Act, clinging to the vestiges of a loyalty to her former employers that she felt more and more they didn't deserve.

It was the timing of this matter that concerned her. Her principal concern should have been Sally. No, her principal concern was Sally, no doubt about it, but she didn't see what she could do to help him at the moment.

So she was free to pursue the puppeteer, and she realized that the prospect had energized her, to the point that she had managed to stay fairly sober in a pub on a Saturday night and not top off her sole pint with an extended nightcap back at the *Cecilia*.

These were accomplishments. It worried her that it took a murder investigation to impose relative sobriety on her life. That would not make for a regularly reliable source of reinforcement, unfortunately, but it had shaken her out of her months-long doldrums, so much so that she found herself whistling as she walked.

Completely inappropriate, Sparks, she thought, but nevertheless it cheered her up, and by the time she arrived at Gwen's house, she was verging on something approaching a good mood.

Gwen herself answered the door when she got there.

'Oh, good, you're here,' she said, holding the door for Iris. 'I have a question I've been wanting to ask you.'

'What's that?' asked Iris as she came in.

'What exactly is garrotting?'

'Goodness. What must the sermon have been this morning to suggest that as a topic?'

'I know it's a way of killing someone,' said Gwen. 'But I don't know exactly what it is. Sally has used the word twice already.'

'Are you assuming I have some expertise in the technique?'

'No, of course not,' said Gwen hastily. 'But you read mysteries and spy novels, and I don't. I imagine you've come across it.'

'It's strangulation with a piece of wire,' said Iris. 'Usually with some form of handle at each end.'

'Oh, dear,' said Gwen, turning pale.

'Don't faint on me now,' said Iris. 'You asked.'

'And Sally recognized the marks right away.'

'Yes.'

'As did you.'

'Yes,' said Iris reluctantly.

'I'm sure Sally didn't kill Mademoiselle Duplessis,' said Gwen. 'But lurking in the back of my mind is that he has killed before, which means that he knows how. And of course, that's true of all our soldiers, but how horrible is it to have that knowledge of yourself? And there is something very different about killing in combat versus whatever Sally did. Whoever launched the mortar shell that killed Ronnie never saw him die. Never saw his face. Women are lucky to have been spared that.'

'Yes,' said Iris.

Something in her tone caused Gwen to look at her sharply.

'Please don't,' said Iris, holding up a finger in warning. 'Not ever.'

'All right,' said Gwen, wondering and not wanting to wonder any further. 'Wire, you said. Any particular sort of wire?'

'Strong enough to do the job without breaking,' said Iris. 'I don't know enough about it to give you a minimum gauge. Why?'

'I was thinking that the most likely suspects for her death would be the others from Paris,' said Gwen. 'She wasn't here long enough to make that sort of enemy.'

'Unless we consider Mr Farrell.'

'No, not him,' said Gwen decidedly. 'He's a difficult man, but not a killer. So either she ran into someone at Ally Pally who murdered her at random, or someone had a reason and took advantage of the location. And had access to wire.'

'Back to the wire again.'

'Yes,' said Gwen. 'What do you think of Legrenzi as a possibility?'

'Legrenzi? The puppeteer?' exclaimed Iris, almost stammering in surprise. 'He had something to do with wire?'

'That Satanic German puppet used wire rather than strings,' said Gwen. 'I was with the boys when he showed it to them. He must keep a coil of it somewhere to repair it. Probably in that miniature theatre of his.'

'If it had to do with something that happened in Paris, why would he wait until now to kill her?' asked Iris.

'I don't know yet. I don't know how he got her into the theatre, or what she did after she left her date with Mr Farrell.'

Should I tell her about Haight and Cosslett? thought Iris. If I don't, we may end up working at cross-purposes.

There's loyalty to the Crown, and loyalty to one's friends.

'Gwen, if I ask you to keep something secret . . .' she began, then she shook her head. 'No, if I ask you to swear on all that you hold holy to keep something secret, will you do it?'

'Of course,' said Gwen without hesitation.

'I am only going to tell you the bare minimum,' said Iris. 'I was given information from someone last night concerning Legrenzi.'

'That he might have killed Duplessis?'

'No,' said Iris. 'About something else. Something that happened during the war.'

'Oh,' said Gwen. 'Well, come into the kitchen, then. I have a feeling that we're both going to need some sustenance for this.'

Iris sat at the kitchen table while Gwen put the kettle on, then pulled some cold chicken from the refrigerator.

'I'm making tea, but if you'd like anything stronger, let me know,' she said as she sliced the chicken.

'Tea would be fine,' said Iris.

The kettle whistled, and Gwen poured its contents into the teapot, then brought everything over and sat down opposite Iris.

'Do you need me to take an oath of some sort?' she asked as she served. 'Is it a blood ceremony?'

'No, your word is sufficient,' said Iris. 'More than sufficient. It always has been, it's just that I've been caught up in my own inability to trust anyone fully.'

'Tell me only what you need to tell me,' said Gwen. 'I won't pry.'

'There was a portion of the war where I was running agents,' said Iris. 'You know about one of them, so I'm sure you had your suspicions about how our relationship started.'

'Andrew,' said Gwen.

'Yes. So this was done primarily through radio contact. This was at a location I can't reveal, and there were others there besides me, including a man who maintained everything. And you've met him as well.'

'Mr Haight?'

'Yes. Which is why I kicked you out of our interview the other day. I had to reassure him that his secret was safe with me.'

'Only now you've revealed it. I'm sorry.'

'No, don't be. I also told him that you were the most trustworthy person I knew, in case I let anything slip.'

Gwen didn't respond other than to reach across the table and grasp Iris's hand for a moment.

'There was a woman who sat next to me,' began Iris.

She summarized the story of Lisette and Theresa. Gwen sat, completely caught up in it, forgetting to sip her tea which had cooled by the time Iris was done.

'That poor woman,' said Gwen. 'And now she's locked herself away from the world and become an addict. She's taken both of our worst experiences and combined them. We should get her to Dr Milford if we can.'

'I agree,' said Iris.

'I wonder how this ties in with the murder,' said Gwen. 'Perhaps Mademoiselle Duplessis knew Legrenzi betrayed Lisette?'

'Maybe,' said Iris. 'But why would he wait until now to kill her if so?'

'I don't know,' said Gwen.

'One other thing, and I don't know what this has to do with anything, but I came in on the tail end of a row between him and Claudine Rivette.'

'They know each other from working together in the Thirties,' said Gwen. 'I'm guessing there was some animosity arising from that experience.'

'It certainly seemed that way. Well, I don't know how that fits in with anything else, so let's stick with the plan for now.'

'Which is to bring this woman in to listen to him?'

'Yes,' said Iris. 'I'm going to speak to Mr Haight about it. It would be nice if we could speak to the other dancers, find out what they knew about her. But that's Mike's territory, and I don't want to step on his toes if I can avoid it.'

'He seems dead set on Sally at the moment. I'm going over there this afternoon. Would you care to join us?'

'Wouldn't I be getting in the way?'

'Not for this,' said Gwen.

She picked up a large piece of paper from the kitchen counter. On it, she had sketched the outlines of Alexandra Palace.

'I want to ask Sally about how she got in Friday night,' said Gwen. 'I can't exactly go back there on my own and wander about.'

'Again, this sounds like Mike's territory.'

'I know. But maybe I'll come up with an angle he hasn't.'

She picked up the plates, washed them and left them in the rack to dry. Iris watched her with amusement.

'You've served me lunch in the kitchen and washed up afterwards,' she observed. 'Had you ever done that for anyone before you bought this place?'

'Ronnie and I raided the larder for many late-night snacks back before he signed up,' said Gwen. 'And God knows I did it on my own when I was pregnant and ravenous. But outside of that, no. I am adding to my household skills daily. I'm even cooking a bit now.'

She grabbed the sketch, folded it neatly and put it in her bag.

'Let's go,' she said.

* * *

Iris spotted the detectives watching the entrance to Sally's building as they came up.

'Should we avoid them?' she asked. 'I know the back entrance.'

'They won't be looking for us,' said Gwen. 'And if they are, who cares? We're not suspects.'

They climbed the stairs to Sally's flat. He answered the door looking unusually dishevelled, his braces pulled up over a shirt that was unbuttoned halfway down, his hair hastily and inexpertly combed. He looked at them blearily.

'Sorry, I was grabbing a kip,' he said. 'Didn't get much sleep last night. Do come in.'

He held the door for them, then pointed to the old green sofa.

'You take that,' he said. 'If I sit on it, I'll nod off inside a minute. Tea?'

'No, thank you,' said Gwen. 'But first . . .'

She stepped forward and hugged him tightly. He closed his eyes, returning the embrace, then opened them to see Iris looking at them with a sad smile.

'Your turn,' he said to her, releasing Gwen.

'I doubt that I can do it as well,' said Iris, coming over to him.

'I am accepting all comfort from all quarters right now,' he said.

Iris embraced him, pressing her cheek into his chest.

'So glad you're not in the nick, mate,' she whispered.

'Not yet,' he said. 'I hear they're expanding one of the cells so I'll fit more easily. Did you catch sight of my newest fans outside?'

'They weren't the most surreptitious sweeneys I've ever seen,' said Iris as she released him. 'But I guess that's the point, isn't it?'

'Have you eaten?' asked Gwen with concern.

'Living on my stored reserves at the moment,' he said. 'I'll make a run for provisions in the morning, give the police a chance to watch me shop and analyse my dietary choices for signs of recent homicidal activity. Now, sit. Discourse. Tell me my fortune.'

'You will meet a tall dark stranger,' Iris intoned.

'That's every morning when I look in the mirror,' he said. 'Tell me something I don't know.'

'I want to ask you about something you do know,' said Gwen, pulling the sketch from her bag and unfolding it.

'That's Ally Pally,' he said, looking at it.

'Correct,' she said. 'Now, you took us through the central entrance under the scaffolding. There is another main entrance by the east tower. And we passed a loading ramp by the west end as I recall.'

'Right,' said Sally. 'That's for the scenery shops.'

'How many other entrances are there?'

'Quite a few,' he said. 'Going all the way around.'

'How many of them are unlocked?'

'Apart from the two main entrances, none of them, or at least that's how it's supposed to be.'

'And the main entrances have someone staffing them at all times?'

'Up until midnight.'

'So if Mademoiselle Duplessis came through one of them on Friday night, someone should have seen her,' said Iris.

'Right. Only neither of the men at the doors did, according to your estimable ex,' said Sally.

'Which means either another door was left unlocked, or someone let her in,' said Gwen. 'I suppose you have keys to all the doors.'

He walked over to a credenza and plucked a key ring from on top.

'They want me to turn them in tomorrow,' he said.

'Who else has keys to the outside doors?' asked Gwen.

'Lots of people,' he said. 'The cleaners, building maintenance, fire brigade staff. And me, Suspect Number One.'

'How could she have got there at night?' wondered Gwen. 'A taxi from the railway station would have been noticed.'

'There is a special bus that runs from Broadcasting House up to Ally Pally and back every half-hour,' he said. 'It's how most of us travel. Some of the bigwigs are allotted enough petrol to drive, lucky sods.'

'How does the scenery shop know when someone's at their door?' asked Iris.

'There's a bell. Someone comes out.'

'But there's no guard at that door?'

'No.'

'Was the scenery shop open on Friday night?'

'No. They usually get done what they need to before airtime. One usually remains at the studios for emergency repairs, but the shop itself is closed down at five.'

'So she was meeting someone, and it was arranged in advance,' said Gwen. 'Or she came with someone who had those keys.'

'And I was working Friday, so that rules me out for the second possibility,' said Sally. 'I am very much in the running for the first, unfortunately.'

'When did she rehearse on Friday?'

'They had an initial try-out of the studio, just to see how their routines fit in the space. That was early afternoon, before we set up for the evening programmes.'

'And after that?'

'They all took the bus back. They're staying at the Langham across from Broadcasting House.'

'Then she goes off to her date with Mr Farrell,' mused Gwen. 'And then somehow gets back to Ally Pally in time to get garrotted in a locked theatre without being seen by anyone.'

'Were there many people working near the theatre on Friday night?' asked Iris.

'Apart from stage crew, no,' said Sally. 'Any office types would have left by five.'

'What about other entrances to the theatre?'

'The original entrances for the audiences have been sealed off from the inside. There's another stage door at the other end, but it was locked and uses the same key, so only the four of us have access.'

'What about from underneath?' asked Iris. 'There's old stage machinery. There must be trapdoors, passages to the orchestra pit, things like that.'

'Sealed up long ago for safety reasons,' said Sally.

'Friday night's programmes,' said Gwen. 'A cooking show, *Kaleidoscope* and *Serenade in Sepia*.'

'You were watching.'

'It was the debut of our new Baird. Could you go over the timing of where you were?'

'The cooking show went first because there were a lot of electrical hook-ups needed for the range and the oven,' said Sally. 'We had to get that pre-set in Studio B. We did that around six. Then we pulled all of the flats and pieces needed for *Kaleidoscope* and pre-set them in Studio A, leaving some outside B. When *Kaleidoscope* started, we pulled the kitchen set into the hall, set up the rest of the *Kaleidoscope* sets in B, then took the kitchen set back to the theatre and started moving the *Sepia* sets to the hallways outside Studio A. Then we pre-set as much as we could while *Kaleidoscope* was finishing up.'

'Sounds like everything was non-stop,' commented Gwen.

'For the most part,' said Sally.

'Did you ever leave the theatre door unlocked, just for the convenience?'

'No,' said Sally. 'We are quite fanatical about that. Once you do something unsafe for convenience's sake, it becomes a slippery slope towards more serious mistakes.'

'And you were working with others?'

'Friday was with Wally Fenton, the assistant stage manager, and two stage hands. And yes, there were moments when I was out of sight of all three of them, so it's not a complete alibi.'

'And the same was true for Fenton,' said Gwen.

'Probably. But neither of us was out of sight for more than a minute or two.'

'How long does it take to garrotte someone?' asked Gwen, trying very hard to make the question sound matter-of-fact.

Sally looked at her for a moment. She returned the look as steadily as she could, but her heart was racing.

'Not long,' he said tersely. 'Done correctly, loss of consciousness happens fairly quickly. Death takes more time, depending on how the garrotte is placed and how strong the killer is.'

She glanced down at his hands before she could stop herself. They were clenched.

'I'm sorry to ask you that,' she said. 'We're trying to help.'

'I know, I know,' he said wearily. 'I'm just tired of being interrogated, even if it's by my friends. I don't know how much you can do given the circumstances.'

'Actually, we're on to a possibility,' said Iris.

'You are? Who?'

'Legrenzi.'

She detailed what they knew. By the end, he was shaking his head.

'It sounds unlikely,' he said. 'But by all means, give it a go. You've pulled off miracles before.'

'We can't set it up until Tuesday at the earliest,' said Iris. 'Stay optimistic, Sally. You'll come out of this fine.'

'Even if I come out of this, I doubt I'll be fine,' he said. 'But that's life, isn't it? One day it's strawberries and cream, the next it's soggy peas. Now, if we're done, I'd like to sleep for about thirty-six hours straight.'

'If you wake up in the middle, call me,' said Gwen. 'Let me know how you are.'

She rose and came over to kiss him. He accepted it without enthusiasm. Iris gave him a quick hug, then the two of them left his flat. Gwen looked over her shoulder to see if he was watching them as far as the stairwell, but he had already closed the door.

'You could have asked me to go on and leave you with him,' said Iris quietly. 'That would have been all right.'

'He didn't want me to stay,' said Gwen. 'Let's go.'

NINE

The two of them still had clients and careers and a business to run, so they showed up at The Right Sort on Monday morning and put some effort into matchmaking. Yet recent events kept intruding into their conversations.

'We should find out what family Mademoiselle Duplessis had,' said Gwen gloomily. 'I feel we should return her fee.'

'She did go on one date,' Iris pointed out. 'Our services were utilized. Work was done. We can't hold ourselves responsible for every terrible thing that happens to our clients.'

'You can be very calculating sometimes,' grumbled Gwen.

'We are spending time and effort investigating her murder, and no one is paying us for that,' said Iris.

'We're doing it to help Sally.'

'I was doing it to help Mr Haight and Mrs Cosslett before you brought Sally into it. No one is reimbursing me for the time I've put in.'

'Except for that pint of stout.'

'Which I restricted to just the one, I'll have you know. And I only had one glass of wine with dinner last night.'

'And after dinner?'

'Only one more before I went out. Virtually sober compared to the last four months. I am focused on our mission. Which reminds me, I need to call Mr Haight. Pass me the telephone, please.'

She rang him up at home. He answered after the third ring, sounding groggy.

'It's Iris Sparks,' she said. 'I found her. The woman at the next desk.'

'You did?' he exclaimed. 'That was quick work.'

'Here's the problem. She doesn't strike me as the most reliable witness, but she would like very much to hear Legrenzi's voice. Could you come up with a credible reason for him to run through his performance tomorrow so she can hear him through a speaker?'

'Of course,' said Haight. 'There's time available in Studio A in the morning. I'll come up with a reason for him to be there. I can have you in the control booth while he's rehearsing.'

'Perfect,' said Iris. 'Let us know what time to be there.'

'Will do, Miss Sparks. And thank you for taking me seriously.'

'Not at all, Mr Haight.'

She hung up, then stared at her desk calendar. Four days since they met Duplessis. Three since she died.

'We could at least send a condolence card,' she said.

'We'll have to ask someone where to send it,' said Gwen. 'We don't know her parents' address in France. And honestly, for them to receive a card from a marriage bureau after their daughter's life has ended like this – I don't know if I would find it comforting or even more upsetting, given all the questions it would raise that can't be answered.'

'Maybe we could send one to her troupe,' suggested Iris. 'They might be the closest thing she has to a family right now.'

'That's a good idea,' said Gwen. 'I keep thinking that we've been in business for just over a year now, and that's the third client we've seen murdered.'

'Let's not put that in our adverts,' said Iris.

Mid-morning, the intercom buzzed.

'Yes, Mrs Billington?' answered Iris.

'There's a gentleman here who wants to speak to the two of you, but he won't say what it's about.'

'Not looking for a bride?'

'He's got a ring already, so apparently not.'

'Did he give his name at least?'

'Avery Conley. He says you've met.'

Iris covered the mouthpiece with her hand.

'Sally's manager is here,' she whispered to Gwen.

'Interesting,' said Gwen. 'Let's find out what he wants.'

'Send him over, please,' said Iris to Mrs Billington.

The suit was herringbone this time, a lovingly maintained relic from before the war. His face seemed to have aged considerably since Saturday, thought Sparks. Seeing a murdered woman can have that effect on some people.

She wondered how her appearance had changed after so many.

'Welcome to The Right Sort Marriage Bureau, Mr Conley,' she said. 'You remember my partner, Mrs Bainbridge.'

'Of course,' he said. 'We met in the cafeteria. How do you do?'

'How do you do?' returned Mrs Bainbridge. 'Please sit. What brings you here this morning?'

'This is somewhat irregular,' he said, sitting across from them. 'I should start by saying the BBC doesn't know what I'm doing here.'

'At the moment, neither do we,' said Sparks. 'I take it you're not in the market for a wife.'

'Got one, thanks,' he said. 'I'm fairly certain she wouldn't approve of me expanding the harem.'

'What, then?'

'As I told you the other day, I am not unaware of your experience in pursuing matters that are complicated and private.'

'Mostly private,' said Mrs Bainbridge. 'We've occasionally made the newspapers.'

'The front page when we do,' added Sparks. 'I take it you want us to put those talents to use.'

'Yes,' he said. 'This matter with Danielli – we're trying to keep it under our hats, naturally, but it's bound to come out sooner or later. Too many people are aware of it. The thing is, I like Danielli. The police seem hell-bent on him as the culprit, but I can't see him doing this.'

'Neither can we,' said Mrs Bainbridge.

'I know. Unfortunately, that detective fellow – Kinley? Was that his name?'

'Kinsey,' said Sparks.

'Right. He seems to lack much of an imagination.'

On the contrary, he has too much of one, thought Sparks.

'I'm worried that his single-mindedness is going to put Danielli up for the charge,' continued Conley, 'and that would look bad for all of us.'

'Especially for Sally,' said Mrs Bainbridge. 'What exactly do you want from us, Mr Conley?'

'To look into it from angles the police aren't considering,' he said. 'The people from France don't know who you are.'

'Madame Rivette and I had lunch together,' Mrs Bainbridge pointed out. 'She knows what I do at The Right Sort. And Monsieur Legrenzi knows we're friends of Sally.'

'But they don't know about your other skills,' said Conley. 'Do either of you speak French?'

'We both do,' said Sparks.

'Excellent,' said Conley. 'Now, we're treating the dancers to an evening at the Cocoanut Grove tonight, trying to get their minds off what's been going on. So what I would like you to do is—'

'Hold up,' said Sparks. 'We haven't agreed to do anything yet. And there's the matter of payment.'

'Payment?' he repeated, puzzled.

'You're asking us to take time away from our regular business,' said Sparks. 'We should be compensated for that.'

'But Danielli is your friend.'

'He is, but why should we be out of pocket because you're too scared to ask your bosses to authorize a private detective and too cheap to pay for one yourself?'

'I just thought—' he started.

'Thought what? That we would do this gratis because we're nice people?'

'Well, I—'

'Because we're women?' asked Sparks, her voice rising.

'We're not so nice, you know,' added Mrs Bainbridge with a serene smile that Conley found strangely unnerving. 'But nice doesn't get results in this sort of thing. And we do.'

'My impression was that you had no need for money, Mrs Bainbridge,' said Conley.

'But I have,' said Sparks. 'And this will require expenses. Taxi fares. Drinks. Possibly a small bribe here and there.'

'Maybe even travel to Paris,' said Mrs Bainbridge wistfully. 'That would be lovely. I've been wanting to see the new fashions there.'

'Come now, you're having me on,' spluttered Conley. 'Be serious.'

'I'm always serious when it comes to fashion,' said Mrs Bainbridge. 'However, we could charge you for London only, and come back for more if it turns out that a trip across the channel is necessary. Miss Sparks, what did we charge the You-Know-Whos for that investigation last year?'

'Eighty pounds plus expenses,' said Sparks.

'Eighty!' exclaimed Conley.

'But it is Sally we're talking about,' said Mrs Bainbridge. 'So I think some discount would be appropriate. Let's say forty pounds. Surely you could find that much in petty cash, couldn't you, Mr Conley?'

He looked at them stony-faced.

'We could recommend an actual private detective if you'd prefer,' she continued. 'Who did we use last year? Oh, yes, Morris Cornell.'

'Excellent man,' said Sparks. 'Pricey, but you get your money's worth. Of course, I don't know if he speaks French as well as we do, and there's only one of him as opposed to the two of us.'

Conley reached into his jacket, pulled out his wallet, and removed four ten-pound notes.

'Do you require a receipt?' Mrs Bainbridge asked as he handed them to her.

'I require results,' said Conley.

'You should add us to the guest list at Ally Pally so we may come and go without needing permission each time.'

'I will,' he said. 'Good day, ladies.'

Gwen waited until his footsteps had faded away, then turned to her partner.

'Calculating *and* mercenary,' she said. 'I like it. You would have done it for nothing.'

'Of course,' said Iris. 'But why not see if we could be taken seriously for a change? The Royals paid for our services, so why shouldn't the hoi polloi? Thank you for following my lead.'

'How should we approach this tonight?' asked Gwen. 'Be ourselves? Be someone else?'

'We were sitting some distance from the dancers in the restaurant,' said Iris. 'They might not have noticed us at all.'

'But Legrenzi came to our table after speaking to them,' said Gwen. 'Some of them might have watched him and seen me. And then you came in afterwards.'

'True enough. The question is: do the dancers know anything more about us than that? I can't see any reason for either Legrenzi or Rivette to have discussed us with them.'

'Legrenzi was mostly flirting with them from what I observed, and I doubt that Rivette would bother speaking to a mere cancan girl, so we will probably be unknown quantities to them. What should we be? Slumming socialites? Office girls on a spree? Starlets on the prowl for fledgling producers?'

'We're too old to pass for starlets, sad to say,' said Iris. 'I vote for the office girls. And if they recognize us from Ally Pally and ask about that, we are in the secretarial pool and came in on Saturday to watch the variety show for fun. That should be enough cover.'

'And then we somehow get them to talk about what happened to Mademoiselle Duplessis,' said Gwen. 'In the middle of a nightclub where they will be trying to forget about what happened to Mademoiselle Duplessis.'

'That's where the drinks come in handy,' said Iris. 'Let me have my half of the money. It looks like we'll be putting it to use.'

Kinsey sat at his desk at Homicide and Serious Crimes Command, going over his notes from his interviews of the staff and visiting performers at Alexandra Palace. His telephone rang.

'Kinsey,' he answered.

'That lady from the marriage bureau wants to speak with you,' said Josie, their receptionist.

'Sparks?' he responded, immediately irritated. 'She's on the line?'

'No, it's the other one. The tall one. And she's not on the line, she's here.'

'Here?'

'Here. Do you want to be rude or polite?'

'Dammit,' muttered Kinsey.

'Polite, then. Are you coming to fetch her, or shall I send her wandering into the warren?'

'Be there momentarily,' he said.

He hung up the phone, then looked at a diagram mounted on an easel next to his desk and draped a cloth over it.

Mrs Bainbridge rose from her chair, smiling as he came in.

'Good morning, Detective Sergeant,' she said. 'So good of you to see me unannounced. I know how busy you must be.'

'Good morning, Mrs Bainbridge,' he replied. 'I assume this is not a social call.'

'Does anyone ever make social calls here?'

'Even policemen have friends,' he said. 'Follow me, please.'

He led her back to his office.

'Please take a seat,' he said as he placed a chair in front of his desk.

'Thank you.'

'Why are you here, Mrs Bainbridge?' he asked as he sat down.
'I would think by now you could call me Gwen,' she said. 'We've known each other long enough.'
'Every time I've seen you, it's been on official business,' he said. 'Is this any different?'
'No, actually.'
'Then we shall be Mrs Bainbridge and Detective Sergeant Kinsey, if you don't mind.'
'Very well,' she said. 'I am here, Detective Sergeant Kinsey, to offer my help in this investigation.'
'Just yours? Not yours and Sparks's?'
'She doesn't know I'm here.'
'Interesting,' he said. 'Is this a betrayal of friendship?'
'Oh, I don't think she'd mind particularly,' said Mrs Bainbridge. 'But given your past difficulties with each other, I thought it would be simpler to keep things on the q.t.'
'And why do you think Scotland Yard requires your help?'
'Because you know we can be helpful. We have been in several other cases, many of which had you stumped or steered in the wrong direction. Why not be gracious and let me add my insights?'
'Add away, Mrs Bainbridge,' he said, holding up his hands in a gesture of conciliation. 'If you come up with anything we haven't thought of, we'll pursue it.'
'Very good,' she said, pleased. 'First, I must ask you a question. That poor woman was garrotted. I suppose you've seen such things before.'
'I have. It's relatively rare, but it does occur.'
'The victim becomes unconscious fairly quickly, I've heard.'
'Heard from whom?'
'Someone familiar with the technique, but who isn't an expert in the – how would you put it? – the medical aspects of the death. How long would it take to actually cause the death of the victim after the loss of consciousness?'
'This will be an unpleasant discussion, Mrs Bainbridge.'
'It's an unpleasant situation, Detective Sergeant. I came here prepared to have the discussion. How long would it take?'
'That would depend,' said Kinsey. 'If it's continued strangulation, several minutes.'
'Several? More than one or two?'
'Yes.'

'Are there ways in which it would take less time?'

'Well, if the windpipe is crushed, or the arteries in the neck are severed, then it could take one to two minutes.'

'I see,' she said, turning pale despite her stated bravado. 'May I ask if either of those happened in this case?'

'They did not. There was superficial bleeding, of course, but the arteries were intact.'

'So the murderer took his time with it to make sure the task was complete.'

'Apparently so.'

'Then it couldn't have been Sally,' she said triumphantly.

She pulled her sketch of Alexandra Palace from her bag and laid it out on his desk.

'She was found here,' she said, pointing to the theatre. 'I have gone over Sally's entire schedule for Friday night. He was never out of sight of anyone for more than two minutes. He didn't have time enough to kill her. You may keep this, if it would be helpful.'

'Never more than two minutes,' said Kinsey. 'That's according to him.'

'Yes,' she said.

'Mrs Bainbridge, you are known to have the ability to read people,' he said. 'Does this happen continuously, or can you turn it on and off like a lamp?'

'I try not to be doing it consciously every minute of the day,' she said. 'It would be too much of a distraction.'

'What do you do when you are friends with the subject?' asked Kinsey.

'Well—'

'When he's your lover?'

She looked at him, shocked into silence.

'You know about that?' she finally asked.

'We interviewed Mr Danielli extensively,' said Kinsey. 'We asked, among other things, how you and Sparks and your children happened to be there. And that led to questions as to his relationship with each of you. He answered honestly.'

'I see.'

'So I ask again, Mrs Bainbridge, when you sought detailed information from your lover, were you reading him while he answered? I assume this was yesterday after we finished with him, so he would have been exhausted and more vulnerable, especially with you.'

'I was reading him,' she said softly, looking down at her lap.

'Did he know that?'

'Maybe. Probably. But I had to know the truth.'

'Was Mr Danielli, in your opinion, telling the truth?'

'I believe so.'

'But are you telling me the truth now?' he asked sharply.

'Yes,' she said, her head snapping up.

'You see, I may not have your much-vaunted ability, but I've been questioning witnesses for many years, Mrs Bainbridge,' he said. 'Witnesses, and suspects. It's what I do, and I fancy myself to be rather good at it.'

'I'm sure you are, Mike,' she said. 'Excuse me, Detective Sergeant Kinsey.'

'So, speaking strictly as a detective, I would not for an instant remove your lover from my list of suspects on your say-so.'

'I suppose that makes sense from your perspective,' she said, the disappointment obvious on her face.

'Not just mine. The Yard's as well.'

'Then I guess I've wasted both our time,' she said. 'Would you like to keep my sketch?'

He reached over to the easel and lifted the drape. Underneath was a scale drawing of each floor of Alexandra Palace, every detail of every room and hallway rendered to perfection. To the right of the drawing was a long list of names, with Duplessis at the top. There was a star marked at the location in the theatre where she was found.

'That's a much better drawing, isn't it?' she commented, deflated.

'We have a chap who trained as an architectural draftsman before joining the force,' said Kinsey. 'He's excellent.'

'Quite professional.'

'As we all are here,' he said. 'That list contains every employee of the BBC working there, as well as all the French visitors and every guest who came to see the Friday night programmes. I've broken down the evening minute by minute, and I can tell you who was with who and who was out of sight and on their own for any length of time. Unfortunately, your Mr Danielli had gaps in his chronology which took more than two minutes, despite his recounting of his whereabouts that night.'

'You're saying he lied.'

'I'm saying he was inaccurate,' said Kinsey. 'Whether it was due to faulty memory or a deliberate attempt to mislead us remains to be seen. But he stays on the list.'

'Fair enough,' she said. 'But he's not the only one.'

'No,' conceded Kinsey. 'Nor have we ruled out the possibility of this being done by more than one person, each then providing an alibi for the other.'

'I hadn't considered that,' said Mrs Bainbridge.

'I have,' said Kinsey. 'As I said, professional.'

'I am duly chastened,' she said. 'May I be permitted another question? Two, in fact.'

'Of course.'

'Did anyone remember seeing Mademoiselle Duplessis there that night?'

'No,' he said. 'Which means someone is lying about that. And the other question?'

'Have you found how she got back there after her date with Mr Farrell?'

'Not yet,' he said. 'We spoke to every cabbie working the local railway stations, and none of them saw her that evening. She could have taken a taxi from London, of course. We're still trying to find anyone who remembers bringing her, but that's not a simple task.'

'No, I guess it wouldn't be,' she said. 'Were any of the French visitors still there Friday evening?'

'None. They cleared out that afternoon. Most seem to have gone out on the town that night.'

'Well, it sounds as if you have matters in hand. I wish you success.'

'Thank you, Mrs Bainbridge,' he said. 'I hope for your sake that it isn't Mr Danielli.'

'It isn't,' she said. 'I have faith in him.'

'How is Sparks?' he asked.

'Excuse me?' she said in surprise. 'Is that relevant to your investigation?'

'No.'

'Then why do you ask?'

'I've never seen her like this,' he said. 'I was concerned.'

'Were you?' she asked. 'Are you that oblivious, Mike? The man she loved was shot down in front of her. It was a terrible blow.'

'I guess I never really believed that she loved him,' said Kinsey. 'Not like . . .'

He stopped.

'Not like she loved you, you were about to say,' she said, looking at him closely.

'I wasn't—'

'My God, the ego of some men,' she said, her temper flaring up. 'Things ended between you how many years ago? And you thought she was incapable of moving on? Did you truly think that you were the irreplaceable summit of her existence?'

'She seemed upset with me when we spoke on Saturday,' said Kinsey. 'Especially when I told her about the baby coming.'

'You and your wife are expecting?'

'We are,' he said. 'I'm surprised Sparks didn't mention it to you.'

'So am I,' she said. 'Interesting. But there's been a lot happening the last few days. I suppose your personal life doesn't rank as highly in our recent conversations as you think it should.'

'I suppose it doesn't,' he said.

'In any case, congratulations to you both,' she said, getting to her feet. 'Your lives are about to change in ways you can't begin to imagine.'

'Any advice?'

'Be there for Beryl and the baby,' she said. 'Your job is not conducive to being a parent. Make it so.'

'My hours are not exactly regular,' he said.

'Neither are a baby's,' she replied. 'Good luck, Mike.'

'Thanks.'

It wasn't until after she had left that he noticed she had stopped calling him by his title.

There was a wardrobe in one corner of their office where they kept a few changes of clothes for emergencies or dates. At five, after Mrs Billington had left, they stood in front of it, contemplating their choices.

'Office girls on a spree, but it's the Cocoanut Grove,' said Gwen. 'Therefore dressier than our daily uniforms. We may have to dance with strange men to keep up with appearances. Are you ready for that?'

Iris reached into the wardrobe and pulled out a black crepe evening gown trimmed with fawn-coloured rayon, then turned to her, holding it against her body, a bright smile on her lips.

'I'm just looking for some fun tonight,' she said breathily. Then the smile disappeared in a trice. 'How was that?'

'Frightening,' said Gwen. 'Let me draw the shades. We don't want to encourage the Toms.'

Iris held the gown out, contemplating it sadly.

'I haven't worn this since last year,' she said. 'It looks more like a costume now.'

'Everything's a costume,' said Gwen. 'I need to call home and let them know I'm going out.'

She picked up the telephone and dialled while Iris pulled down the shades and started changing.

'Bainbridge residence,' came Millie's voice.

'Millie, it's Mrs Bainbridge,' said Gwen. 'How are you?'

'Fine, ma'am,' said Millie. 'What may I do for you?'

'I'm going out this evening, so let Rachel know there will be one less for dinner.'

'Yes, ma'am. Have a good time.'

'Could you put Ronnie on?'

'Of course, ma'am.'

She heard her calling upstairs, then a sound like a small avalanche as Agnes yelled from a distance, 'No running in the house!'

A moment later, she heard shoe leather skidding to a stop, and she quickly held the handset away from her ear as Ronnie cried, 'Hello, Mummy!'

'Hello, my darling boy,' she said. 'How was school today?'

'It was all right,' he said. 'We learned about animal families.'

'Ah, that must have been interesting.'

'I knew them all already,' he said. 'What's interesting is that the things we think of to say what they are don't say what all of them are. There are mammals that fly, and birds that swim!'

'That's true,' said Gwen. 'There are even flying fish, although I don't think they really fly. Are there fish that can walk?'

'I don't know,' said Ronnie. 'I don't think any of them have proper legs.'

Iris held up her hand.

'Wait a second, I think Iris has some information for you,' said Gwen.

She handed over the handset to Iris, who sat on the corner of the desk.

'Hello, young scholar,' said Iris.

'Hello, Iris!'

'I hear you have a question concerning taxonomy,' she said.

'Yes! That's the word we learned today. Mummy wants to know if there are fish that can walk.'

'Well, I happen to know that there is one called the walking catfish,' said Iris.

'Gosh! And it walks?'

'Slithers, more accurately,' said Iris. 'But it can crawl on land from one body of water to another. I think they live in Southeast Asia, but that's the extent of my knowledge.'

'I can't wait to tell Miss Ellingsworth!' he burbled. 'Thank you, Iris.'

'You're quite welcome. Now let me put your mother back on the telephone.'

'Ronnie, Iris and I will be going out for dinner,' said Gwen. 'I wanted to let you know. Mind Agnes, and blow me a kiss.'

'I will, Mummy,' he said. 'Have a good time.'

She smiled as she heard the kiss, and made one in response.

'Goodnight, dear,' she said.

She hung up, her smile lingering. Then it faded.

'What's wrong?' asked Iris.

'Oh, I gave some advice to someone about raising children, and I'm realizing that I'm not qualified to do that,' said Gwen. 'Ronnie is being raised by a committee. As was I. Not everyone can afford that. Especially not average working mums.'

'We weren't an average family,' said Iris. 'Mum was let go from her teaching position when she had me. That launched her into full-time suffragism and crusading for birth control. And now she's an MP. Daddy was a not particularly successful businessman, so I was left on my own for most of the time, obsessed with books and beetles. And I worked out, more or less.'

'Would Dr Milford agree with that?'

'My traumas came from the war,' said Iris. 'Well, most of them did. Watching my parents' marriage founder certainly took its toll. But in any case, I don't think there's any single right way to raise a child. Ronnie is a marvellous one, so let the committee carry on its good work.'

She glanced at her watch.

'I vote a light supper before we hit the club,' she said. 'Enough to slow down the alcohol. Let's go.'

* * *

The Cocoanut Grove was only a ten-minute walk from their office, but Iris, flush with money and wanting to save wear on her good shoes, flagged down a taxi after they finished eating.

'We should arrive there in style,' she said to Gwen as they got in.

'Agreed,' said Gwen.

They were at the club entrance on Regent Street in no time at all. The doorman nodded politely as they came up, then smiled broadly as he saw their faces.

'Sparks, as I live and breathe,' he said. 'It's been a while. And is that Mrs Bainbridge with you?'

'Hello, Herman,' said Sparks. 'Who's playing tonight?'

'Sid Phillips has the house band,' he replied. 'He's got Jill Allen singing with him.'

'I don't know her,' said Mrs Bainbridge. 'Is she any good?'

'All I hear is what comes through the door when I open it,' he said, opening it for them. 'But the snatches of song have been lovely. Have a wonderful evening, ladies.'

'Thank you, Herman,' she said.

They checked their coats in at the cloakroom.

'Should we get a table?' wondered Mrs Bainbridge as they approached the hall.

'Let's see where our ladies are, and take it from there,' said Sparks.

They came into the club, keeping to the side rather than making an entrance to be seen. Sid Phillips, a thin, balding clarinettist, was up on the bandstand, which was covered by a sloped roof decked with red faux pantiles and flanked by a pair of stylized palm trees. The palm motif was echoed on the pillars and the walls, while dolphins and seahorses cavorted in silhouette over the bar. It was a Monday-night crowd, smaller than normal, and the evening jackets intermingled with uniforms – dress for the British officers, and whatever was clean for the Americans. The women were mainly clad in pre-war gowns that had survived, chiffon dominating. But there was a group of women at two tables near the bar wearing frocks with dangerously plunging necklines and more soft, voluptuous fabric than any ration-abiding Brit could obtain legally.

'That's them,' said Sparks. 'Shall we?'

'Wait,' said Mrs Bainbridge, nodding toward a similarly Gallic-looking woman sitting by herself at a small table near the back. 'Do you recognize her?'

'Can't say I do,' said Sparks.

'She was the woman crying outside Alexandra Palace as we drove away.'

'Interesting,' said Sparks. 'Good. We'll divide and conquer. You're the more sympathetic one. You take Lonely Crying Girl, and I'll dive into the pack.'

'How are you going to do that?'

'I,' declared Sparks, 'have a plan. We'll meet up in an hour. Good hunting.'

'Same to you.'

Sparks walked determinedly toward the troupe, glanced over their outfits, her eyes widening, then hurled herself into their midst like a bowling ball into a set of ninepins, shrieking, 'Oh, my God! Those frocks are fabulous! Where did you get them? You must tell me! Immediately!'

'We brought them with us,' said one of the dancers, laughing. 'From Paris.'

'*Vous êtes françaises? Magnifique!*' exclaimed Sparks. 'I read about this new Dior collection in *Harper's Bazaar*! I've been dying to find out more. I must go to Paris at once and buy everything I can. Tell me everything!'

'Ah, but our English is not very good,' said one of the others.

'*Ça ne fait rien!*' said Sparks with a broad smile. '*Je parle français!*'

Mrs Bainbridge was almost at the table where her quarry sat when she was beaten to her by a somewhat drunken American soldier. Even with the band playing 'I'm Keeping Company' and the chatter around her, she could catch the gist of the conversation. It started with a request to dance, to which the woman shook her head. Then it turned ugly.

'Look, mademoiselle,' he began, his voice rising with each syllable. 'I damn near crawled across your country inch by inch under fire so you could sit in a swanky club. The least you could do is dance with me.'

He grabbed her wrist as she began to protest vehemently. Mrs Bainbridge moved in quickly, stepping around him, crying in French-accented English, 'Josette, there you are! I've been looking for you everywhere.'

She threw her arms around the startled young woman, whispering in French, 'Call me Cécile. I'm your cousin. I'll rescue you.'

'Cécile, *ma chère cousine*,' the woman said immediately, rising to return the embrace.

The soldier released his grip, looking at the two of them angrily.

'But who is this?' asked Mrs Bainbridge, still holding on to the woman, looking at the man curiously.

'I do not know,' said the woman in heavily accented English.

'Ah, monsieur, I apologise,' said Mrs Bainbridge. 'My cousin and I have this date together. We have not seen each other since before the war. Forgive us.'

'I want to dance with her,' he said petulantly.

'I am sure there are many women here who would happily dance with a handsome soldier like you,' said Mrs Bainbridge. 'Ask an English girl. They will dance with any man in uniform. But leave us to our reunion, *s'il vous plaît*.'

He glared at her. She drew herself to her full height, which with her heels was some three inches taller, and smiled down at him. He mumbled something and walked away.

'Are you all right?' Mrs Bainbridge asked in French.

'Yes,' said the woman. 'Thank you. Your accent – are you Swiss?'

'English,' said Mrs Bainbridge, 'but I spent a few years in a Swiss boarding school perfecting my French. I guess the accent rubbed off. My name's Gwen.'

'Mireille,' said the woman.

'Would you like a drink? That was an upsetting experience, I'm sure,' said Mrs Bainbridge.

'I am trying not to spend too much,' said Mireille.

'Then you're in luck,' said Mrs Bainbridge, signalling a waiter. 'I am.'

Sparks quickly seated herself at the centre of the group and peppered them with questions, starting with the latest Paris fashions, but moving on to what they were doing in London.

'The cancan!' she said with a giddy laugh when they told her. 'You all must have legs longer than my entire body. It's a good thing we're sitting down.'

'Do you dance?' asked one of them.

'Not really,' she said. 'Certainly not like any of you.'

'A pity,' came a man's voice from behind her. 'I was about to ask if you would dance with me, mademoiselle.'

She turned slowly in her chair to see Legrenzi smiling at her, his hand held out in invitation. Around her, she sensed sudden tension among the troupe.

She smiled and placed her hand in his.

'I'd love to,' she said.

TEN

'Forgive me for being intrusive,' said Mrs Bainbridge as the waiter arrived with a bottle of wine and poured it. 'But it seems strange that you came to a nightclub to be alone.'

'I did not want to come,' said Mireille with a sigh. 'They made me.'

'Who did?'

'My friends,' she said, nodding toward the troupe. '*Non*, not really my friends. My co-workers.'

'Where do you work?'

'I am a dancer,' she said. 'At Casino de Paris. We are in London to perform on a television programme.'

'Really? I saw a show at Casino de Paris before the war. Maybe I saw you.'

'*Non, non*, I only started there in 1943.'

'So you've been high-kicking for four years. I admire your endurance.'

'It is a living,' said Mireille with a shrug.

'Why did your friends make you come here if you didn't want to?'

'We are being forced to cheer ourselves up,' she said, looking over at her troupe disdainfully. 'Look at them. Laughing like nothing has happened. The last place I want to be is in another nightclub, dancing.'

'Why do you need to be cheered up?' asked Mrs Bainbridge.

'One of us . . .' she began. Then the tears started coming. 'My friend. My only friend there. She was murdered. She survived the entire war and Occupation only to be murdered in London.'

'Oh, my dear girl,' said Mrs Bainbridge, taking her hand sympathetically. 'I am so sorry. What happened?'

'We do not know, exactly,' said Mireille. 'We found out on Saturday. We were finished with lunch, then they told us to wait in a rehearsal room. Then suddenly the police were there, and they took us one by one to speak to a detective.'

'It must have been a frightful shock,' said Mrs Bainbridge, refilling the other woman's glass.

'I could not stop crying,' said Mireille. 'I ran out of that office with the detective and all the way through that long, long building until I found myself outside. I don't even remember doing it. And when I stopped crying, I had to go back through that door and walk all the way back to finish talking to him. And he didn't even care what I had to say once he found out I didn't see her after her date. He only wanted to know about Friday night.'

'She had a date? In London? With whom?' asked Mrs Bainbridge, trying not to sound overeager.

'She found a place, some business that said they could find her a husband here,' said Mireille. 'She was so excited about it. Can you imagine such a ridiculous thing? How desperate people must be in England to need an agency to find them love.'

'These are strange days,' agreed Mrs Bainbridge. 'Why did she want to get married here instead of Paris?'

'Something happened at her last job,' said Mireille. 'She wouldn't talk about it much, but she had to leave. She wanted to get out of Paris, but it was too dangerous, too difficult, so she came to us. It was right after I had started, so we became friends. The two new girls. Even four years later, the others call us the two new girls. Now I am the only one.'

'Did you ever find out what happened at that other job to make her flee?'

Mireille looked over Mrs Bainbridge's shoulder and shuddered.

'He happened to her,' she said with contempt. 'And now he's here.'

Mrs Bainbridge turned to face the dance floor, which was filling up as the band played 'After You've Gone', Phillips's clarinet wailing over the sax section as the drummer launched into a break on woodblocks and cowbell.

There was Marcel Legrenzi, resplendent in a tailcoat that matched the one his marionette counterpart had worn in its tiny puppet world. And in his arms was Iris.

'You are a better dancer than you pretended,' commented Marcel as they glided through the other couples on the dance floor.

'You know how to lead a woman quite well,' she replied. 'But one would expect that from a puppeteer.'

'I have many talents,' he said. 'I can juggle, tumble, walk the high wire, and play seven instruments, some well, some not.'

'Impressive. Puts my typing skills to shame.'

'Is that what you are?' he asked sceptically. 'A typist?'

'Oh, no, not just a typist,' she said. 'I can also file and take shorthand. And you thought you were accomplished.'

'Forgive me,' he said. 'I am surprised to see a secretary, even such a talented one, show up at a club like this.'

'I 'ave come all ze way from Spain so I can dance ze tango weeth you,' she said. 'Well, ze foxtrot at ze moment.'

'I am flattered that you remembered my performance,' he said.

'I enjoyed it very much,' she said. 'Is the show like that when in Paris?'

'Ah, it is longer and more elaborate,' he said, grinning wolfishly. 'Perhaps too risqué for an English girl like you.'

'I can handle risqué,' she said. 'Maybe I'll see it there someday.'

'Hmm.'

'What?'

'It's just that seeing you here tonight reminded me of something,' he said.

'Really? Of what?'

'Before the war, if I see a pretty woman, and then I see her two more times, I know it is a sign she is someone I will make love to.'

'Lucky for me this is only our second encounter,' she said.

'Third,' he said.

'How do you figure that?' she asked. 'There's here, and when we met in the studio on Saturday.'

'And when you were listening to my conversation in the hallway with Madame Rivette,' he said.

He smiled, but there was no warmth in it. She felt a shiver run down her spine. He sensed it, his hand at the small of her back, and the smile grew colder.

'But during the Occupation,' he continued, 'when we lived under the thumb of the Germans, when I saw a pretty woman appear in my life three times, I knew something very different.'

'What was that?'

'That she was a spy,' he replied. 'And do you know what I would do then?'

'What?'

'I would still make love to her,' he said. 'Would you like to know why?'

'Tell me,' she said, looking up at him like a mouse watching a snake for its next move.

'Because then I knew that she would die happy,' he said.

'Well, lucky for me the war is over,' she said.

'Is it?'

'Last I heard. And I would count our momentary encounter in the hallway as a continuation of our first meeting, not a separate event.'

'Perhaps,' he conceded. 'Still, your appearance here strikes me as more than a coincidence.'

'You're a very suspicious man, monsieur,' she said. 'Why are you worried about an ordinary little no one from the secretarial pool?'

'I have survived because I am a suspicious man,' he said. 'So, as much as I have enjoyed our dance, I hope for your sake that there will be no further encounters between us. And you had better make certain there are none, *chérie*.'

There will be one more tomorrow, she thought. I'd better make certain I live through it.

'Who is he?' asked Mrs Bainbridge.

'His name is Legrenzi,' said Mireille. 'He is a vile toad of a man. A marionnettiste. He works at another club in Paris. There was no reason for Jeanne-Marie ever to see him again, but then we get chosen for this show in London and suddenly he is back in her life. And now she is dead.'

'Do you think he killed her?' asked Mrs Bainbridge.

'It must be. It was no accident that it happened after he saw her again.'

'But why would he want to do such a thing? Did she tell you what happened between them?'

'It was after she left the Opéra Ballet,' said Mireille. 'She came to a nightclub looking for work as a dancer, but that man saw her and immediately demanded that she become part of his act. He had a woman already working for him, but he fired her and hired Jeanne-Marie.'

'Good heavens! Just like that? What was the reason?'

'She told me he said she reminded him of someone he once knew,' said Mireille. 'She said it was fun, at first, acting with the little puppets, but he became obsessive.'

'Were they lovers?' asked Mrs Bainbridge softly.

'It was never love,' said Mireille. 'In Paris during the Occupation, many people did many things because of necessity. For survival. But it became too much for her, and one day, she packed her things and left. And came to us.'

'Why didn't you tell the police all of this?'

'I tried,' she said bitterly. 'But that detective, he talked to me again this morning. He had investigated. Legrenzi left the studio with the rest of us on Friday afternoon, then went straight to the hotel bar and never left it.'

'If that's the case, how do you think he did it?'

'I don't know how,' said Mireille, looking out at Legrenzi and Sparks on the dance floor. 'But he has ways. He pulls the strings like a spider on its web, and all the little flies are trapped and devoured.'

'Why would he do it?' asked Mrs Bainbridge. 'Why now, after all these years?'

'Because no woman would work with him again after her,' said Mireille. 'She was his final love. He must have seen her as a curse. And when he learned her plan to find a husband here, it must have driven him mad.'

'How did he find out about that?' asked Mrs Bainbridge.

'He saw her at the studio,' said Mireille. 'He tried to ask her to forgive him, and she threw it in his face. "No more of you!" she shouted. "I am going to stay in London with a new man, an Englishman, and you will be out of my life for ever." She told me about that when we came back to the hotel and she was changing for her date.'

'Did she tell you what he said to that?'

'No, the telephone rang while she was telling me. She picked it up, then said to me, "It's him. I must go." And she left.'

The tears, fuelled by the wine Gwen kept pouring, flowed again.

'That was the last time I ever saw her,' she said.

'What time did she leave?' asked Gwen.

'I don't know, maybe three o'clock.'

'Then I don't see how this Legrenzi person could have done it, especially with so little time,' said Mrs Bainbridge.

'It was him,' insisted Mireille. 'I know this. I know it with every bone of my body.'

* * *

Legrenzi brought Sparks back to the troupe's table, then kissed her hand, smiling up at her as he felt it flinch. Then he left, waving to the dancers. Only a few returned his wave, and those only tentatively.

Sparks saw her partner looking at her from across the room and idly scratched her nose in response, then turned back to the table.

'So tell me about Marcel,' she said to the dancers. 'He seems interesting.'

'You don't want to be with that one,' said one of them. 'He flirts, but he does not love.'

'Just my type,' said Sparks. 'Tell me more.'

She wants to meet me later, thought Mrs Bainbridge, recognizing the signal. She must be worried about Legrenzi seeing us here together. I hope I'm far enough from the dance floor for him to have missed me in the crowd. He was dancing with another woman now, staying close to the bandstand as a rhumba played.

Might be my best chance to sneak out unobserved, she thought.

She glanced at her watch.

'I'm afraid I'm going to have to call it a night,' she said to Mireille. 'Look, if you need a sympathetic ear to listen some more, call me tomorrow night, or any night you like.'

'I don't even know you,' said Mireille. 'Why are you so sympathetic?'

'Sometimes strangers are the ones you can talk to,' said Mrs Bainbridge, jotting down her number on a page from her notebook, then tearing it off and handing it to her. '*Bonne soirée*, mademoiselle. It was a pleasure having a conversation in French, by the way. It's been a while.'

She left, making her way around the back tables rather than cutting past the dance floor. She didn't see Legrenzi anywhere, but she didn't want to risk being seen waiting for Iris. She retrieved her coat and hat, then hailed a taxi and went home.

The house was quiet when she came through the front door. She wanted to wait up for Iris in case she was coming there. Until then, there was one thing she had heard from Mireille that had piqued her curiosity.

She went up to her room and into her walk-in closet. Up on a shelf in the corner was a box she hadn't opened in ages. She retrieved it, then went back downstairs into the parlour and sat down. She hesitated for a moment, then lifted the lid.

Inside were the keepsakes from her honeymoon. She and Ronnie had taken the train to Rome, then travelled through Italy before returning by way of Paris. She had kept ticket stubs, railway passes, postcards and photographs. And programmes from every club and theatre they had gone to.

It would have been tempting to dive down the rabbit hole of some of her happiest memories, but she wanted to find a specific souvenir before Iris showed up. She felt vaguely discomfited looking at them so soon after taking her relationship with Sally to a more intimate level, but this was part of helping him, so she set aside that emotional conflict, saving it for her next session with Dr Milford, and started digging through everything.

The Parisian memorabilia were on top, fortunately. She flipped through the programmes, poring over each as fragments of songs, cascades of plumes and knockabout clowns surfaced in her memory, one after another.

She found the item she was searching for: a thin lavender booklet with a lupine emcee in top hat and tails leering out at the viewer, beckoning them to enter a dark, forbidding doorway behind him.

She opened the booklet and ran her finger through the small grainy photographs of the performers until she saw the one she was looking for.

She was still staring at it when she heard a soft rap at the front door. She ran to open it before anyone in the house woke. Iris stood there, her cheerful outfit and makeup in stark contrast to her bleak expression.

'Get in before you frighten the neighbours,' said Gwen, holding the door open.

Iris came into the parlour, tossed her coat and hat on to one of the armchairs, then collapsed on to the couch, shivering.

'I don't scare easily,' she said. 'But that man really gave me the willies.'

'Mireille thinks he may be our killer,' said Gwen.

'Mireille? That's her name?'

'Yes.'

'I think she may be right,' said Iris. 'Only a feeling. And the fact that he threatened me and wasn't even subtle about it.'

'The problem is he couldn't have done it,' said Gwen.

'Why not?'

'Apparently Mike verified he was at the hotel bar for the rest of Friday, from the moment he returned, drowning his sorrows.'

'What sorrows?'

'Let's trade stories,' suggested Gwen.

When they had finished, Iris slumped back against the armrest, rubbing her eyes.

'If Mike is right, it can't be him,' she said. 'Yet Legrenzi feels like he's a killer. He had no compunctions about trying to put the fear of God into me.'

'Lucky you're an atheist,' said Gwen.

'And to think I got all prettied up for tonight,' said Iris ruefully. 'I even danced with a man for the first time since – since Archie died, and he turns out to be this loathsome thing. And I was constantly remembering that of the last three men I danced with before tonight, two ended up dying. If I believed in curses, I'd be thinking I've become one.'

'Give it time, dear,' said Gwen, grabbing her ankle, the closest thing she could reach, and giving it an affectionate squeeze.

'How much?'

'As much as it takes. But you'll dance again, I promise you. Now sit up. I have something to show you.'

'I was wondering what those were all about,' said Iris as she sat up and glanced at the pile of programmes.

'July, '39,' said Gwen. 'The grand finale to the honeymoon was a week in Paris.'

'Looks like the two of you did it up quite thoroughly.'

Gwen opened the programme and pointed to a photograph. It was of a marionette theatre with a top-hatted little puppet grinning up at a beautiful, brunette woman who looked back at him with adoration.

'Duplessis?' wondered Iris. 'No, it couldn't have been in 1939. Wait – is that Madame Rivette?'

'It is,' said Gwen. 'Eight years younger and a brunette. More importantly, the puppet looks just like the Marcel puppet Legrenzi has now.'

'The little theatre isn't the same one,' Iris noted.

'No, but those can be replaced. As can puppets. As can women.'

'What are you thinking?'

'Legrenzi told us on Saturday that another man stole his technique for the exploding puppet. Ronnie and I saw this act, and there was dialogue between the puppet and the woman that was quite intimate. I wonder if that other puppeteer stole not only Legrenzi's designs, but his lover as well.'

'Rivette.'

'They definitely have some history to them, complete with an underlying tension.'

'I did catch the tail end of a row between them on Saturday,' said Iris. 'I didn't hear what it was about, but he was quite bothered that I knew about it.'

'And when he hired Duplessis to be in his act, it was because she reminded him of someone. Now that I've seen this older picture of Rivette before she went blonde, I can see a resemblance.'

'Yes,' said Iris, peering at it. 'So we may be looking at an obsessive. That would clearly be a motive. Which leaves the simple problem of how? And if he killed Duplessis, could Rivette be next?'

'That's a disturbing thought. Should we warn her?'

'I don't see how we can, based on what we know,' said Iris, chewing on her lip. 'If it was him, we still haven't figured out how he got to Duplessis after her date with Mr Farrell, and how he got her to Ally Pally, and got inside without being observed, all while maintaining his position at the hotel bar. Maybe the man at the bar was a clever full-sized puppet double with a trick hollow leg.'

'As for getting inside unobserved, I had a thought,' said Gwen.

'What?'

'Mireille said she ran through the building and outside to cry. That's where we saw her, at the end by the scenery loading dock. But then she said she went right back in to go and speak to Mike. Which means that door didn't lock behind her on Saturday.'

'Which means it may also have been unlocked on Friday,' said Iris. 'We should tell Mike that much at least.'

'Agreed. But let's see what happens when your former colleague hears Legrenzi's voice tomorrow morning, in case that gives us more to bring to the table.'

'I'm looking forward to that more than ever now that I've seen this side of Legrenzi,' said Iris grimly. 'The puppet play's the thing with which we'll catch the conscience of the puppet king!'

'You've completely spoiled the iambic pentameter,' complained Gwen. 'Look, it's late. Would you like to stay here? The guest room is already made up.'

'I live less than ten minutes' walk,' Iris reminded her. 'I'll be fine.'

'I don't like the idea of you walking back alone when you've been so recently threatened. Why don't I walk you back?'

'Then who walks you back? It becomes that problem with the fox, the chicken, the worm and the boat, and I always mess that one up.'

'I have an idea. Let me get my coat.'

They walked out together, then turned right until they reached Carlton Hill. There was a policeman standing on the corner, whistling softly.

'Constable Merrick, is that you?' Gwen called.

He turned and smiled when he saw her.

'Mrs Bainbridge, is it?' he said. 'Out late for a Monday, aren't you?'

'I am. This is my friend, Miss Sparks. She lives over on the canal, and I was wondering if you could walk her back.'

'Of course.'

'See you in the morning,' Gwen said to her partner. 'The world must be peopled!'

'The world must be peopled,' replied Iris.

Merrick offered his arm, and she took it.

'I never thought of this as part of a policeman's duties,' she commented as they walked.

'Can't say it's in the manual,' he said, 'but protecting the public is what we do, and you are a member of the public.'

'I'm grateful, Constable.'

'And may I add that it's an honour to meet you, Miss Sparks,' he added.

'How is that?'

'Oh, word about your exploits with Mrs Bainbridge has trickled down to the rank and file,' he said. 'The two of you have outdone the Scotland Yard lads a few times, and we all like to see them taken down a peg once in a while, just to keep them humble.'

'That was never our intent,' said Iris.

'No, of course not,' he said. 'It's an ugly business any time a murder happens. But every time it did, you and Mrs Bainbridge took it on full force with no hesitation, and that's something.'

'Truth be told, there was hesitation every single time,' she said.

'Well, you're not fools, so there should be some, I suppose, but you went ahead in spite of it. If you don't mind me saying, I think it's admirable.'

'I appreciate that, Constable. And the company.'

'Not at all, Miss Sparks. May I ask which is harder? Solving murders or matching marriages?'

'I've never thought about that,' said Iris, smiling at the unexpectedness of the question. 'I would say that love is more complicated than murder. Murder is usually an impulse. Love should last for ever.'

They came up to the canal.

'That's mine,' she said. 'The *Cecilia*.'

'Ah, you're watching it for Mr Hollister.'

'Something like that. Thank you for getting me here safely.'

'You're quite welcome, Miss Sparks,' he said. 'I'll stay until you get in the door.'

On the one hand, she felt she didn't need the protection. On the other, she had been imbibing while interrogating an entire troupe of dancers. And there was a mad marionnettiste on the loose. She walked up the gangplank to the boat, unlocked the door and made sure it was otherwise unoccupied, then waved to Merrick who touched his truncheon to the brim of his cap and walked away.

Their leftover funds from the payment from Conley were more than enough to allow for a taxi to take them and Theresa Cosslett to Ally Pally. They passed under the scaffolding to the main entrance, waving up to Ernie who was back at his task of unpuzzling the stained-glass window. He waved back, then held a piece of green glass up to the sun, causing his face to turn slightly froggish.

Haight was waiting for them at the front desk. He gave a slight nod of recognition as he saw Cosslett, who gave him a hesitant smile in return.

'Come this way,' he said, leading them down a corridor. 'I don't think there's a chance he'll see us. He's getting his theatre together, then I'm going to help him move it to the studio.'

'What cover story did you give him?' asked Iris.

'That I wanted to tinker with the positioning of the microphones to get better sound quality. I do, in fact. We've been experimenting with stereophonic sound – well, no time to explain all that. Anyhow, I'm putting the three of you in the control room. I've turned on one of the cameras as well as the sound system, so you'll be able to see him as well as hear him. I'll meet you there after he's set up.'

He led them into the control room, a cramped cluster of consoles with several television monitors set up on the wall opposite. There was also a small window looking out into Studio A. One of the monitors showed the studio from the centre Emitron camera.

'Don't touch anything,' he warned them.

'We won't,' promised Iris.

He left them there.

'He hasn't changed,' whispered Cosslett. 'He was always so fussy about our radios.'

They watched the monitor intently. There was a sound of a door opening, then they saw the marionette theatre roll into the centre of the screen, with Legrenzi and Haight appearing at the left side pushing it.

'Let me see,' came Haight's voice as he looked at the studio floor. 'You were about here.'

He moved the theatre over a few inches until it was centred precisely in the camera, then grabbed a case from a nearby chair and removed a pair of microphones and two coils of cable.

'We were getting some overlap between the two,' he said to Legrenzi as he opened the door to the theatre. 'I want to make some adjustments in the positioning so there'll be no distortion. Are you all right with turning your head toward each mike when you're voicing the puppets on that side?'

'Of course,' said Legrenzi.

It was the first time they heard him speak. Iris and Gwen glanced over at Cosslett, who was frowning.

'That isn't his voice,' she whispered.

'He has more than one,' replied Iris. 'Wait for it.'

Haight emerged from the theatre, then went around the back to connect the cables.

'Don't you need others to help you?' asked Legrenzi.

'Not for this,' Haight called from the rear. 'I could run the whole show by myself if I had to. Don't tell the rest, or they'll get worried I might take their jobs.'

He came back around.

'Will you give me the timing?' asked Legrenzi. 'The director wants it even shorter now. I have cut some lines.'

'Certainly,' said Haight. 'I'm going to the control room. You get set, then I'll give you the intro and mark it from when you start.'

'Very well,' said Legrenzi.

He disappeared into his theatre while Haight walked off camera. They heard the door open and shut. A few seconds later, Haight came into the control room.

'Absolute quiet,' he told them. 'He can only hear us when I use this microphone, but I need to speak to him. I'll turn it off when he starts his show.'

They nodded solemnly. Haight sat at a console, toggled a few switches, then pulled a microphone towards him and pressed a button.

'Monsieur Legrenzi, can you hear me?' he asked.

'*I can*,' came Legrenzi's voice through the speakers.

'I'm going to adjust the levels,' said Haight. 'Try the right microphone first, then the left.'

'*Hello to you, Monsieur Haight, my invisible audience of one*,' said Legrenzi.

'Good,' said Haight. 'Now the other one.'

'*Hello, Monsieur Haight*,' said Legrenzi in a sepulchral tone. '*This is the voice of Doom!*'

Gwen shuddered at the sound. Cosslett was staring at the screen, listening intently.

'Very well, let us begin,' said Haight. 'I have my stopwatch at the ready. Ladies and gentlemen, the BBC is proud to present Monsieur Marcel Legrenzi and his Marionettes!'

On screen, the curtains parted, revealing Legrenzi's tiny alter ego.

'*'Allo, 'allo!*' he said, the high squeaky voice startling shrill in the control room. '*I am Marcel! 'Ow do you do? Welcome to Paris*, mesdames et messieurs. *My apologies for my appearance, I was not ready for you. I 'ave special surprise – tonight, we go dancing! But first, I must put on ze right clothes.*'

Dancing, thought Iris. Even that puppet makes it sound creepy now.

They heard him singing the snippet of 'Top Hat' as the Marcel in evening clothes popped out.

'*So, ze night, eet eez young!*' cried Marcel. 'Cherchons les femmes!'

Here it comes, thought Gwen.

The Devil appeared.

'*Marcel, Marcel!*' came the German-accented voice. '*Eet eez I! Ze Devil!*'

Cosslett stood bolt upright, both hands going to her mouth to suppress a squeak of terror.

'*Ze Devil? But you sound German.*'

'Natürlich. *What else would ze Devil sound like?*'

'It's him,' breathed Cosslett.

'*Zat makes sense. Why are you 'ere?*'

'*I 'ave come for your soul!*'

'Oh, my God!' cried Cosslett.

'Non, *not tonight You can 'ave eet tomorrow, but tonight, I go dancing.*'

'*Dancing?* Wunderbar! Ich komme mit!'

'Are you certain?' demanded Iris.

'Absolutely certain,' said Cosslett.

'So am I, now that I'm hearing it again,' said Haight.

'Non, non, *you will get een my way.*'

'What do we do now?' asked Gwen as the Devil sang behind her.

'*Stop! You will not come wiz Marcel.*'

'We can't go to the police with this,' said Iris. 'I'll contact the people who deal with war crimes.'

'*You cannot stop me.*'

'Not good enough,' said Haight grimly.

'*But I can.*'

'What else can we do?' asked Gwen.

'*Bompbompbompbompbompbomp bomp bomp bom!*' sang Legrenzi.

Then came the boom of the cannon, which made them all jump.

'I'm not going to wait around for some two-year enquiry,' said Haight.

'What do you propose?' asked Gwen. 'You can't take matters into your own hands.'

'Gwen's right,' said Iris. 'I'm not saying he doesn't deserve – what's that?'

She stopped. There were gasping sounds coming through the speakers.

'Why isn't he going on with his routine?' wondered Iris.

'Look at the screen!' cried Gwen.

The two puppets, the tailcoated Marcel and the exploded Devil weren't moving. They lay, partially collapsed, on the tiny stage, their control bars dangling visibly from the top of the proscenium.

There was a pounding noise, then the door to the theatre opened and Legrenzi fell through it, landing on the studio floor, clutching his chest.

'He needs help,' said Haight, moving towards the door.

'Wait!' cried Iris. 'Are there exhaust fans in there?'

'Yes,' replied Haight. 'Why?'

'Switch them on,' she said. 'I think it's gas of some kind.'

He went over to another panel and flipped two switches. Seconds later, the thrum of two giant fans came through the speakers.

'He isn't moving,' said Gwen, looking through the window.

Haight went over to a storage bin at the side of the control room, opened it, and removed a gas mask.

'Call for help,' he said, pulling it over his face.

Iris picked up the telephone and started dialling. Gwen watched the screen as Haight came in and knelt by Legrenzi, checking for a pulse. He looked up at the camera and shook his head.

'He's dead,' whispered Gwen.

'Good,' said Cosslett.

ELEVEN

'What the hell were you two thinking?' shouted Kinsey. The partners sat in front of the desk, mute and glum. 'Well?'

'We were trying to get Legrenzi's voice through the speakers,' said Sparks reluctantly.

'Why?'

'So that someone could identify him.'

'Your Mrs Cosslett,' said Kinsey.

'Yes.'

'Who has clammed up completely after muttering about the Official Secrets Act,' said Kinsey. 'Are you a signatory, Mrs Bainbridge? I'm assuming Sparks is.'

'Would I tell you if I were?' replied Mrs Bainbridge.

'If you are not, then any failure to provide me with answers to my questions will be regarded as hindering a police investigation and will subject you to arrest,' he said.

'That sounded like an official warning, didn't it, Miss Sparks?' commented Mrs Bainbridge.

'It did,' said Sparks. 'Mike, this whole thing was my idea. How much do you know about Legrenzi?'

'He's a puppeteer, or was,' said Kinsey. 'He was performing at Le Carnaval des Monstres in Paris, came over for this television programme with its rapidly dwindling cast, and is now dead because some very clever person put a glass vial with a fumigant mixture inside a rubber bulb connected to a puppet cannon. The moment he stepped on it, the gas was released.'

'Cyanide poisoning,' said Sparks.

'Exactly so. It was smart of you to tell Mr Haight to activate those fans, or he might have suffered the same fate. Mrs Bainbridge, why did you want Mrs Cosslett to see his performance?'

'Not to see him,' said Mrs Bainbridge. 'To hear him. More specifically, to hear one of his voices.'

'Voices? You mean one of his puppets?'

'Something happened during the war,' said Sparks. 'A betrayal. I don't know all the details, but a woman was killed, and Legrenzi had something to do with it. Mrs Cosslett heard his voice just after the woman was killed.'

'How did Cosslett hear the voice?'

'Over the radio,' said Sparks.

'I see. Some wartime espionage matter, I suppose. And you thought Legrenzi was the man who killed this woman?'

'Enough for me to bring Mrs Cosslett in to listen to him.'

'And now he's dead.'

'That wasn't part of the plan,' said Sparks.

'Convenient, though, wasn't it?'

'He knew Duplessis,' said Mrs Bainbridge. 'They worked together. They were lovers, or something like lovers, during the war. Did you know that?'

'I learned it from one of the dancers,' said Kinsey. 'We looked into him, of course, but his alibi was solid.'

'More liquid than solid, from what we heard,' said Mrs Bainbridge. 'Besides verifying that he was at the hotel bar, did you find out why he was drinking like that?'

'It wasn't important at the time,' said Kinsey. 'We were trying to pin down where everyone was. You seem to think Duplessis's murder had something to do with the other French performers, but none of them was anywhere near here on Friday evening. Legrenzi was at the bar along with the acrobats, the cancan troupe had gone out to the Stork Club, and Rivette was being squired from one club to another so that producer fellow could get her in front of as many newspaper cameras as he could. None of them could have killed Duplessis.'

'You haven't got anywhere with that one, have you?' said Sparks.

'I've hit a wall, to tell you the truth,' he admitted. 'No one saw anything, no one is lying in any way we can pin down.'

'Go ahead and ask us for our help, Mike,' said Sparks. 'You know you want to. It's all right, we won't tell anyone.'

He looked back and forth at the two of them, then sighed.

'Ladies, would you mind if I picked your brains on these matters?' he asked.

'There, that wasn't so hard, was it?' replied Sparks. 'Of course you may, Mike.'

'In fact, there is one small point I may be able to clear up,' added Mrs Bainbridge. 'How she might have got back in the building unobserved.'

'That would be useful to know. How?'

'One of the dancers told me that the entrance by the loading dock was unlocked on Saturday. Maybe it was kept unlocked for the convenience of whoever works down at that end. Or maybe someone tampered with the lock so Miss Duplessis could come in without passing by any security.'

'That would be possible if she came in that way,' he said, pulling his notebook out and consulting it. 'That end has the workshops for scenery and costumes and the like. The people there work regular hours. All of them had gone home except for a standby painter and carpenter who stayed by the studios for any emergency repairs needed during the broadcast. I wonder why that dancer didn't tell me the door wasn't locked.'

'She may not have realized its significance,' said Mrs Bainbridge.

'And you made her cry,' said Sparks.

'Ah, Mademoiselle Boucart,' said Kinsey. 'She was more upset than any of the people I interviewed. That actually made me suspect her more, but as I said, all of the French performers were accounted for Friday night.'

'Could any of them have killed Legrenzi?' asked Mrs Bainbridge.

'His marionette theatre was stored in a rehearsal room, according to one of the stage managers. Anyone here could have gained access to it, French or English.'

'But not Sally on this one,' she said.

'What makes you think he's been excluded?' asked Kinsey. 'This was a booby-trap. It could have been set up any time after Legrenzi last rehearsed his show on Saturday. It was waiting for him up until the moment he stepped on that bulb. Brutal. It could have killed anyone in the vicinity. We're lucky it wasn't in a crowded room somewhere. No, Mrs Bainbridge, your Mr Danielli is still on the list of possibilities. In fact . . .'

He flipped through his notebook, then tapped an entry, making a small grunt of recognition.

'Friday night, during the broadcast, only one person went from the studio area into the basement,' he said.

'Who?' asked Mrs Bainbridge.

'Danielli,' he said. 'One of the performers in the variety show couldn't find her wig, and he ran down to the costume shop to fetch another one. He had keys, of course.'

'Of course he had keys,' said Mrs Bainbridge in chagrin. 'And by telling you about the unlocked side door, I've just made it easier for you to pin this on him.'

'I'm afraid so,' said Kinsey.

'Promise me you'll give me visiting privileges after you lock him up, will you?' she said.

There was a knock on the door, and Harvey poked his head in.

'We found something,' he said.

'What?' asked Kinsey, motioning him in.

'This was in that puppeteer's theatre,' said Harvey, placing an evidence bag on the desk. 'There's a toolbox in there, filled with strings and wire and glue and odds and ends. This was underneath all of it.'

He upended the bag, and a length of wire fell on to the desk, its ends wrapped around a pair of wooden dowels.

'So that's what a garrotte looks like,' said Mrs Bainbridge, leaning forward to view it.

'Looks like there might be some dried blood on it,' said Harvey. 'The lab boys should be able to determine that.'

'If that's the case, then the man who absolutely could not have killed Duplessis had the murder weapon,' observed Sparks.

'Are these ladies helping us now?' asked Harvey.

'I'd rather have them on our side at this point,' said Kinsey. 'You think someone planted it to cast suspicion on him, Sparks?'

'I do.'

'So do I,' said Mrs Bainbridge. 'I'm not an expert on wire, but that looks like . . . what's the word they use for thickness again?'

'Gauge,' said Sparks.

'Yes, gauge. This wire is a thicker gauge than the wire he used for that Devil puppet.'

'Did you see any wire in that toolbox that matched this?' asked Kinsey.

'No, come to think of it,' said Harvey. 'There was a spool of the finer stuff that matched up with some of the puppet wires. And another thing – I searched that theatre on Saturday when we were looking for the weapon, and the garrotte wasn't in there then. I'd swear to that.'

'So someone wanted to frame him, then decided to kill him after,' said Kinsey.

'Or there were two different killers working independently,' said Sparks. 'What happens now?'

'See if you can convince Cosslett to talk to me,' said Kinsey. 'Or I'll talk to whoever she requires permission from to talk. And don't arrange any more stunts like this without going to me first.'

'We won't,' promised Mrs Bainbridge. 'May we go, then? And may we take her home? We promised her we'd get her back safely.'

'I certainly can't vouch for the safety of this place,' said Kinsey wearily. 'Take her home. We now have to talk to every single employee again.'

As they came out of the office, they saw Avery Conley waiting for them at the end of the hallway. Before they could reach him, however, another voice shouted his name.

'Freddie?' he said, turning to his right. 'What are you doing here?'

'I just got word that my marionnettiste has been murdered!' came the voice of Freddie Oakes, the producer. 'What in God's name is going on here?'

'There are detectives trying to figure that out as we speak, Freddie,' said Conley.

He made a brief gesture to the women to remain out of sight. Sparks tried a door next to her. It was unlocked.

'In here,' she whispered.

They quietly ducked into what turned out to be a cleaner's cupboard, closed the door, then pressed their ears against it.

'They're going to want to talk to you about it,' said Conley.

'Me? Whatever for?' asked Oakes.

'To rule you out as a suspect, I suppose. Find out what you know and all that.'

'Ridiculous,' sputtered Oakes. 'I'm producing the show! He was supposed to be the comedy segment, not to mention the transition to the girls. What am I supposed to do about it now? I've got five minutes of dead air to fill.'

'Your grief over a fellow man's death becomes you,' observed Conley. 'You've got two days to fix it. Give the singer another song, figure out another transition. I'll authorize whatever extra rehearsal time you need. In the meanwhile, get the performers on the next bus up here so they can go through the interrogations again.'

'They won't be happy about it.'

'At this point, I would be shocked if any of them were,' snapped Conley. 'But any one of them who doesn't co-operate will most likely jump to the top of the suspect list. Start making those calls, Freddie.'

They heard Oakes's grumbling receding into the distance. A moment later, there was a rap on the door. Sparks opened it.

'Well, I did hire you to clean up this mess,' commented Conley as he saw them standing amidst the mops, brooms and buckets.

'We seem to have made it worse,' said Sparks. 'Now there are two people dead, and Sally's no closer to being in the clear.'

'What's the next step?'

'We take our witness home, then put our heads together and regroup,' said Mrs Bainbridge. 'One question. Who here might have access to that form of poison?'

'Anyone, in theory. They've had perennial problems with rats in the basement,' said Conley. 'We've had the place fumigated more than once.'

'I'm so glad we didn't know about that when Sally gave us the tour,' said Mrs Bainbridge with a shudder. 'Very well, Mr Conley. We'll get back to you when we come up with something.'

'Please make your next stratagem less lethal,' he said.

'We'll do our level best,' said Sparks.

They telephoned for a cab, then located Mrs Cosslett, who was seated near the security desk at the central entrance.

'How are you holding up?' asked Sparks.

'I'm shaking like a leaf,' she said. 'I was, and I can't believe I'm saying this, absolutely exhilarated when I realized he was dead. All my nightmares have been centred around that single night four years ago. But now that it's over and done with, I want nothing more than to go home, take a pill, and go to sleep for a month.'

'What are you taking?' asked Mrs Bainbridge.

'Quinalbarbitone.'

'Ah, I remember it well. I was on it for a while.'

'You were? Why?'

'My own terrible experience,' said Mrs Bainbridge. 'I was institutionalized for several months. The pills did help me sleep. Too well, in fact. I was terrified about giving them up.'

'But you were able to?'

'They switched me to Veronal when they released me, then I gradually tapered down until I was able to stop entirely. The psychotherapy continues on, thankfully.'

'Do you still have nightmares?'

'Yes,' said Mrs Bainbridge. 'But less and less as time goes by. What does your doctor say?'

'I don't go to a doctor,' confessed Cosslett.

'You don't? Then where are you getting your quinalbarbitone?'

'I have . . . someone,' she said.

'I see,' said Mrs Bainbridge.

She pulled out her notebook, scribbled down a name and number, then tore out the page and handed it to her.

'This is the number for my psychiatrist,' she said. 'He's a good man. I've been going to him for a few years, and he's helped me considerably.'

'I go to him, too,' said Sparks.

'You shouldn't be treating yourself,' said Mrs Bainbridge. 'You don't know how, and the drugs may only be postponing the worst rather than preventing it.'

'Think about it, won't you, Theresa?' asked Sparks.

'But the nightmare is dead, now,' said Cosslett. 'The worst part of my life is gone.'

'It's never that simple,' said Mrs Bainbridge. 'Your mind could react in ways you can't possibly foresee. You don't have to do this alone. Please take my advice.'

The cab pulled up outside. The three women crossed under the scaffolding. Mrs Bainbridge turned to wave to Ernie, who waved back. Then they got into the cab and headed back to the city.

No one spoke until they reached St Pancras. The cab stopped at the entrance to the alley.

'Wait for me,' said Sparks. 'I'm going to walk her to her door.'

'Of course,' said Mrs Bainbridge.

As they walked down the alley, Cosslett said softly, 'What do you want to know that you can't ask in front of her?'

'About Lisette,' said Sparks. 'Did you ever learn where she was working?'

'She kept that from me for security,' said Cosslett. 'As did the higher-ups on my end.'

'What sort of information was she giving you?'

'High-level details from the occupying command in Paris,' she said. 'From more than one source. She was running a network.'

'How were they getting this information?'

'How does any woman winnow secrets out of a man?' replied Cosslett as she went through the door to her building. 'Goodbye, Miss Sparks. I'll ring you when I wake up, just to let you know I have.'

They sat at their desks at The Right Sort, staring at the open door and the view of the stairwell beyond.

'This was a disaster,' said Gwen. 'I was so sure Legrenzi was behind Mademoiselle Duplessis's death.'

'He may still have been involved somehow,' said Iris. 'What did we confirm? That he was either a Nazi or collaborated with them.'

'He seemed so French,' said Gwen.

'A German spy in Paris would have been able to pass as French. Hell, I could pass for French. Or German.'

'Was that originally the plan for you?' asked Gwen.

'It was a plan,' said Iris. 'Things went wrong. As plans involving me frequently do.'

Gwen pulled out her notebook and started writing.

'What are you doing?' asked Iris.

'Jotting down all the details from today while they're still fresh in my memory. Mike said Sally ran down to the costume shop Friday night during the broadcast.'

'Correct.'

'So that would have been sometime between eight thirty and ten, most likely. If he was the one who unlocked the door and let Duplessis in, that would have had to be by some prior arrangement.'

'But he went down there because one of the performers misplaced her wig. Although . . .'

Iris stopped.

'I don't like where this idea is going,' she said.

'Sally could have purposely hidden that wig to give himself a reason for going down there,' said Gwen. 'To let Duplessis in for a secret rendezvous.'

'You can't possibly suspect Sally.'

'I don't,' said Gwen. 'But Mike does, and I'm sure he's thought about this. Opportunity for unlocking the side entrance, means of accessing the prop storage area – both could have been Sally. Along with his access to Legrenzi's puppet theatre.'

'Motive,' insisted Iris. 'He doesn't have one.'

'No, he doesn't,' agreed Gwen. 'Who would have a motive to kill Legrenzi?'

'Besides Cosslett, Haight, and anyone connected to British intelligence or the Parisian Resistance?' asked Iris. 'Rivette for whatever happened in the past, or your new friend Mireille could have done it for revenge.'

'I don't think she would have been as open with me if that were the case.'

She finished writing her notes, then flipped through the notebook, scanning it intently.

'There's something I've missed,' she said. 'It's in here, or buried in my brain somewhere I can't reach. I need to let it simmer for a while. Pass me the telephone, would you?'

Iris handed it over. Gwen dialled a number.

'Sally, it's me,' she said. 'I'd like to come over if you don't mind. No, Iris won't be with me. Good, I'll be there in half an hour.'

She hung up, then fetched her coat and hat.

'I guess I'm not going to be with you, then,' said Iris. 'Have fun.'

'What are you going to be doing tonight?'

'The usual. Boat, book, bottle, bed.'

Gwen looked at her oddly for an instant, then shook her head.

'I'm doing it again,' she muttered. 'I have to keep it turned off somehow. Whatever you're really planning, be safe.'

'I'll try. But you know me and plans.'

'Be safe anyway,' said Gwen as she put on her coat. 'See you tomorrow.'

Sally opened his door for Gwen, who walked in shedding her coat and hat, her notebook and pencil already in her hand.

'No kiss hello?' he asked as he collected her things.

'Not yet,' she said. 'Sit over there, please.'

He complied, looking at her curiously as she sat across from him, staring at his face with an intensity he had only seen directed at others before now.

'Did you go to any of the shops during the broadcast Friday evening?' she asked.

'You're doing that reading thing,' he said in shock.

'Answer the question, please,' she said.

'But you're treating me like a suspect!' he protested.

'I'm trying to save your life, Sally. Answer the question.'

'Yes.'

'Why?'

'One of the singers on *Serenade in Sepia* couldn't find her wig,' he replied. 'I went to the costume shop to get one for her.'

'Did you see anyone in the basement on the way there or on the way back?'

'I already told Kinsey all about this.'

'Now, tell me,' she demanded, the intensity of her gaze increasing.

'No, I didn't see anyone,' he said.

'Thank God!' she said, sagging against the back of her chair.

'You actually thought it might have been me,' he said in astonishment.

'No.'

'But you weren't absolutely certain.'

'Absolute certainty is an indulgence I can't afford right now,' she said. 'I'm sorry, Sally, but I have to be objective.'

'I'm not sure I like you being so objective where I'm concerned.'

She came over, sat on his lap, then kissed him long and hard.

'There,' she said when they came up for air. 'Does that feel objective to you?'

'Not at all,' he said. 'I feel much better about things now.'

'Good,' she said. 'Now, let's go into the bedroom and throw my last shreds of objectivity to the winds.'

* * *

Colton made his way from the station to his house slowly. The leg wasn't doing well today, and the codeine he took to dampen the pain seemed less and less effective lately. He thought he might go back to the morphine again. He didn't like how it disrupted his bowels, but the leg was demanding priority.

He finally reached his door and hooked his cane over his forearm while he fumbled for his keys. He opened the door and stepped inside gingerly, holding on to the frame until he could close it again. He threw his coat and hat on to the coat tree, then went into his study and turned on the light, revealing walls with bookcases running along them, a desk by the window, and a pair of leather-covered armchairs. A small, brunette woman was curled up in one of them, looking at him.

'Took you long enough,' she said. 'I expected you twenty minutes ago.'

He held up his cane.

'If I'd known you were coming, I would have picked up the pace,' he said, limping over to the desk and sitting heavily in the chair behind it. 'Lieutenant Sparks, isn't it?'

'Miss Sparks, now,' she said. 'I've been out for a few years.'

'So I've heard,' he said. 'How did you know where I lived?'

'I followed you home from school one day,' she said. 'I always like to know who I'm working for. You were remarkably easy to tail, I was shocked to find out. Not that you would have noticed me. Nobody could spot me following them when I'm on my game, which I very much was back then.'

'That's appalling behaviour for a subordinate. Which leads me to the obvious question of why are you here now?'

'Something's come up, Major Colton,' said Sparks.

'And you know my name,' he said with a sigh. 'By the way, it's Colonel, now.'

'Ex-colonel, if we're being accurate,' she said. 'You were asked to resign six months ago.'

'You're surprisingly well-informed,' he said. 'Tell me what you want, then get the hell out of my house.'

'A man died this morning,' she said. 'A Frenchman named Legrenzi.'

'Never heard of him.'

'We have reason to believe that he was actually German, a former Nazi spy. He was identified as the man behind the death of a Frenchwoman working for us, code-named Lisette. You remember that night at Eynsford? The night Lisette was betrayed and killed? I'm trying to find out more about that operation.'

'I may not be working for the old firm any more, but the Act still applies to me,' he said. 'As it does to you.'

'It does, but I think that we could come to some agreement that would help us stop a killer while keeping your name out of it.'

'Are you offering to bribe me, Sparks?'

'Not at all,' she said. 'I'm offering to keep what I know about you quiet.'

'Are you?' he replied, amused. 'I can't think of a single thing that you could possibly know that I should be worried about.'

'There's the drug dealing,' said Sparks.

'I've done no such thing,' he said sharply.

'Of course you have. You were handing out pills right and left to the ladies at Eynsford. Even I popped a methamphetamine or two thanks to you.'

'Those were Army issue to help keep the lot of you awake and alert during wartime,' he said.

'And then the other pills to help us sleep after,' said Sparks. 'The problem is that you've continued doling them out since the war. How many of the Eynsford ladies are still coming to you for their unauthorized doses? How many of their friends?'

'Stuff and nonsense,' he scoffed. 'Do you think you can prove these reckless allegations?'

'I think the police would be fascinated with what I've learned about you,' she said. 'But I'm willing to keep mum if you tell me what I need to know.'

'Generous of you,' he said. 'Unfortunately, I find myself unable to trust you or your offer. But I can still obtain your silence.'

He opened a desk drawer and pulled out a revolver.

'She broke into my house and attacked me,' he said, pointing it at her. 'She left me no other choice. A pity, Detective. She sank so far after leaving the service.'

He pulled the trigger. There was a loud click.

She held up her right fist, then opened it. A handful of cartridges poured on to the other upturned palm.

'I'm still at the top of my game, Mr Colton,' she said, getting to her feet. 'First thing I did when I broke in here was to search for weapons. I have the box of spare cartridges in my coat pocket, so don't bother looking for them.'

He put the gun on the desk, then limped around it, holding his cane up with his left hand.

'I may not be at the top of my game any more,' he said. 'But you're still just a little girl pretending to be a spy.'

'Stop being overdramatic,' Sparks said wearily. 'I came to talk, not fight. And that cane won't even up things between us.'

He gripped the cane's handle with his left hand, then pulled a narrow sword from it.

'I stand corrected,' said Sparks.

TWELVE

Don't get cocky, Sparks, she thought. He may only have one good leg, but he's a trained British soldier, and she had a feeling he carried that sword because he knew how to use it.

Check your terrain, woman! she could hear Gerry Macaulay shouting in her mind.

Small room, not much space for manoeuvring. There was about four feet between the armchairs and the desk, five feet behind her to the bookcases at the far wall. No other way out besides the door or the bay window behind the desk, and there was an angry man with a sword in between her and both.

She hadn't ever trained against swords. Guns, yes. Knives, of course, but their longer cousins were not considered common enough during this last global fracas to waste time worrying about, and she was neither blue-blooded nor masculine enough in her upbringing to have had fencing lessons in her past.

And those were only useful when you also had a sword. Whatever other advantages she might have over Colton, he had a sharp steel point twenty inches closer to her very penetrable self than anything she could bring to bear against him.

But she did have a knife.

He took a step towards her. She twirled between the armchairs, reaching into her bag with her right hand, then pulling it out and flipping it open with one well-practised motion.

'Stay where you are,' she warned him.

He smiled and held his arms out, the sword and the cane parallel to the floor.

'Go ahead,' he said. 'I am offering you the first strike. Throw your little knife, Sparks.'

She remained motionless.

'Not so easy to kill a man when he isn't putting up any resistance, is it?' said Colton.

'I don't want to kill you,' she said. 'I want you to talk.'

'But I want you to be silent,' he said. 'Very well, if you won't accept my offer, I withdraw it.'

He pointed the sword at her again. She stepped back, waiting for his move.

He feinted towards her, not moving his feet, and she shifted behind the armchair to her left.

It's all about the footwork, she thought. He'll have to lunge from the good leg. The left one.

As he began the thrust, she grabbed the sides of the armchair and toppled it to the right. Colton stopped short, and she quickly stepped behind the other armchair and sent it crashing into the first, creating a low, uneven wall between them.

'Pardon me for unlevelling the playing field,' said Sparks. 'Feel free to jump over them.'

'Damn you!' he shouted.

He grabbed at the arm of one of the chairs, but couldn't get a good grip while clutching the cane.

Forget the knife, thought Sparks. There are less lethal weapons available.

She shoved it back into her bag, then reached behind her, grabbed a book from a shelf, and threw it at him. He blocked it with his arm, but she used both hands to hurl book after book in his direction. He couldn't block all of them, and the effort turned him red with rage. He lurched over the armchairs, stumbling as he did so, and she took advantage of that to make a running leap past his left.

He managed to bring the cane up enough to trip her, but she used her forward momentum to heave her body at the desk, catching the top with her right hand to keep from hitting the floor. She pulled herself up and rolled across it, scattering a pair of ornamental quill pens in the process, but was able to grab the gun lying there.

Colton propped his cane against the floor and forced himself to an upright position, then turned to see Sparks calmly loading his revolver with the cartridges from her coat pocket. She slapped the barrel into place, then pointed it at him.

'You shouldn't have left this here,' she said. 'Sword beats knife, but gun beats sword. You've now tried to kill me twice with two different weapons in the space of a minute, so I'm feeling less and less charitably inclined towards you. Drop your weapon.'

'Or you'll do what, Sparks?' he scoffed. 'Kill me with my own gun before I tell you anything?'

She pointed it at his left leg.

'That's the good one, correct?' she asked. 'How long did it take for the right to recover from the last bullet?'

He looked at the gun, then lowered his sword.

'It never has,' he said.

'I found these in your desk as well,' she said, pulling a pack of syrettes out of her coat pocket. 'Morphine, I'm guessing.'

'I need those,' he said, desperation flashing across his face.

'I'm sure you do,' she said. 'If you don't tell me everything, I will smash them one by one. I'll return them when you're done talking. Which can't happen until you start talking. And you still haven't dropped the sword.'

He let go, and it settled on to the Persian rug.

'Mind if I sit?' he asked.

'Leave those chairs as they are,' she said. 'You can perch on an arm.'

He lowered himself awkwardly on to one of the overturned armchairs, then stretched his bad leg out, massaging it with both hands.

'Once the adrenaline wears off, the pain comes back in earnest,' he said, grimacing.

'Poor you,' said Sparks. 'Let's pick up the conversation at the point just before you tried to kill me, and to hell with the Official Secrets Act. I think it matters to you as much as drug laws do.'

'It does matter to me, oddly enough,' he said. 'It's something I can cling to when all else has crumbled. I can say with some fragment of pride, "Yes, I did my bit for the war, gammy leg and all." Why, if you needed my information, didn't you go through official channels?'

'There's a killer running loose, a friend of mine is in jeopardy, and time is of the essence,' said Sparks. 'And I'm out of favour with the old firm, so the channels have been cut off.'

'I know how that goes,' he said. 'So, Lisette. Lisette and Albertine. Lisette is dead and Albertine is a shell of her former self.'

'What happened to Lisette?'

'We never got the full story.'

'Who was she?'

'A performer at a cabaret in Paris,' he said. 'Once France was occupied, Paris more or less resumed business under the Nazis, and they wanted French nightlife and entertainment. And French girls. They found them just as enticing as we do, so we recruited them. Operation Showgirl, we called it. There were several of them, all from different clubs and theatres, using their charms to get as close to the Nazi High Command as they could, and that was very close indeed. More secrets came through pillow talk than any other clandestine operation we could set up there.

'The woman we called Lisette was in charge after another woman was exposed and fled. All of the gathered information was funnelled through her.'

'What was her real name?'

'Never knew, never needed to,' he said with a shrug. 'We couldn't risk blowing her cover, so she was only Lisette. It's too bad. There would have been a medal or two coming her way had she lived.'

'I'm sure that would have been adequate reward,' said Sparks. 'You had no inkling as to who betrayed her?'

'It wasn't from our end, I can tell you that much,' he said. 'They were thorough with Albertine. And with me. She broke, I didn't, but neither of us was to blame.'

'There was no investigation by the French?'

'The French could spend several lifetimes investigating every collaborator they had, and most of them they'd rather not find. Lisette's death was never a priority.'

'Poor thing,' said Sparks. 'All that she did for us is forgotten, dead and buried. And the few left to remember her didn't even know her name. What about the nightclub where she worked? Could there still be anyone there who might have any information about her?'

'Maybe. Who knows? It was four years ago, those people move around, and times were chaotic. Are you planning to take the boat across the Channel, Sparks? I hear Paris is lovely this time of year. Chestnuts in blossom, holiday tables, and all that.'

'It's a possibility. What was the name of the club?'

'Café des Loups. Rather decadent place from all reports, which made it catnip to the Germans and perfect for the operation.'

'How many women were involved in Operation Showgirl?'

'A dozen or so. All of them wiped out, executed. Lisette was the last to go.'

'Then there may have been Vengeance visited upon someone today,' said Sparks.

She tossed him the pack of syrettes, then held up his pistol.

'I'll leave this on your front step,' she said. 'Unloaded, in case you're still contemplating using me for target practice. I'm giving you a pass on the drug dealing, Colton, but I strongly recommend you get out of it. If you cross my path again, I won't hesitate to turn you in.'

He started to rise, but she pointed the gun at him and he sank back on to the armrest.

'No need to stand on my account,' she said as she walked to the door. 'It would take a great deal more than that to convince me you're a gentleman.'

She disappeared. A moment later, he heard the front door open and close. He reassembled his sword-cane, then limped back outside. Sparks was nowhere to be seen. The gun, as promised, was on the front step. He checked the cylinder to confirm it was empty, then shoved it into his waistband and went back in.

With a great deal of effort, he righted one of the armchairs and collapsed into it. Then he removed one of the syrettes from the pack and rolled up his sleeve.

Gwen, having satisfied her curiosity among other things, returned home at eight thirty. Millie came to meet her at the door.

'Rachel saved you some dinner,' she said. 'You're just in time to read to Ronnie if you'd like to do that first. And there are two messages for you.'

'From whom?' asked Gwen as Millie took her coat and hat.

'Miss Sparks called an hour ago. She said she would swing by later and see if you were in. She wanted to tell you something.'

'Good. What was the other one?'

'A Miss Mireille Boucart. She sounded French.'

'She is French. What did she want?'

'She asked if you could call her at her hotel,' said Millie, handing her a note with a telephone number.

Food, child, murder investigation, thought Gwen. Priority?

Obvious.

'Ask Rachel to put my dinner out on the table,' she said. 'I'm going up to read to Ronnie. I'll need you to stand guard in case Miss Sparks comes by.'

'Certainly, Mrs Bainbridge. I'll listen to the radio, if you don't mind.'

'Of course not. It's the house radio/television, so any time you like.'

She went upstairs to find Ronnie already in bed while Agnes was taking a book down from a shelf.

'Mummy! You missed dinner,' said Ronnie accusingly.

'I am so sorry, my darling boy,' she said, coming over to kiss him. 'There was something complicated happening at work. I shall have my dinner cold as punishment, but at least I get to read to you. Where are we in *The Little White Horse*?'

'Maria has rescued a hare from the hunters,' he said. 'Her name is Serena. Could I have a pet hare, please?'

'Oh, no,' said Gwen. 'They don't make very good pets, and they would eat all the vegetables and flowers in the gardens.'

'But Maria has one, and her family doesn't mind.'

'The Merryweathers live in the country, dear. Hares don't do well in London. I'll take over, Agnes, if you don't mind.'

'I don't,' said Agnes. 'Ronnie thinks I need to fall in love with an old parson now because the governess in the book does. I don't know any, unfortunately.'

'Are you matchmaking now, Ronnie?' asked Gwen. 'Maybe I should bring you into the office to help us.'

'I'd like to,' he said seriously. 'Then I'd get to see Iris.'

'Well, we'll have to arrange another visit soon. Let's read now. Say goodnight to Agnes.'

'Goodnight, Agnes!'

'Goodnight, Ronnie,' said Agnes as she left the room. 'Sweet dreams.'

Gwen read the chapter until she saw Ronnie's eyelids at half-mast. Then she tucked him in and kissed him softly on the cheek. He murmured something unintelligible, and closed his eyes.

She turned off the lamp and left, closing the door quietly behind her. Then she took the note with Mireille's hotel number from where she had tucked it into her belt.

Food? Murder investigation?

Her stomach rumbled, but her cold supper would stay for the length of a telephone call. She went downstairs. Her ladies were in the parlour, listening to the radio. Some soprano was singing with the BBC Theatre Orchestra, but the women were chattering over it.

Good, she thought. I don't need them to know what's going on.

She went to the telephone and dialled the number, then asked to be put through to Mademoiselle Boucart.

'*Oui?*' came the dancer's voice.

'Mireille, it's Gwen Bainbridge.'

'Oh, Gwen,' said Mireille. 'Thank you so much for calling. I don't know who else I could speak to.'

'What's the matter?'

'That man we were talking about? Legrenzi, the marionnettiste?'

'Yes?'

Mireille dropped her voice down to a horrified whisper. 'He was murdered today! At the studio!'

'My word,' said Gwen. 'Do they know who did it?'

'*Non*, and that is why I am so frightened,' said Mireille. 'Someone may be trying to kill all of us, and I do not feel safe here any more. Could I come and stay with you until we return to Paris? I do not know anyone else in London.'

'Of course,' said Gwen immediately. 'I have a guest room you can use.'

She gave her the address.

'*Merci*, Gwen,' said Mireille. 'I cannot thank you enough.'

'We'll see you soon,' said Gwen.

She hung up, then went to the parlour. Millie looked up at her immediately.

'Millie, Mademoiselle Boucart will be coming to spend the night,' Gwen informed her. 'Possibly two or three. The guest room is already made up. She can have that. Please let me know when she arrives.'

'Very good, Mrs Bainbridge,' said Millie.

Dinner, thought Gwen as she left them. At last.

She was starving now. Not surprising, she thought, given her recent exertions. Between those and her daily self-defence regimen, she was hungry as only a tall, active woman during rationing could be. She found a plate of cold chicken and celery salad waiting for her in the kitchen, and with no one else there to see her, she wolfed it down in a most unladylike fashion.

She washed her plate and silverware, not wanting to bother Rachel with the chore, and poured herself a tall glass of water.

She heard the doorbell from the front of the house and went back to find Millie greeting Iris warmly. Gwen looked at her partner closely, noting the signs of dishevelment in her clothes, the flushed complexion, and a liveliness in her eyes that she hadn't seen there for months.

'Am I correct in guessing that you would like something stronger than tea this time?' she asked as Millie collected Iris's coat and hat.

'Quite correct,' said Iris. 'Much to tell.'

Gwen led her back to the kitchen. Iris sat at the table while her partner pulled out a bottle of whisky and two tumblers and poured each of them a drink. Then Gwen took another look at Iris's face and added more to hers.

'I can think of two reasons why you might look like this right now,' she said, sliding Iris's tumbler across to her. 'Both involve physical encounters. Unfortunately, my first guess is that you've been in a fight.'

'I'm afraid so,' said Iris, forcing herself to sip the whisky rather than gulping it down. 'Don't tell Ronnie. I don't want to set a bad example.'

'Are you all right?'

'I'm fine,' said Iris. 'Quite jazzed at the moment, in fact. Not getting killed was just the thing I needed.'

'Getting killed?' exclaimed Gwen. 'Exactly how close were you to getting killed?'

'Closer than expected,' said Iris. 'Which led to the subsequent exhilaration.'

'I see. And the other fellow? As in, but I should see the other fellow? How exhilarated is he feeling at the moment?'

'Not very, I should think.'

'In hospital?'

'Uninjured, apart from his dignity. I left his room in shambles, though.'

She took a longer sip this time, swirled it around her tongue, then swallowed it, leaning back with a sigh of contentment.

'Mind you, I've left rooms in shambles in some non-violent encounters,' she said.

'And I'm sure you'll be telling me those stories,' said Gwen. 'Right now, I want to hear about this evening.'

'This comes under the "oath of secrecy" part of our relationship.'
'Noted.'
Iris recounted her evening's combat.
'My God, Iris!' said Gwen, aghast, when it was done. 'What if he had come in with the gun in his pocket instead?'
'Once I found the one in his desk, I assumed that would be it,' said Iris. 'If he had produced a second one, I would have talked my way out of it.'
'Or not,' said Gwen. 'You didn't talk your way out of the one-sided swordfight.'
'Well, I survived,' said Iris. 'The question is, what to do with this? We still don't know Lisette's real name. I've been thinking we should go to Paris and ask there.'
'Or you could go to the Brigadier,' said Gwen. 'He might have information this Colton fellow doesn't.'
'I've burned that bridge,' said Iris. 'Repairing it would come at a price I can't even begin to pay, and my sense of Colton is that he was telling the truth.'
'I'm sorry I wasn't there to see him,' said Gwen. 'Look, I have Mademoiselle Boucart coming over soon.'
'Here? Why?'
'She is understandably concerned about her safety, so I've offered her the guest room. Maybe she knows something about Operation Showgirl.'
'We could ask, I suppose,' said Iris.
The front door rang.
'That will be her,' said Gwen. 'You stay here. I'll bring her.'
By the time she reached the front hall, Mireille was standing inside, gawking as Millie relieved her of her coat, a suitcase resting by her feet. Rachel and Agnes were still sitting on the couch, looking out at her curiously.
'You have servants!' exclaimed Mireille in French.
'Only three,' said Gwen. 'This is Millie, who will take your suitcase up to the guest room. The other two are Rachel, our chef extraordinaire, and Agnes, who looks after my son for me.'
'You have a son,' said Mireille. 'Then there is a Monsieur Bainbridge?'
'There was,' said Gwen. 'He didn't survive the war, I'm afraid.'
'I am sorry,' said Mireille. 'But you must be rich to have all this!'
'I am, in fact,' said Gwen. 'May I offer you some tea?'
'*Merci*,' said Mireille.

'Come with me. Millie, lock up, would you?'

'Would you like me to make the tea, ma'am?' asked Rachel.

'No, thank you. I can boil water with the best of them. And goodnight, ladies. Thank you for getting me through another day.'

There was a chorus of 'Goodnights' from the trio as Gwen led Mireille to the rear of the house.

'I offered tea because I am English,' said Gwen. 'But my friend and I are having a nightcap if you'd prefer whisky.'

'I have never had whisky,' said Mireille as they entered the kitchen. 'Perhaps . . .'

She stopped short as she saw Iris sitting there.

'Mademoiselle Mireille Boucart, this is my friend, Miss Iris Sparks,' said Gwen.

'You,' whispered Mireille, pointing at her with one trembling finger. 'You were there last night. At the club.'

'Yes,' said Iris. 'You have a good memory.'

'You danced with him,' she said, her voice rising. 'You danced with Legrenzi!'

'I did,' said Iris. 'But—'

'And now he's dead!' cried Mireille. '*Mon dieu!* You killed him!'

'Good memory, poor logic,' said Iris.

Mireille turned on Gwen.

'This is a trap!' she shouted. 'You killed Jeanne-Marie! You killed Legrenzi! And now you've lured me here to join them.'

'We're doing nothing of the kind,' protested Gwen. 'Please let us explain.'

Mireille dashed to the kitchen counter and grabbed a knife from a rack.

'I will not go quietly!' she shouted.

'Quiet has not been part of your repertoire,' agreed Iris as she got to her feet, an eager glint in her eyes. 'But if you don't put that down, I will show you one of the nastier parts of mine.'

'Both of you, settle down,' commanded Gwen. 'I will have no fighting in my house.'

'But I'm already warmed up,' said Iris.

'Sit down, Iris,' ordered Gwen.

'Yes, Mother,' she muttered, retaking her seat and picking up her tumbler.

'Mummy?' came a small voice from the hallway.

They looked to see Ronnie standing there, looking agog.

'Who is that lady?' he asked. 'Why does she have a knife?'

'Mireille, this is my son, Ronnie,' said Gwen. 'Ronnie, this is our new friend, Mademoiselle Mireille Boucart. She's been looking for a new kitchen knife and wanted to see what ours was like.'

'You shouldn't play with those,' said Ronnie sternly. 'You could hurt yourself.'

'From the mouths of children,' said Iris.

Agnes and Millie came dashing up behind him.

'Is everything all right, Mrs Bainbridge?' asked Millie, eyeing Mireille combatively. 'I heard shouting.'

'Everything is fine,' said Gwen. 'Isn't it, Mireille?'

Mireille glanced at each of the company in turn, finally settling on Ronnie.

'*Oui*,' she said, replacing the knife in the rack. 'It is a very nice knife. I shall have to get one for my kitchen.'

'Are you one of the dancers from Paris?' asked Ronnie.

'I am.'

'We're going to watch you on our new television,' he said.

'That is very sweet of you,' said Mireille. 'I hope you enjoy it.'

'Now, you get back to bed, Ronnie,' said Gwen.

'Yes, Mummy,' said Ronnie. 'Could I get a goodnight kiss from Iris?'

'Nothing would please me more,' said Iris, coming over to him and kissing his cheek.

'Come, Ronnie,' said Agnes. 'I'll tuck you in.'

The two ladies left with Ronnie, Millie casting a doubtful glare over her shoulder at the Parisienne.

'Right,' said Gwen. 'Come sit, and we'll start over. First order of business is to pour you that whisky.'

'And I could use a refill,' said Iris, holding up her glass.

Gwen poured for all of them, then held up her glass.

'To Jeanne-Marie,' she said.

They clinked glasses.

'Why were the two of you at the club last night?' asked Mireille.

'We're looking into Jeanne-Marie's murder,' said Iris.

'Are you police? Detectives?'

'No to the first, and occasionally to the second,' said Gwen. 'Mostly, we run a marriage bureau.'

'A marriage bureau? The one Jeanne-Marie went to?'

'That's us,' said Gwen. 'The Right Sort Marriage Bureau.'

'How do you become detectives there?'

'Quite accidentally, I assure you,' said Gwen.

'But we're rather good at it, as it turns out,' added Iris. 'Now, we have some questions for you.'

'The policeman already asked me questions.'

'We have more,' said Iris. 'They're about Paris during the war.'

'Why?'

'Because we think what's happening now has something to do with what happened then,' said Iris.

'Very well. Ask your questions.'

'This would have happened in mid-1943,' said Iris. 'Did you hear about a number of showgirls and other female performers from different clubs and theatres being taken away by the Nazis?'

'There was one from our club,' said Mireille. 'Her name was Yasmine. She was from Morocco. She was a – I don't know how you would say it in English – *une danseuse orientale.*'

She got up from the table and writhed her torso for a moment.

'A belly dancer,' said Gwen.

'God, I wish I could do that,' said Iris. 'Why was she taken?'

'She had become lovers with a German captain,' said Mireille. 'He would pick her up in his car every night. Then one evening before the show, they came for her. After they took her, they questioned everyone there.'

'About what?' asked Iris.

'About whether we had seen her passing information to anyone. We told them we knew nothing about that, and they left us alone. But we never saw her again.'

'Was this before or after Jeanne-Marie came to work at your club?' asked Gwen.

'She came just after,' said Mireille. 'There were several women taken from her club. She was afraid the Germans would think she was part of them.'

'Was she?' asked Iris.

'Maybe, maybe not,' said Mireille. 'She never told me any more about it.'

'What was the name of that club?'

'Café des Loups,' said Mireille. 'I've never been there. It had a reputation for having the women perform . . . favours for the more affluent gentlemen, even before the war. And especially after the Occupation.'

'And that was where she performed with Legrenzi?' asked Iris.
'*Oui*. May I ask you both a question?'
'You may.'
'Did Jeanne-Marie say why she wanted to come to your marriage bureau?'
'She wanted to get married to an Englishman,' said Iris. 'She said she didn't want to return to Paris.'
'Does it cost very much?'
'Our initial fee is five pounds,' said Iris. 'Twenty more if you marry another one of our clients.'
'I am surprised she would spend money like that,' said Mireille. 'She did not have much.'
'She had a fair amount with her when she came to the office,' said Iris. 'And she wanted us to speed the process along as much as possible. Normally, we like to put more time into these matches, but she said she wasn't choosy.'
'It was quite extraordinary,' said Gwen.
'She was so happy that you arranged that meeting so quickly,' said Mireille. 'She spoke of nothing else when she changed back at the hotel that afternoon.'
'I wonder why it went wrong then,' said Gwen.
'Did it?'
'The gentleman rang me up after their dinner to say that she said she had only gone to us because she wanted to make an old lover jealous, and that she was going back to him. Then she walked out. She must have gone to Alexandra Palace after that.'
'I know of no old lover other than Legrenzi,' said Mireille. 'She would never go back to him. That is very strange. She would have told me. We told each other everything.'
'And Legrenzi was in the hotel bar from Friday afternoon until late,' said Iris. 'The dead man is innocent, at least of that murder. I can't think of anything else to ask you.'
'Let me show you to your room,' said Gwen. 'What time shall we wake you tomorrow?'
'I have to rehearse early,' said Mireille. 'They are changing everything now.'
'I'll make sure you get to your bus,' said Gwen. 'Iris, I'll have to pass on walking with you to the shop tomorrow. Wait here a minute, if you would.'
'Of course.'

Gwen took Mireille up to the guest room. Millie had already laid out a towel and flannel for her. Gwen pointed out the bathroom and left her there.

'Interesting,' said Gwen when she returned to the kitchen. 'When I mentioned Café des Loups to Legrenzi, he denied working there.'

'If I were a former Nazi collaborator who had betrayed and killed my fellow employees, I wouldn't be too forthcoming about linking myself to where it happened,' said Iris.

'You think someone amongst the French avenged the ladies of Operation Showgirl?'

'It's a strong possibility,' said Iris. 'Maybe even someone here who had something to do with them. Mrs Cosslett was certainly enthusiastic about the idea.'

'Maybe,' said Gwen dubiously.

'What's your theory then?'

'I have a notion that I want to pursue further before I put it up for examination,' said Gwen. 'If you don't mind running the shop tomorrow morning, I am going to look into it.'

'Can do,' said Iris. 'Going anywhere dangerous?'

'Back to Ally Pally,' said Gwen. 'So yes.'

'Well, I'm going back to the boat,' said Iris, getting to her feet. She wobbled for a moment.

'Is that the whisky, or are you coming down from your evening's exhilaration?' asked Gwen.

'A bit of both,' Iris admitted.

'Right,' said Gwen. 'Constable Merrick will be walking you to the *Cecilia* again.'

She walked Iris as far as Carlton Hill, where the policeman was once again walking his beat.

'Good evening, ladies,' he said as he saw them. 'Does Miss Sparks require the pleasure of my company again?'

'I do, if it won't be too much trouble,' replied Iris.

'None whatsoever,' he said. 'But we must stop meeting like this. People will talk.'

She laughed, surprising herself. It felt good to laugh.

'Let them talk,' she said, taking his arm. 'Goodnight, Gwen.'

'Goodnight, Iris.'

Merrick chatted quietly about whatever topics came to mind, mostly his observations of the denizens of the neighbourhood, until they reached the *Cecilia*. Iris thanked him profusely, entered the narrowboat, and collapsed headlong on to her bed without removing a single piece of clothing. She was asleep in seconds.

She awoke at dawn, her head throbbing. She turned on the hot-water heater, changed into her exercise togs and forced herself to climb to the roof. The workout cleared her head somewhat, and she permitted herself a brief shower, which went a long way further towards making her feel human again.

She made tea and toasted a single slice of bread, indulging in a precious spoonful of orange marmalade from her dwindling supply. Then she changed into a blue Utility suit that hadn't been slept in recently and walked out to face the world once again.

She stopped short on the gangplank as she saw the Bentley parked in front of her, the engine idling. A tall, well-built man in his thirties was standing by it, looking straight at her.

Right, she thought.

She walked up to him.

'You looked better in uniform, Sergeant Carruthers,' she said.

'So did you, Lollipop,' he replied.

He opened the rear door. She looked inside. An older man sat in the back, wearing a grey suit, a trilby hat on the seat beside him.

'Get in, Sparks,' he said, still facing forward.

'I don't know if I want to,' she said.

'No games, Sparks,' he said. 'It's too early in the morning. Get in.'

She slid in beside him. Carruthers closed the door, then got in behind the wheel.

'Hello, Brigadier,' she said.

THIRTEEN

The Bentley pulled away from the kerb.

'Where are we going?' asked Sparks.

'To Mayfair, of course,' said the Brigadier. 'That's where your office is, isn't it?'

'Goodness! Are you looking for a wife? I don't know if we have anyone that old at the moment.'

'Nothing like that, Sparks.'

'Then this isn't a professional call, is it?'

'I'm afraid not. At least, it isn't one for you.'

'Well, unless we're taking the long route to Mayfair, I suggest that you tell me what you want.'

'Hmm, where shall I start?' he said. 'I received a request through back channels from Scotland Yard last night. A detective by the name of Kinsey. I believe you know him.'

'You know that I do,' said Sparks, all playfulness gone from her voice.

'You still blame me for destroying that relationship, don't you?'

'I blame myself more,' she said. 'I accepted that assignment knowing what I was getting in to. But you offered it to me knowing how eager I was to prove I would do anything for the firm, even sleeping with an enemy, so I do blame you, too.'

'It was unfortunate what happened,' said the Brigadier.

'Are you expressing an actual regret, sir?'

'Not at all. If I had to do it all over again under those circumstances, I would have made exactly the same plan, and asked you to be the one to implement it. And it worked perfectly well. Until it didn't.'

'End result: one dead Spaniard, one dead engagement, one me on Mike's permanent suspect list,' said Sparks. 'I've always wondered if he would have forgiven me if he knew the truth.'

'If you're asking me to reveal it to him, the answer is forever no,' said the Brigadier.

'Well, we've all moved on, haven't we?' said Sparks. 'So Mike reached out through official channels to ask what?'

'The message began, "A French marionnettiste was murdered by poison gas at Alexandra Palace this morning",' said the Brigadier. 'One of the most bizarre openings to a message I have ever seen. But then I found out that you were involved, and things became less surprising once I knew that.'

'What did he want to know?'

'About a woman who worked for us, code-named Albertine. You worked next to her when you were handling Major Stanton's mission.'

'I remember her.'

'Apparently you remembered her well enough to bring her into this investigation of yours,' he said sharply.

'I did.'

'I've lost count of how many rules you broke doing that. Even speaking to her about those experiences violated the Act.'

'The police have made Sally – excuse me, Captain Danielli – their prime target,' she said.

'So I understand.'

'Even if you owe me nothing, you owe him,' she said. 'England owes him. Maybe I broke your rules. No – no "maybe" about it. I broke them knowingly and willingly because I was helping Sally. And if I had to do it all over again under these circumstances, I would have made exactly the same plan, and would have asked Mrs Cosslett to be the one to implement it. And it worked perfectly well. Until it didn't.'

'No, it didn't,' agreed the Brigadier.

'What did Mike want from you? Specifically?'

'He wanted us to authorize Mrs Cosslett to tell them what she knows. And for you to do the same.'

'Are you granting it?'

He pulled a silver case from his jacket, removed a cigarette, and tapped it against the lid. He held the case out to Sparks, who shook her head. He replaced the case, then lit the cigarette and inhaled the smoke. She waited.

'My inclination is to deny permission,' he said.

'Sir, I must ask you—'

He held up his hand to stop her.

'However, I am going to override my instincts in this case,' he said. 'It is Danielli's neck on the line, as you said. But I think it was the oddity of it being your ex-fiancé making the request that convinced me. It stirred up something, a need to make some form of amends to both of you, even if I can't restore what had been.'

'That sounds suspiciously like a regret, sir.'

'Maybe so,' he said. 'I shan't be making a habit of it if it is. Cosslett only, though. No need for you to enlighten him any further about your part in our operations.'

'What about Operation Showgirl? Is there anything more you can tell me about it? It seems to be linked to this matter.'

'It wasn't my operation,' he said. 'France wasn't my territory back then.'

'But you know about it now, don't you? I imagine the first thing you would have done once you got the request from Mike would be to pull the file.'

'Files from failed operations are frequently hard to locate,' he said. 'People would rather they stay buried.'

'Who was running things in France back then?'

'Can't tell you, Sparks,' he said. 'Besides, the fellow's dead.'

'Is there a file somewhere with Lisette's real name?' she persisted. 'Someone at our end must have known who she was. Who recruited her, or her predecessor? Someone from here must have gone in to set things up at some point.'

'Your ex is working under the theory that this marionnettiste was killed to avenge her death,' said the Brigadier. 'A theory suggested by you.'

'Yes.'

'What I gleaned from what little I heard about it at the time was that we sent a man into Paris immediately after Dunkirk fell. He was to set up rings to gather information, anticipating that the Germans would come for that city next, then get the hell out. One of them was Showgirl.'

'Is he still alive?'

'I could find out for you,' said the Brigadier.

'I would be grateful, sir.'

He turned to look directly at her for the first time.

'In the years that I've known you, Sparks, I don't think I've ever seen you this – I'm trying to come up with the appropriate word.'

'Polite?' she suggested. 'Although I will accept stunningly beautiful.'

'Subdued,' he said.

'I am most certainly not that,' she said vehemently, but even as she did, she felt the lack of the necessary force to sell it.

'Not that it matters,' he said. 'You're not working for me.'

'No. Nor will I.'

'We won't bother repeating that particular conversation,' he said. 'But we have kept tabs on you since our last encounter. I know about your loss. My condolences. I only met Mr Spelling the one time, but he struck me as a capable man.'

'Oh, Archie was capable of many things,' she said with a fond smile.

'Was his death the reason you're now holed up in a boat on the Regent's Canal?'

'The convents wouldn't take me.'

'It must be nice to be able to keep the world at bay,' he said wistfully. 'Hard to do in London.'

'I didn't shut it out entirely. You showed up. But I've grown to like it there. And the walk to the office keeps me trim.'

'As do your martial arts exercises. I'm glad to see you've kept up with them.'

'You watched me?'

'We were waiting for the opportune moment to intercept you.'

'Very enjoyable,' added Carruthers, holding up a pair of binoculars with his free hand.

'I'm not sure I like the idea of you watching me like that,' said Sparks. 'A lady likes her privacy when she's exercising.'

'Then the lady shouldn't do it on the roof of a narrowboat,' said the Brigadier. 'And here we are. The famous marriage bureau. Go and match your clients, Sparks. But if you ever want something more interesting and worthwhile to do, I might have something for you.'

'A continuing no,' said Sparks as Carruthers came around to open the door for her. 'I find my current life both interesting and worthwhile. Thanks for the lift, sir. And the information. Call me here when you find out who the recruiter was.'

'Will do,' said the Brigadier.

He watched her go into the building without looking back. Carruthers got back in and put the Bentley in gear.

'I wonder who's lonelier,' he said. 'The people she's matching, or her?'

'Her, of course,' said the Brigadier. 'The others are at least trying.'

Ernie, the architect, got to Ally Pally around the same time Iris was dropped off at The Right Sort. He had taken a room in Muswell Hill for the duration of the job, renting by the week, thinking he wouldn't be there that long, but the rose window was a massive thing, and he was figuring out how to put it back together all by himself, so the weekly rent was stretching on past what he had hoped for.

But living there saved him on transport, and living in the city proper wouldn't have done his purse any better. It was a pleasant walk up the hill to Ally Pally, and if he felt particularly in need of inspiration, he would set his alarm clock for half an hour before dawn, then watch the sunrise from atop the scaffold, sipping tea from his thermos, reminding himself that it was good to be alive after all he'd been through.

This was not a sunrise morning, though. He put his lunchbox and thermos, along with his satchel, into the large bucket resting by the foot of the ladder with a rope connecting it to the top, climbed up to the platform, then hauled the bucket up and placed it against the wall just below the gaping hole that had once been a secular spectacle of stained glass.

There was a large tarpaulin spread across the wooden planks that made up the top level of the scaffolding. He rolled it up and contemplated his progress, walking carefully around the pieces of glass he had placed in the various sectors of the giant circle he had laid out. Then he pulled a photograph from his satchel and compared it to the patterns that lay before him.

The bus from the BBC headquarters trundled up the hill and pulled up in front of him, disgorging a mixed flock of secretaries, scenery artists and switchboard operators, now enhanced with a gaggle of young lovelies who chattered away in French.

'Yo, ladies!' he called from up high, and some of them looked up and waved back.

Which was all he could hope for, given their relative positions.

It would have been nice if one of them, out of curiosity, would climb up to see what he was accomplishing. Because it was wonderful, he thought as he looked at it.

Yellow, he thought as he studied one sector. A piece of yellow was needed. He went to the bucket where he had the yellow pieces stored and pulled out a handful, then laid them out by the sector where he had begun. He picked up one of the larger ones, pausing to look through it as the last of the passengers disappeared under his platform, then at the vista in front of him, momentarily turning the world yellow.

The bus pulled away. Various men, important or wealthy enough to merit cars of their own, made their way from the car park to the two front entrances. None of them looked up to acknowledge his existence. He didn't work for them, so he did not matter to them. The exception to that rule had been Danielli, the tall man, who would venture up the ladder during his lunch hour to see what progress Ernie was making, or just sit with him on the edge of the platform, their legs dangling as they ate, like a couple of schoolboys on break, but with the best view in a hundred miles.

The yellow piece wouldn't fit into the sector he was looking at, but the curve of one edge looked familiar. He spotted the corresponding piece two sections over and placed this one by it.

There, he thought. Another one done and it only took me – he consulted his watch – six minutes. At this rate it will take me . . .

He looked at the bucket filled with yellow pieces, then at the other buckets, each filled to the brim with other colours, and decided to forgo the calculation.

Around nine twenty, he noticed a taxi coming up the drive. Nothing unusual about that, but then it stopped short by the end of the building.

Odd, he thought. Even if someone was going to one of the workshops, they would still have to check in by entering one of the front doors. He reached into his satchel and pulled out his binoculars, focusing them on the taxi.

Then the woman got out, and Ernie revised his opinion as to what was the best view in London. She was tall, blonde, and gorgeous. And, for some reason, she was staring at the side door to the lower level.

Then she turned and saw him watching her from on high. He hastily thrust the binoculars back into the satchel, hoping she hadn't seen them, then looked back to see her still looking at him. She smiled and waved.

Tentatively, in case he was mistaken as to whom she was directing it (but there was no one else to wave at, was there?), he waved back. Then she began walking in his direction.

Well, she must have figured out she couldn't go through the side door, he thought. This had nought to do with him. He shouldn't let himself be distracted. That window wasn't going to reassemble itself.

He let himself be distracted. He was looking – no, he was staring at her like she was an incoming V-2 homing in on his perch atop the scaffolding, and there was nowhere he could hide.

Stop staring at her, Ernie, he admonished himself. She wouldn't be coming all the way here to see you, so stop acting like some daft bimper. You're not impressing anyone like this. Get back to work.

Reluctantly, he pulled more pieces from the bucket and laid them out. Out of the corner of his eye, he saw the woman come up to the scaffolding, then disappear under it.

She's going inside, he thought. Of course she is. That's where everything important is.

He waited to hear the door open and shut, for the vision of beauty to walk out of his life as mysteriously as she had walked into it.

But he did not hear the door open and shut. Instead, there was a very faint trembling in the floor beneath him, then the sound of someone ascending the ladder.

Ascending his ladder!

That can't be, he thought in astonishment, but a moment later, the radiant crown of blonde hair rose into view followed by the rest of her. She saw him outright goggling at her now, and her smile grew even broader.

'Request permission to come aboard,' she said.

'Miss, you shouldn't be coming up here!' he protested. 'It isn't safe.'

'It looks sturdy enough,' she said as she climbed on to the platform, looking around. 'In any case, it has to be me coming here. My partner, who is afraid of nothing else, is terrified of heights.'

'And you're not?'

'I've skied the highest slopes at St Moritz and Gstaad,' she replied. 'This is an anthill by comparison. My name is Gwen Bainbridge, by the way. You're Ernie, correct?'

'Ernie Spashett,' he said, stammering. 'You're one of Sally's friends. You were with him the other day, along with a brunette woman and a pair of young boys.'

'Exactly right,' she said. 'What an excellent memory you have!'

She turned to gaze out towards the city proper.

'Glorious,' she pronounced. 'You're a very lucky man to have this as a backdrop for your job. The window behind my desk overlooks a construction site, and the noise and the dust are singularly lacking in aesthetics. I envy you your view.'

'It's lovely, as long as it isn't raining,' he said.

'Yes, I'm sure that's an inconvenience,' said Mrs Bainbridge. 'Do I detect a dash of Cornwall in your speech, Mr Spashett?'

'Ayes, miss,' he said. 'From Penzance. And please don't sing anything. I've heard every song from that ever since I went upcountry.'

'I'm sure that must be tiresome,' she said.

She looked down at the pieces of glass partially assembled, then back at the gaping round hole behind her.

'Do they think you can put Humpty Dumpty back together again?' she asked.

'They want me to try,' he said. 'First, I have to see how much of the glass survived. It's like putting together the world's biggest jigsaw puzzle.'

'You don't work for the BBC, I take it.'

'No, miss,' he replied. 'I joined the Ministry of Works as an architect. This is my first job since I was demobbed.'

She looked at him more closely. He was younger than her. He couldn't have been more than twenty-four, with a cheerful, slightly narrowed face, ears that stuck out, and hair that had grown accustomed to being out in the wind.

'Where did you study?' she asked.

'At the Guildhall in St Ives until I signed up. And now with the ministry.'

'What does an architect do in the military?' she wondered. 'Design barracks and hangars and the like?'

'That would have been a much more pleasant experience than the one I had,' he said sombrely. 'I was a pilot in the RAF. I flew Halifaxes.'

'I'm not sure what those are,' she said. 'But my son's friend, the one who was with us the other day, could tell me all about them.'

'It's a bomber, miss. Four-engined, good old boat. I flew missions over France and Germany from '42 until the end. Didn't design so much as a ridge tent the entire time.'

'So this height is nothing to you, either,' she said, chastened. 'Nor are my Swiss mountains.'

'I hear they're quite spectacular, miss,' he said.

'Thank you for your service, Mr Spashett,' she said. 'What will this be when you're finished?'

'This is what was there,' he said, showing her the photograph.

The original rose window was a stylized representation of the sun, its rays spreading out through wedges capped by large yellow diamonds containing smaller orange diamonds alternating with simple cross shapes, all of it encircled by a blue field that deepened from the pale to near-violet.

'Lovely,' she pronounced. 'I like that it's a sun, not a cross. Something almost pagan about that.'

'It's still religious in its way,' he said. 'This palace was built to be a place of community, a place of escape, a place of contemplation, and they put it on the highest elevation they could find. They didn't need to put in a rose window, but they did. I studied cathedrals, and the windows always fascinated me. I wondered if Christopher Wren or Jean de Chelles had visions of what the designs would be like, or if they just put a great big round hole in the wall and said, "Here, lads. Put something pretty in there."'

'What if there isn't enough glass surviving to preserve it?'

'I don't think there will be,' he said. 'Too much of it is browjans.'

'What are those?'

'Sorry, that's Cornish. Fragments, I should have said. But if there's not enough, I'm going to redesign it.'

'I like puzzles,' she said. 'May I have a go?'

'Certainly, miss. But first, tell me this.'

He picked up a yellow piece and handed it to her.

'I'm reassembling it with the outer face looking up,' he said. 'If I was in Penzance, I'd be asking if you could tell which face of the piece is allycumpooster because you don't want it backsyfore?'

'Meaning?' she asked, laughing.

'Which piece is all right, because you don't want it wrong side out.'

'Let me see,' she said, holding it up to her eyes and twirling it.

Then she traced her fingers lightly over the two surfaces.

'This side faces out,' she pronounced. 'It looks and feels as if it's been through the storms over the years.'

'Very good, miss.'

She walked around the perimeter of the sun, then stopped and knelt before it, placing the piece carefully into one of the diamonds.

Like a goddess remaking the universe, he thought, watching her reverently.

'Well done, miss,' he said.

'Thank you,' she said, rising. 'Now, speaking of puzzles, I'm working on a rather complicated one myself, which is why I've come to you. Have you heard about what's been happening inside?'

'Just what Jimmy at the desk told me. I only come into the building to use the lav, pardon my saying it. He told me there was a woman killed here Friday night. One of the Frenchies.'

'And a man was killed here yesterday. Also a Frenchman.'

'That's horrible,' he said. 'But why are you asking me about it?'

'Have the police spoken to you?'

'No, miss. I guess since I wasn't working Friday night, they didn't bother.'

'But you were working Friday afternoon, weren't you?'

'I was.'

'Did you see the French ladies leave on the bus?'

'Yes, miss. I was taking my lunch right about then. I remember giving them a wave.'

'Did you, by any chance, see one of them come back later that afternoon in a taxi? And get dropped off down at that end of the building where I was dropped off?'

She was looking at his face with a sudden intensity that he found distinctly unnerving.

'No, miss, I didn't,' he said, and her face fell.

'Damn,' she said. 'I was certain she had come back.'

'One of them did come back,' he said. 'But it wasn't in a taxi.'

'She did?' exclaimed Gwen. 'Was she on foot?'

'Oh, no,' he replied. 'She was in a car. One of the fellows who works here was driving. He parked in the lot down there. I had my binoculars with me.'

He pulled them out.

'Souvenir from piloting,' he said, holding them out to her. 'Always on the lookout for anything coming from any direction. And I like looking at birds.'

She looked through them, bringing the end of the building into clear focus.

'Was she a brunette?' she asked quietly.

'Yes, miss.'

'Would you recognize her picture if you saw it?'

'I would.'

'One more thing,' said Gwen.

She pulled out her notepad and handed it to him, opened to a sketch of a man's face. He looked at it carefully.

'You've taken lessons,' he commented.

'I have. Do you recognize him?'

'That looks like the man,' he said. 'I don't know his name, but I've seen him coming and going. Bit of a tuss, as far as I'm concerned. Never says hello when I do.'

'Mr Spashett, the police may need you to come in and repeat all of this,' said Gwen. 'May I get your number?'

'I would give you my number even if the police didn't need it,' he said, grinning shyly, jotting it down on her notepad. 'It's my landlord's. I don't have a telephone of my own. And call me Ernie, please.'

'Thank you, Ernie,' she said, taking it back. 'Good luck with the window. I hope you get the chance to redesign it. I think it will be marvellous. Goodbye.'

He held her hand and helped her negotiate her way back on

to the ladder. She climbed down carefully, then disappeared under the scaffolding.

This time, he heard the door open and shut.

Ah, well, he thought. Then he picked up another yellow piece and went back to rebuilding the sun.

Gwen went up to the man sitting at the front desk.

'I'm Mrs Bainbridge,' she said, showing him her ident. 'I believe Mr Conley added me to the list. Is he in his office?'

'Yes, madam. That's all the way down to the right. Room 113.'

She followed the corridors to the right tower, where the administrative offices were located. She found Conley at his desk. He looked up at her in surprise.

'Mrs Bainbridge,' he said, rising to guide her to a chair. 'This is unexpected. Are you here to make a progress report?'

'Not so much a report as a request,' she said. 'Will there be a run-through of *Across the Channel* before it airs?'

'More than one, I believe,' he said. 'They're rearranging the running order and adding another number for Mademoiselle Rivette.'

'When will the run-through be?'

'Tomorrow. Mid-morning.'

'Excellent. May I borrow your telephone?'

'Certainly,' he said, sliding it across his desk.

She pulled out her address book, looked up a number, then dialled.

'Detective Sergeant Kinsey, please,' she said. 'It's Mrs Bainbridge calling. Hello, Detective Sergeant. I've found something you've missed. Could you and your partner meet me at our office in an hour? Very good. I'll see you there.'

'What did you find?' asked Conley.

'Something impossible,' she said, dialling another number. 'Hello, Saundra. Put me through to Miss Sparks, would you? Iris, brace yourself. Mike's coming over in an hour. No, I invited him. I'm calling a cab now, but be nice to him if he beats me there.'

'Are you going to tell me?' asked Conley in exasperation.

'Not until we've confirmed everything,' she said. 'I'm going to call you later when I know who's coming.'

'Coming where?'

'To the rehearsal, of course,' she said, dialling a number for a cab service.

* * *

Iris couldn't concentrate on work at all after Gwen's call. She glanced at her watch every two minutes, willing it to go faster, yet dreading Detective Ex's arrival.

The telephone rang. She resisted the reflex to snatch it from its cradle, allowing Mrs Billington to do her job. A moment later, the intercom buzzed. She forced herself to answer it calmly.

'There is a Mr Petheridge for you,' said Mrs Billington. 'He's not one of our clients.'

'That's fine, Saundra. Put him through.'

A second later, the Brigadier's voice came on the telephone.

'I have a name for you,' he said.

'Go ahead,' she said, grabbing a pencil.

She wrote it down.

'I don't know what he's doing currently,' continued the Brigadier.

'That's all right,' said Iris. 'I do.'

Fifteen minutes later, Gwen came through the door.

'I think I have the who and the how,' she said triumphantly. 'Still working on the why.'

Iris held up a piece of paper. On it was written: FREDDIE OAKES.

Gwen stared at it in astonishment, then reached into her bag and pulled out the sketch she had shown to Spashett. It was of Oakes.

'That's a good likeness,' said Iris.

'How did you know?'

'I was visited by the Ghost of Wartime Past,' said Iris. 'The Brigadier was waiting outside the *Cecilia* this morning.'

'Oh, dear,' said Gwen, hanging up her coat and hat. 'How much trouble are you in? And am I included?'

'Don't know, and possibly,' said Iris. 'I've told you too much.'

'Then you might as well tell me more,' said Gwen as she sat behind her desk.

'Oakes worked for British Intelligence during the war. He was sent into Paris to organize spy rings, including one involving cabaret performers and dancers.'

'He certainly knows that world,' said Gwen. 'Sounds like he was a good choice for the assignment. So there was a connection between him and the women who were betrayed by Legrenzi. That sheds some light.'

'It would support the revenge theory,' said Iris.

Gwen shook her head.

'I don't think it was that,' she said.

'What then?'

'I think that may be Mike and DS Harvey coming up the stairs. Let's wait for them.'

A moment later, Kinsey appeared in the doorway, Harvey at his shoulder.

'Please, join us,' said Mrs Bainbridge. 'Thank you for coming at such short notice.'

'Hello, Mike,' said Sparks. 'DS Harvey.'

'Mrs Bainbridge, you claim to have found something we've missed,' said Kinsey, ignoring Sparks's greeting.

'Yes,' said Mrs Bainbridge. 'Two things, in fact.'

'We have questioned every single person working in that building,' he said vehemently. 'As well as every one of the French performers. I have verified their stories as to their whereabouts Friday night, cross-checked them against each other, and eliminated every single one of them as a possible killer with the exception of Mr Danielli. I have maps, I have diagrams, I have photographs, fingerprints and metallurgical comparisons of the wire in the garrotte with every wire we could find in the place. Tell me what I've left out.'

'Two things that point to Freddie Oakes,' said Mrs Bainbridge.

'And there is much to know about Mr Oakes,' said Sparks. 'You'll be getting all this through official channels at some point, but what you're about to be told is that he worked in intelligence during the war and recruited showgirls and performers in Paris to insinuate themselves into the beds of the occupiers. The women he recruited were ultimately betrayed and executed.'

'All right, that's interesting,' said Kinsey. 'Oakes didn't mention that aspect of his life when he spoke to us. Another Official Secrets Act intervention, I suppose.'

'More likely concealing something worse,' said Mrs Bainbridge. 'I think he killed Mademoiselle Duplessis.'

'Impossible,' said Kinsey. 'He had an alibi. There is no way he could have been in Ally Pally with Duplessis that night.'

'No, there isn't,' agreed Mrs Bainbridge. 'You're correct, it's quite impossible. Now, here's the first thing you missed. You interviewed everyone inside the building. But not everyone outside it. There was a man working on restoring the rose window. His name is Ernie Spashett.'

'He's not on the employee lists,' said Kinsey.

'Nor would he be. He's with the Ministry of Public Works. He virtually lives on that scaffolding in front of the central entrance.'

'And I suppose he knocks off at five when the light's no good,' said Kinsey. 'Why does he matter for Friday night?'

'Because on Friday afternoon, he saw one of the Frenchwomen return to Alexandra Palace and go in the side entrance. I think it was Jeanne-Marie Duplessis. And she was with Freddie Oakes.'

'Oakes still couldn't have killed her,' insisted Kinsey. 'He was the most documented man in London that night. He was gadding about with that *chanteuse* at all the hot clubs. Every maître d' and every tabloid photographer in town verified that.'

'You're quite right, of course,' said Mrs Bainbridge, beaming at him. 'Which is why you are also completely wrong about everything. And I'm willing to bet—'

'Here it comes,' said Sparks.

'I am willing to bet you tuppence,' continued Mrs Bainbridge, 'that you have neglected to do one very important, basic thing in this case.'

'What's that?' he asked.

She wrote something down on a piece of paper, folded it in half, then held it towards him. He reached for it, but she pulled it away from his grasp at the last second.

'Do we have a bet, Detective Sergeant?' she asked, holding it up.

'Tuppence? Yeah, I can afford that' he said. 'The bet is on, Mrs Bainbridge.'

She handed it to him. He opened it, read what was written, winced, then handed it to Harvey.

'I guess we go back to Mr Farrell now,' said Harvey as he read the note.

'I guess we do,' said Kinsey.

Ted Farrell was at a lathe, turning legs for kitchen chairs at the furniture factory where he worked, when Alf came over and tapped him on the shoulder.

'Couple of detectives want to talk to you, Ted,' he shouted over the noise. 'What've you done now?'

Farrell looked up to see Kinsey and Harvey standing at the top of the stairs. He sighed and shut off the machine, then went to join them, wiping his hands on his apron.

'Why do you got to be bothering me at work?' he asked. 'Haven't you caught the bloke yet?'

'We neglected to do one thing,' said Kinsey. 'Mind stepping into the office for a moment?'

'Am I in trouble?' he asked. 'Do I need to get my union rep?'

'Nothing like that, I assure you,' said Kinsey. 'It will just take a minute.'

He looked back at Alf and shouted, 'Won't be long.'

Alf shrugged, and Farrell followed the two detectives to the office. They closed the door, and Kinsey reached into his satchel and removed a photograph, which he placed on the desk.

Farrell peered down at it and winced.

'Who's that?' he asked.

'You don't know?' asked Kinsey.

'Nope.'

'Guess you just lost tuppence,' Harvey said to Kinsey.

'Guess so,' said Kinsey.

FOURTEEN

Kinsey pulled up in front of their building in a grey Wolseley Eight saloon at nine fifteen the next morning. The two women were waiting in the foyer, and came out as soon as they saw him.

'Just you?' asked Sparks as he came around to open the door.

'Harvey is collecting our other guests,' he said. 'Speaking of which . . .'

He reached into his pocket, pulled out two pennies, and handed them to Mrs Bainbridge.

'Sweets for Ronnie,' she said, putting them in her bag. 'Where shall we sit?'

'You take the front,' said Sparks. 'You have longer legs.'

And that won't put me right next to him, she thought.

They got in, and Kinsey put the car in gear.

'I didn't know the Yard had Wolseleys in any colour other than black,' commented Sparks.

'We don't always want to signal our presence,' said Kinsey. 'I have ten men in plain clothes coming in separate cars. Mr Conley is having Oakes into his office for a meeting at ten so we can slip in without being seen. Harvey is bringing in the rest of our guests. The rehearsal starts at ten thirty. We'll start Phase One at ten fifteen.'

'Which is me,' said Mrs Bainbridge. 'Iris, I'm going through a phase! How exciting!'

'Are you certain about this?' Sparks asked her.

'I am,' she replied. 'And help won't be far away, will it?'

'One scream, and we'll be there in twelve seconds,' promised Kinsey.

'What if she can't scream?' asked Sparks.

'If she stops talking, we'll be there in six seconds,' said Kinsey.

They continued discussing their plans until they reached Muswell Hill. Kinsey parked in the car park reserved for visitors. There were several other Wolseleys mixed in with the rest of the vehicles.

'Is that Spashett?' asked Kinsey as they walked up to Alexandra Palace.

'It is,' replied Mrs Bainbridge, waving to the architect.

He waved back, this time making no effort to conceal the binoculars in his other hand. They walked to his ladder and looked up. He peered back down from the edge of the platform.

'Good morning, Ernie,' said Mrs Bainbridge. 'Could you come down and meet someone?'

'Of course,' he said, quickly descending the ladder. 'Good morning. Ernie Spashett, Ministry of Public Works.'

'Good morning, Mr Spashett,' said Kinsey, pulling out his identification. 'Detective Sergeant Michael Kinsey, Scotland Yard. You already know Mrs Bainbridge. This is Miss Iris Sparks, my . . . er, Mrs Bainbridge's business partner.'

'How do you do, Miss Sparks?' said Ernie. 'You came in with Mrs Bainbridge and Mr Danielli on Saturday.'

'I did,' said Sparks.

'Mr Spashett, we require your help in a police matter,' said Kinsey. 'It will take perhaps an hour or so of your time.'

'When?'

'Right now,' said Kinsey. 'I promise to square things with your ministry over missing work.'

'To tell you the truth, I think the ministry has completely forgot I'm here,' said Spashett, grinning. 'I don't mind the break. It sounds more important.'

'In the short run, it is,' said Mrs Bainbridge. 'Art, of course, is for the ages.'

'Come with us, Mr Spashett,' said Kinsey. 'We'll tell you your role inside.'

Oakes emerged from Conley's office feeling peeved. The meeting had been about several petty expenses, most of which vaguely masked entertainment for the visiting performers, not to mention himself, which he felt were perfectly justified given the amount of work he had put into organizing this production. He deserved some amusement as recompense. And the free publicity he had generated by taking Mademoiselle Rivette to those clubs was worth the cost in champagne and taxis.

He muttered harsh words about Conley as he walked, so annoyed that he didn't notice the woman until he was almost on top of her.

'Oh, hullo,' he said, his mood altering in an instant. 'You're Danielli's friend, aren't you? We met the other day before everything went topsy-turvy.'

'Yes, I remember it quite well,' she said. 'I'm Gwen Bainbridge. You mistook me for an actress, which was very flattering.'

'On the contrary, I think beauty should be put out there for all to see,' said Oakes. 'Especially beauty like yours.'

'I can't tell you how much that means to me,' said Mrs Bainbridge. 'I've been thinking about what you said ever since our meeting. Do you really think I could be on the stage?'

'Stage, television, even film,' he said grandly. 'Do you have representation?'

'Oh, dear, do I need it?' she asked. 'I've never done anything like this before.'

'Well, it doesn't matter right now,' he said. 'Where do you think your talents lie? Did you do any acting in school?'

'Goodness, yes, but I was so much taller than the rest of the girls that I always played the male roles,' she said with a laugh.

'That was certainly a waste,' he said, eyeing her roguishly. 'Although I wouldn't have minded seeing a love scene between you and the ingénue.'

'Now, now, Mr Oakes,' she said, wagging her finger at him playfully. 'Don't be naughty. But come to think of it, I did memorize one of Joan of Arc's speeches from the Shaw play. Do you have time for a quick audition?'

He glanced at his watch. He wasn't really needed for the rehearsal, he thought, and this was promising to be some unexpected fun.

'I think I could squeeze you in,' he said.

'Lovely,' she said. 'Now, as to where? Both of the studios are being used. What about the old theatre?'

'Where that poor woman was killed?'

'Oh, I'm sure the police are finished with it by now,' she said, sliding her arm into his. 'Besides, I think it would give the whole thing an extra frisson, don't you?'

He allowed himself to be led down the halls as she chattered away. The two of them finally fetched up against the stage door. She tried the doorknob.

'Blast, it's locked,' she said in chagrin. 'I wonder if there's another way in.'

'No need to fret, my dear,' he said, reaching for his keychain.

He sorted through his keys until he found the one he was looking for, then he unlocked the door and held it open for her.

'So you do have a key to that door,' said a voice from behind him. 'Interesting.'

Oakes whirled to see Kinsey, Sparks, and a pair of plainclothes constables coming toward them.

'He was a stage manager here before the war,' said Mrs Bainbridge. 'I imagine he forgot to turn in his keys when he joined up.'

'Something you failed to tell us when we interviewed you,' said Kinsey. 'We were under the impression that there were only four men with keys to this particular door, but here you are.'

'What of it?' asked Oakes.

'Mr Spashett, would you join us, please?' Kinsey called.

The architect came out of a door in the hallway.

'Do you recognize this man?' asked Kinsey.

'Yes,' said Spashett. 'He works here.'

'Of course I work here,' said Oakes in exasperation.

'And he was the man I saw coming in the side entrance on Friday afternoon with the Frenchwoman,' continued Spashett.

'Now, hold on,' protested Oakes.

Kinsey ignored him, reaching into his satchel for a photograph. He showed it to Spashett.

'Was this the woman?' he asked quietly.

Spashett looked at the photograph and turned slightly pale.

'Oh, dear,' he said. 'Yes, that was her. Poor girl.'

Kinsey turned the photograph around to show it to Oakes. It was a close-up of Duplessis, taken as she lay on the floor of the theatre where she had been found.

'Mr Oakes, I am placing you under arrest for the murder of Jeanne-Marie Duplessis,' said Kinsey as the other policemen moved in. 'Take him to the Yard, gentlemen. Use the exit to the right end of the building. We'll speak with him further.'

They quickly handcuffed Oakes.

'This is absurd!' he shouted as they led him away. 'I was nowhere near here that night!'

Kinsey looked at his watch.

'Ten twenty-seven,' he said. 'Perfect timing. On to Phase Two. Mr Spashett, we'll let you go for the moment, but we'll get you to come down to make a statement later.'

'May I watch Phase Two, whatever it is?' pleaded Spashett.

'I'm afraid not,' said Kinsey. 'It's going to be crowded enough as it is. Sparks, Bainbridge, with me. Quick march.'

'Thank you, Ernie,' said Mrs Bainbridge as they passed him.

The three walked quickly to the corridor by Studio A and the control room. Conley was waiting for them. He nodded as he saw them and knocked softly on a door. It opened, and out came Harvey with Theresa Cosslett.

'Go all right?' asked Harvey.

'It did,' said Kinsey. 'Hello, Mrs Cosslett. Are you ready to watch some more television?'

'I still don't know why you want me here,' said Cosslett.

'We don't want to influence you in advance,' said Kinsey. 'So we'll be keeping you in the dark for the moment. Mr Conley, please lead the way.'

Conley led them to the control room, then opened the door.

'Mr Postlethwaite, I'm bringing in some people to observe,' he called inside. 'Carry on as if they weren't here.'

'Very good, Mr Conley,' replied the director.

Postlethwaite was sitting at a console, looking up at the monitors with the feeds from the cameras from both studios, six in all. On Camera Two was Claudine Rivette, waiting in front of the cancan dancers who were standing in a line wearing leotards and rehearsal togs and looking bored. On Camera One was Maurice Highmore, immediately recognizable by the famous moustache. He was clad in an ordinary suit rather than the dinner jacket he wore when on the air, and was smoking a cigarette in a long black holder. The third camera was on the band, who sat waiting for things to commence.

The visitors crammed together behind the crew. Sparks noticed Haight working the sound and gave him a slight nod. He nodded back, then turned to his console.

'Can everyone hear me?' said Postlethwaite into a microphone. 'Give me a wave.'

Hands went up at all three cameras.

'Good,' he said. 'First one's for love, then we go for timing. Cameras?'

'Camera One ready.'

'Camera Two ready.'

'Camera Three ready.'

'Music ready,' called the music director from the bandstand.

'Sound ready,' said Haight.

'Quiet, everyone,' said Postlethwaite. 'Camera Three to start. Five, four, three . . .'

He left the last two silent, then the drummer began a crescendo on the tympani, and the band launched into 'The Last Time I Saw Paris'.

Both Sparks and Mrs Bainbridge suppressed the urge to hum along.

'Camera One,' murmured Postlethwaite.

Highmore, his cigarette held at a jaunty angle, smiled ingratiatingly into the camera.

'Paris,' he intoned. 'The City of Lights, the fashion capital of the world, and most of all, the City of Love. Too long has England been denied its pleasures, and we willingly went to war to restore it to freedom. Yet even now, so many of its treasures remain inaccessible to the average Englishman. So tonight, ladies and gentlemen, or should I say *mesdames et messieurs*, BBC Television is proud to bring a few of those treasures to you in a brand-new variety programme we are calling – *Across the Channel!* First up, *un bouquet de jolies fleurs*, and wait till you see the stems on these roses!'

'Camera Two.'

Rivette, in contrast to her dramatic posture of the ballad performance they had seen on Saturday, had on a bright, gay smile, her arms out in a welcoming gesture, while behind her, the troupe from Casino de Paris formed a living frieze of flirtatious poses.

The band struck up a lively tune as Rivette cried out, "Allo, London!' and the troupe echoed her with multiple, high-pitched "allo's' with kisses blown to the cameras.

'Two close in on Rivette,' said Postlethwaite. 'Three to the dancers.'

Rivette's face gradually filled the monitor as she sang, '*Lorsque demain tu reviendras dans ton village*', while the dancers swung their hips and shifted their arms through a series of come-hither gestures, managing to dance more without moving their feet than most people could do moving them.

Sparks never looked at them, keeping her eyes on Theresa Cosslett the entire time. Cosslett's expression started with fascination as she watched the full process, but as Rivette continued to sing, it changed to astonishment, then horror. Sparks nudged Mrs Bainbridge as Cosslett put her hands to her mouth as she had when she first heard Legrenzi's Germanic devil. Only this time, it looked as if she was going to scream.

Sparks went over to her and whispered something in her ear. Cosslett nodded, then Sparks turned back and nodded to Kinsey, who nodded back and whispered to Conley.

The song was coming to its close. Rivette's final note was an octave up, her face triumphant and glorious. Postlethwaite leaned forward to issue his next command, then stopped and looked up in annoyance as Conley tapped him on the shoulder.

'I'm in the middle of rehearsal,' he snapped.

'Sorry, Barry,' said Conley. 'Hold everything for a moment.'

'Now, Theresa,' said Sparks. 'You know what to do.'

'Right here, Mrs Cosslett,' said Haight, motioning to his microphone.

Hesitantly, Theresa Cosslett approached the microphone. Haight pressed a button at its base, and she leaned towards it.

'Lisette, this is Albertine,' she said. 'Lisette, this is Albertine. It is good to hear your voice again.'

On Camera Two, Rivette's bright smile disappeared, replaced by a look of shock.

'*Non, non*,' she whispered. '*Ce n'est pas possible!*'

'*Ce qui n'est pas possible c'est que tu sois en vie*,' said Cosslett.

'What the devil is going on?' demanded Highmore.

The sound of his voice snapped Rivette back to her surroundings. She looked around the room as everyone there, the musicians, the cameramen and the dancers, stared at her.

She suddenly broke for the studio door and flung it open, ready to flee down the corridor. Then she stopped.

In the corridor facing her was Legrenzi's puppet theatre. As she stared at it, mesmerized, the curtains on the miniature stage parted, revealing the red devil marionette, its painted eyes staring at her.

'*Guten Tag*, Claudine,' it growled. '*Ich bin gekommen, um deine Seele zu holen!*'

She screamed in terror.

'You!' came a man's voice to her left. 'What are you doing here? They told me you were dead!'

She turned. There was a small cluster of people standing in the hallway, looking at her. In the centre was a short man, staring at her in confusion.

'Do you recognize this woman, Mr Farrell?' asked Kinsey, standing next to him.

'Well, she's the one I had dinner with Friday night, isn't she?' replied Farrell. 'The one you said got murdered after she walked out on me to go meet her tall man. Only you're not murdered at all, are you? And you've gone blonde. You were brunette on Friday.'

'She was wearing a wig,' said Mrs Bainbridge. 'Mr Danielli, you had to fetch a replacement wig from the shop on Friday night because one went missing. Do you recall what colour it was?'

'I do,' said Sally, emerging from the puppet theatre, eliciting another shriek from Rivette. 'It was brunette.'

'It was a good plan, Claudine,' said Mrs Bainbridge. 'You and Oakes found out from Mademoiselle Duplessis where she was going for her date before the two of you killed her. Then you went in her place wearing that stolen wig, making it appear that she was still alive through the dinner hour, after which you left, became blonde again, changed into a more memorable outfit, and spent the rest of the evening out on the town with Oakes establishing your alibis.'

'Why would I want to kill her?' asked Rivette.

'Because she knew you had betrayed your spy ring to the Nazis during the war,' said Mrs Bainbridge. 'She had a large amount of cash on her when she came to us, more than one would expect from a cancan girl here for a one-week engagement. Blackmail money, I'm guessing. But she was asking for more, wasn't she?'

'It was Oakes,' whispered Rivette. 'He killed her. Then he made me help him.'

'You're a very helpful woman, aren't you?' commented Kinsey. 'You also helped Monsieur Legrenzi into an early grave.'

'He helped you fake your own death on the radio during the war,' said Sparks. 'Unfortunately for you, someone here recognized his voice. And now someone has recognized yours.'

'Where is she?' demanded Rivette.

Cosslett stepped forward.

'Hello, Lisette,' she said. 'I always thought if I ever got to meet you that you would be beautiful. And you are.'

Rivette looked at her, a sneer forming on her face.

'I always thought if I ever got to meet you, that you would be an insignificant little nothing,' she said contemptuously. 'And you are.'

Cosslett reeled back as if she had taken a blow to the chest. For a moment, it seemed as if she was going to collapse. Then she took a deep breath, collected herself, and walked up to Rivette.

'Well, that may be,' said Cosslett, looking her in the eyes. 'But I'm the insignificant little nothing who's brought you down.'

Rivette stepped toward her, but Sally's hands clamped down on her arms before she could make another move.

'And I'm the much taller nothing you tried to set up for the murder,' he said. 'Hold still so the nice detective can arrest you.'

'Mademoiselle Rivette,' said Kinsey, approaching her while pulling a pair of handcuffs from his coat pocket. 'I am charging you with the murders of Jeanne-Marie Duplessis and Marcel Legrenzi. I will be escorting you to Scotland Yard to make a statement.'

He handcuffed her and took her away.

'We have to go, too,' said Mrs Bainbridge to Conley. 'Long day still ahead of us.'

'We'll send you our bill later,' added Sparks. 'Some miscellaneous expenses. Cab fare and drinks, mostly.'

'Well worth it to get Danielli back,' said Conley. 'Which reminds me. Danielli, put that box of puppets somewhere safe until the police pick it up for evidence.'

'Can't,' said Sally, casually leaning against it. 'I'm suspended.'

'I've just unsuspended you,' said Conley. 'Get back to work, you sluggard.'

'Yes, sir. Thank you, sir,' said Sally, making an exaggerated bow. 'Oh, Mrs Bainbridge?'

'Yes, Mr Danielli?' she said, coming over to him.

'I'm employed again. I can afford to buy you a drink. A very late drink.'

'It's a date,' she said.

She leaned in closer and whispered, 'It's a pity, really. I enjoyed seeing you right after I finished work.'

'This won't be for ever,' he promised.

'Nice Legrenzi impersonation, by the way,' she said. 'Call me later.'

She, Sparks and the rest of the witnesses left with Detective Sergeant Harvey. Sally trundled the puppet theatre down the corridor, leaving Postlethwaite and Conley standing together.

'What are we going to do about the show?' asked Postlethwaite. 'We've just lost the headliner. All we have left are the acrobats and the cancan girls.'

'Same thing we always do whenever things go wrong,' said Conley. 'We'll put on some cartoons.'

Oakes sat at one side of a long table, his hands cuffed in front of him. Regarding him from the other side were Kinsey, Harvey, Sparks and Bainbridge. A shorthand stenographer sat at the end of the table, pad in hand.

'What are they doing here?' asked Oakes, glancing at the two women.

'Special consultants to Scotland Yard,' said Kinsey.

'I thought they ran a marriage bureau,' said Oakes.

'As I said to you before, no woman is anything all the time,' said Mrs Bainbridge.

'When did you first meet Claudine Rivette?' asked Kinsey.

'Before the war,' answered Oakes. 'I would go to Paris whenever I could. I saw her with Legrenzi at Café des Loups when she was just starting up. I knew right away that she was destined for greater things, and I thought I could help her career along.'

'You were just a stage manager then,' said Kinsey. 'How did you think you could help her career?'

'I knew I was destined for greater things as well,' said Oakes. 'I had an eye for talent. And beauty. She had both in abundance. I made my introductions, and we began seeing each other whenever I was in town. Had it not been for the damn war, things might have progressed nicely for us.'

'The damn war upset quite a few people's plans,' said Kinsey. 'Tell us about Operation Showgirl.'

'Don't know anything about it,' said Oakes immediately.

Kinsey reached into a folder and removed a letter.

'This is from your former command,' he said. 'It releases you from the Official Secrets Act for the purposes of this investigation.'

He turned it so Oakes could read it from his side of the table.

'I'm surprised they would do that,' said Oakes when he was done.

'Given that the woman who betrayed the operation to the Germans is in our custody, they are more than happy to see her get what's coming to her,' said Kinsey. 'Tell us about it.'

'I went into Paris right after Dunkirk,' said Oakes. 'Claudine was the first person I saw. She hid me, helped recruit the others, then she got me to the Resistance when I had to get out. Saved my life.'

'When did you fall in love with her?' asked Mrs Bainbridge.

'Who says I did?' he replied, attempting a smirk but not quite pulling it off.

'I do,' she said.

He looked down at the table.

'From the moment I saw her,' he said softly.

'Yet you recruited her to seduce German officers,' said Sparks. 'How could you do that to a woman you loved?'

'Because we were at war,' snapped Oakes. 'And sometimes we do terrible things to the people we love when there's war.'

Kinsey found himself glancing at Sparks. She wouldn't meet his eyes.

'Did you know she had given up Showgirl to the Germans?' asked Kinsey.

'Not at the time. I thought she had died with the rest of them. Then when I went back to Paris with my unit, I found out she was alive. I put two and two together.'

'But you didn't turn her in,' said Kinsey.

'No,' said Oakes miserably. 'She took me straight back to her room when I saw her, and after that I had no intention of giving her up.'

'Why didn't you just bring her back to London after the war?'

'It would have raised red flags with my unit,' he said. 'I had the job waiting for me at the BBC as a producer once I got demobbed. I knew if I could bring her here as a performer, it would appear as the normal course of things.'

'And the womanizing rogue you've appeared to be was an act?' asked Sparks.

'A shabby role in a long-running show,' he said. 'Sorry to disappoint you.'

'Tell us about Jeanne-Marie Duplessis,' said Kinsey.

'She accosted me as soon as the troupe arrived,' he said. 'She wasn't part of Showgirl, but she knew someone who I had recruited, and recognized me from back then. And she had figured out Claudine's part in everything. First she demanded money, and my help in finding a way to stay in London. I gave her what I had on me. I had heard about The Right Sort from Haight, so I sent her there.'

'Then what?'

'She wanted more money,' he said. 'She came to me Friday morning. She had heard Claudine and me speaking to a reporter while I was puffing her up as a secret heroine of the Resistance. Duplessis threatened to blow up everything we had planned for so long. So I told her I would have to get to my bank, and that I would pick her up that afternoon. And I sweetened the deal by saying I knew another producer who could help her establish her career here, and that he would be at Ally Pally.'

'That's how you lured her there?' asked Kinsey.

'Let me be clear,' said Oakes. 'Everything that happened after that was done by me. Claudine didn't know about the blackmail, or my intention to kill Duplessis.'

Kinsey glanced over at Mrs Bainbridge. She shook her head slightly.

'It's good of you to admit to everything,' said Kinsey. 'And I appreciate your efforts to minimise Mademoiselle's role. Why did you kill Legrenzi?'

'He suspected Claudine after Duplessis's death. And he knew about what happened in Paris. He was a threat, so he had to go.'

'How did you kill him?' asked Kinsey.

'Poison gas,' said Oakes. 'In his puppet theatre.'

'We know that,' said Kinsey. 'But precisely where in the theatre?'

'Excuse me?' asked Oakes, looking uncertain for the first time.

'The mechanism of the death. How did you arrange it?'

'I . . . that is to say,' he began, his voice shaking. 'I don't quite remember where I put it.'

'And the garrotte? What did you do with that after you killed Duplessis?'

'Threw it in the woods down the hill,' he said. 'Can't think where. I was in a bit of a haze right after.'

'Sorry, Mr Oakes,' said Kinsey, standing and knocking on the door. 'You can't save her.'

'But it was me!' shouted Oakes. 'I killed both of them! It was me!'

Two constables came in and took him out of the room. His shouts continued as they escorted him away to a cell.

'You got all of that?' Kinsey asked the stenographer.

The man nodded.

'Right, let's bring her in,' he said.

'Here, you'll need this,' said Mrs Bainbridge, handing him the programme from the Café des Loups. He put it in his folder.

Rivette still wore the frock she'd had on for the rehearsal, a deep blue satin number that was gathered in folds across her bosom and at one hip. Her makeup was still camera-ready, but appeared exaggerated and garish in the ordinary light of the interrogation room. She winced as the WPC escorting her handcuffed one wrist to the arm of the chair.

'Is that really necessary?' she asked.

'It is,' said Kinsey as the WPC took a seat nearby.

'You have already talked to Monsieur Oakes,' she said.

'We have.'

'Then you know that I did not kill anyone,' she said defiantly.

'You assisted him in manufacturing an alibi,' he said.

'Does that carry the same penalty?' she asked.

'It supports the theory of a prior conspiracy,' said Kinsey. 'There was planning going on.'

'On the contrary, he came to get me while I was in my dressing room after he killed her,' she said. 'He showed me the body. I was shocked. He threatened to blame me for it. Everything I did after that, I was still in that state of panic and fear. But I did not kill her.'

'That might work with a jury,' conceded Kinsey.

'There, you see,' she said, smiling slightly.

'One small problem,' said Kinsey. 'Oakes couldn't tell us how Legrenzi was killed. That took someone with an intricate knowledge of the workings of his puppet theatre. And you had that knowledge.'

He slid across the programme, opened to the picture of her with the marionette. She glanced at it, then shrugged.

'Do you think your English jury will convict me?' she asked.

'I think we have enough,' said Kinsey. 'But if they let you off, the French government is now very interested in your part in the apprehension and execution of several Parisian Resistance members by the German occupying forces.'

Her smile faded.

'The way I see it,' he continued, 'if an English noose isn't in your future, a French guillotine will be. It doesn't matter much to me either way.'

'Do you still have family living in France?' asked Sparks.

Rivette looked at her for the first time, then nodded slowly.

'Much less shame in being a murderess than a collaborator,' said Sparks. 'Given the choice, I'd go for the noose.'

She looked across at all of them, then nodded again.

'Tell us why Legrenzi was killed, Mademoiselle Rivette,' said Kinsey. 'We already know you and he faked your death in 1943, which means he also had information that could be used to blackmail you. Was that the reason?'

'He was angry about Jeanne-Marie's death,' said Rivette.

'He still cared for her?'

'He cared for no one but himself,' she said bitterly. 'But he felt it would draw too much attention to us, and people might start looking into our pasts. You didn't know Marcel the way I did. He was the true traitor to the ring, and forced me to give up the rest if I didn't want him to expose me to the Germans. He threatened me on Saturday after he found out about the murder, and I became afraid of what he might do. So I struck first.'

'Where did you place the vial containing the gas pellet?' asked Kinsey.

'In the bulb for the little cannon,' she said. 'I thought he would be alone when it happened. He was obsessive about rehearsing. I did not think there would be others about when it happened. I am glad no one else was hurt.'

'And the garrotte?'

'I took it from Freddie after he killed Duplessis. Then when I planted the pellet in Marcel's theatre, I hid the garrotte in his toolbox. I thought that would point to him as the murderer.'

'I'm satisfied,' said Kinsey, nodding to the stenographer. 'Type that one up first, then we'll have her sign it. Take her back.'

The WPC uncuffed her from the chair, then cuffed her again and escorted her from the room. The stenographer followed them.

Kinsey leaned back in his chair, rubbing his forehead with the heels of his palms.

'Now, Mrs Bainbridge,' he said. 'I would like you to explain how you figured this all out.'

'It was several small things,' she replied. 'Most of them I didn't even consider at first because I was so set on Legrenzi as the killer.'

'What was the first?'

'Something Mireille Boucart said nagged at me. She was with Jeanne-Marie Duplessis before she left the hotel on Friday. There was a telephone call for Duplessis. She answered, said, "It's him," and left. But that was at three o'clock.'

'Ah,' said Kinsey.

'Exactly. Why would she be leaving for a dinner date at three? And that popped back into my head, and I wondered where she could have gone at that time and for what purpose? And I thought the only other place she had been to since she arrived was Alexandra Palace, so it must have been either there or to meet someone she had met there.'

'But you knew Farrell said she had met up with him for their dinner date.'

'Yes,' said Mrs Bainbridge. 'That was the sticking point for all of it. It was impossible. So I thought, what do I have to change to make the impossible possible? And I realized that either Mr Farrell had to be lying, or it was someone else having dinner with him while poor Jeanne-Marie was already dead. I figured you had verified Mr Farrell's dinner engagement.'

'We did,' said Kinsey. 'The restaurant staff remembered him as well as the brunette who walked out on him halfway through.'

'But it occurred to me that every first date we generate at The Right Sort is a blind date. He wouldn't have known what Jeanne-Marie looked like. And even had we provided some general description, there was a resemblance between the two women.'

'Our first thought was that Legrenzi originally hired Duplessis because he was still obsessed with Rivette, and she reminded him of her,' said Sparks.

'But the reverse was also true,' said Mrs Bainbridge. 'Especially when Rivette had been a brunette. And you yourself brought up that a wig had gone missing that night.'

'I did,' said Kinsey. 'But its significance escaped me. I was focusing on Danielli's presence in that part of the building that night. Oakes and Rivette stole the wig for her impersonation. How did you rope Oakes into your thinking?'

'If it was Rivette, then Oakes was her very prominent alibi that night,' said Mrs Bainbridge. 'And Sally had mentioned he had been a stage manager there before the war, and I wondered if he had kept his keys. Then I confirmed it was him when I showed my sketch to Mr Spashett.'

'That was a long shot,' said Kinsey.

'Yes, but it had to have been one of the staff at the BBC involved, because if this had been precipitated by someone Duplessis knew in Paris, it would have happened there and long before this.'

'So you came to Ally Pally to talk to Spashett.'

'Not specifically,' said Mrs Bainbridge. 'I wanted to look at the side entrance and see who might have seen her come back that way. Then I saw Mr Spashett watching me from his eyrie, and I thought that he was someone you might not have interviewed because he didn't work for either the BBC or Alexandra Palace. After talking to him, I knew how and who. Iris provided the why.'

Sparks shifted uncomfortably in her chair as Kinsey and Harvey looked at her.

'No,' she said. 'Can't talk about it. You have what you need.'

'We do,' said Kinsey. 'Thank you both, ladies. We'll get you a ride back.'

'I'd rather walk,' said Sparks.

'Me, too,' said Mrs Bainbridge.

'Then I'll show you out,' said Kinsey.

He paused at the door to the driveway, and there was a moment when they thought he was going to say something. Then he shook his head, opened the door, and nodded politely as they left.

It was mid-afternoon. The two women stopped once they passed through the arched entrance to Victoria Embankment.

'Rather late to be getting back to the office,' said Gwen.

'I'm not in a matchmaking mood,' said Iris. 'Shall we ring Saundra and tell her to close up shop?'

'Let's.'

They found a phone box, and Gwen telephoned the office. When she emerged, her partner was looking gloomy.

'What is it?' asked Gwen.

'This is going to sound selfish,' said Iris.

'Go on.'

'This little adventure of ours kept me from thinking about my own situation,' said Iris. 'Now that it's over, I'm feeling a bit of a letdown, and I hate the idea that it takes something this horrible to bring me back to life.'

'Give it time,' counselled Gwen.

'Is that what finally did it for you?'

'Time, Dr Milford, work. And you.'

'Me more than Sally?'

'I'm still waiting to see how things go with him,' said Gwen. 'It's wonderful to have a lover, but a friend is what gets one through in life, I've decided. You got me through my days with the black dog, and I will do the same for you.'

'Shall we find another murder to investigate?'

'Good heavens, no!' said Gwen with a laugh. 'But let's treat ourselves to something fun with what's left of Mr Conley's money.'

'Aren't you having drinks with Sally?'

'Not until late. What would you like to do?'

'Anything,' said Iris.

'We could come back to my place and see what's on television,' offered Gwen.

'Anything but that,' said Iris.

CODA

For a change Gwen was the more hung-over one the next morning. Iris mercifully kept her silence during the walk to Mayfair. By the time they reached The Right Sort, they were feeling marginally better.

Their mood plummeted again when they opened the door to their office to find the Brigadier sitting behind Sparks's desk.

'That's my chair,' said Sparks irritably. 'Nobody sits on it except me.'

He pointed at the guest chair in front of the desk without saying anything. Sparks remained standing, glaring at him, while Mrs Bainbridge hung up her coat and hat.

'I take it you want the door closed for this conversation,' she said.

The Brigadier nodded. Mrs Bainbridge went over and shut the door, then sat in the other guest chair in front of her own desk.

'Why don't you sit, Miss Sparks?' she suggested. 'We'll let him have his petty little power position for now.'

Reluctantly, Sparks sat in front of her desk, her coat still on, her arms crossed in front of her.

'I won't ask how you got in,' she said. 'I'm sure you've picked your share of locks in your prime, even if that was a long time ago.'

'The old skills never leave you,' he said. 'Rather enjoyed it, I must say.'

'Where's your minder?' asked Sparks.

'Minding things,' said the Brigadier. 'Now, let's talk about you.'

'Should I be here?' asked Mrs Bainbridge.

'You are the essential part of this conversation, Mrs Bainbridge,' said the Brigadier. 'I must ask you to stay.'

'I'm the essential one?' she said, puzzled.

'Get to the point, sir,' said Sparks. 'We have work to do.'

'As do I,' he said. 'I've been holding back on one of my responsibilities for several months now.'

'Which one?'

'The one where I have you arrested and prosecuted for multiple violations of the Official Secrets Act, going back to your little stunt working for the Royals.'

Sparks took a deep breath, then let it go.

'Guilty as charged,' she said. 'Of course, our little stunt ended up helping your greater plan.'

'It did,' he said. 'And every time you or Mrs Bainbridge have run afoul of the laws, you have somehow managed to bring someone to justice who otherwise might have evaded it. So I have held back.'

'You must find that very frustrating, sir,' said Sparks. 'I take it this time is different.'

'This time my superiors, and yes, I do have superiors, have become involved, thanks to your detective's request for classified information. And they are looking more closely at you, and wondering why I haven't acted more responsibly.'

'Why haven't you?' asked Mrs Bainbridge.

'Why?' he repeated. 'Because I value Sparks's abilities too highly. They shouldn't be wasted in a prison cell because of some absurdly absolutist enforcement of the laws. But now I am required to act by men whose orders I cannot ignore. And there is only one solution for it.'

'So, at long last, this is it,' said Sparks with a sad smile.

'It is,' he said.

He reached down and picked up a briefcase, then placed it on the desk in front of him. He opened it and removed two sets of documents.

'Mrs Bainbridge, I am going to ask you to read these over, then initial each page and sign at the end,' he said, holding them up. 'Sparks, you will be the witness.'

'What are those?' asked Sparks.

'As you are apparently incapable of withholding classified information from Mrs Bainbridge,' he said, 'I have no other choice but to make her a signatory to the Official Secrets Act. That way, I can assure my superiors that I have sealed the leak. Or dammed the flood in your case.'

'You can't make her do that!' protested Sparks. 'She doesn't work for you. Or any branch of the government.'

'Hush, Iris,' said Mrs Bainbridge, taking the documents from him. 'He's doing this to protect you.'

'Exactly right,' said the Brigadier. 'Take your time. If you have questions, ask before you sign.'

'No, no, this is all very clear,' said Mrs Bainbridge as she perused them. 'Tell me – would this allow me to speak to Mr Danielli about his war?'

'It would, in fact,' said the Brigadier.

Mrs Bainbridge read them through twice, then reached for a pen from her desk. She initialled and signed the pages where indicated, then passed them on to Sparks, who added her initials and signatures. She slammed them down on her desk in front of the Brigadier, who did not flinch. He calmly countersigned, then handed one of the sets to Mrs Bainbridge.

'Keep this somewhere safe and secure,' he said.

'Of course,' she replied.

He put the other into his briefcase, closed it, and rose.

'There is one more piece to this,' he said.

'I knew it,' muttered Sparks.

'Neither of you work for me,' he said. 'That is something that may prove useful down the line. I may call upon your services at some point.'

'Will we have the option of refusing if that happens?' asked Sparks.

'You know the answer to that, Sparks,' he said. 'Good morning, ladies. Have a fruitful day of matchmaking.'

They watched as he opened the door and left.

A moment later, Mrs Billington poked her head through the doorway.

'Who was that?' she asked. 'He wasn't in the appointment book.'

'A potential suitor,' said Gwen. 'He's still thinking about it.'

'Why are you sitting in front of your desks?'

'Sometimes you need a change of perspective,' said Iris, getting to her feet and hanging up her coat. 'Let's all get back to work, shall we?'

'So you're both actually going to be spending the day at the office?' asked Mrs Billington. 'Not gallivanting about helping Scotland Yard?'

'That's done,' said Gwen.

'And Mr Danielli is safe?' asked Mrs Billington anxiously.

'He is,' said Gwen, smiling. 'Thank you for asking.'

'That's a relief. You have a ten o'clock.'

'We'll be ready,' promised Gwen.

Mrs Billington left, closing the door behind her.

'I'm sorry I've dragged you into this,' said Iris as she sat at her desk.

'Don't be,' said Gwen. 'It may be the best thing that could have happened to us.'

'How so?'

'Because you've been holding back the entire time we've been friends,' said Gwen. 'I've told you about the worst parts of my life, but you haven't done the same.'

'I have Dr Milford for that,' said Iris.

'He's a therapist. I'm your friend. It's different. Every time you've told me you can't talk about some aspect of your past, I could see that eating away at you.'

'If I told you everything, you would despise me,' said Iris.

'I wouldn't,' said Gwen. 'I won't. I think I've guessed most of it by now. It would have to be something truly awful for you not to confide in me. You killed someone during the war, didn't you?'

Iris went still.

'Listen to me, Iris,' continued Gwen. 'Whatever happened must have been terrible, but it can't change my opinion of you.'

'Which is what?'

'That you're a good person, a brilliant woman, and a brave one,' said Gwen. 'Whatever you did, I'm sure it was done for the war, and the war was a terrible time. My husband killed, and was killed doing it. Sally has killed. Hell, my own hands are no longer clean. The murderers we've caught may swing for it in the end, and I've caused all that.'

'I'm not ready to talk to you about it,' said Iris.

'I know,' said Gwen. 'But when you are, I'm ready to listen. Now, go wipe your cheeks, darling. We need happy faces for our ten o'clock.'

Iris hadn't even realized she'd been crying. She grabbed the key to the ladies' lav and walked quickly down the hall so Mrs Billington wouldn't notice her face.

When she returned, she had achieved some semblance of cheerfulness.

'Better,' pronounced Gwen. 'Now, one more thing. I would like us to go on a double date this Saturday.'

'I am nowhere near ready for that,' said Iris.

'I understand,' said Gwen. 'But these are gentlemen you cannot possibly refuse. Trust me.'

After work, they had a quick drink at the Five Hats, then walked to Maida Vale together. They parted with their usual exchange of watchwords and went their separate ways.

Iris slowed as she approached the *Cecilia*. Sitting on the rail of the foredeck, watching her approach, was Mike Kinsey.

'This can't be anything good,' said Iris as she crossed the gangplank to him.

'Good, bad, I don't know any more,' he said. 'I have come to express my thanks for your help during this past investigation.'

'You're welcome,' said Iris. 'Is Gwen next on the gratitude tour? Her place is a ten-minute walk.'

'And also . . .'

He stopped, then took a deep breath.

'It's been obvious for some time that you worked for some branch of Intelligence,' he said. 'Maybe you're still working for them, for all I know. The incident that drove us apart, when I caught you cheating on me with that Spaniard, I finally realized had to have been part of some operation.'

Iris didn't respond. She merely waited.

'So I wanted to tell you that I forgive you,' he said, almost forcing it out.

'I don't need your forgiveness,' she said. 'I apologized to you last year, and it took you until now to accept it. Go live your life, have your baby, and don't bother worrying about me any more.'

'I should be asking your forgiveness, shouldn't I?' he said forlornly.

'It wouldn't do me any good at this point,' she said. 'Goodbye, Mike.'

'I thought maybe . . .' he started.

'Don't say anything that will lead to more apologies later,' she said. 'Get off my boat, Mike. Now.'

She went inside the saloon and closed the door behind her. Then she listened until she could hear his footsteps crossing the gangplank to land.

She checked her supplies. There was one bottle left from Archie's basement. A pinot noir.

Seems like a good time to celebrate, she thought as she reached for it.

On Saturday morning, the Bainbridges' Bentley pulled up alongside the *Cecilia*. Nigel got out to open the rear door, and Ronnie and John spilled out, yelling, 'Argh! Ahoy, Captain!'

'Welcome, mateys,' called Iris from the foredeck. 'Are ye ready to take to the high seas?'

'Aye aye, Captain Iris!' they cried.

'Walk, don't run on that gangplank,' cautioned Gwen as she emerged from the car carrying a picnic basket. 'Thank you, Nigel.'

The boys clambered on board and Iris put life jackets on to each, fastening them securely.

'Wait,' said Gwen, pulling a camera from her bag. 'A picture of the three of you.'

They posed for a moment as she took two shots.

'Now, I will go down the ladder first,' Iris instructed them. 'You two come down slowly and carefully, and sit together in the stern. Gwen will be in the bow, and will be responsible for warding off any shark attacks.'

'There are no sharks in fresh water,' said John.

'That's what they want you to think,' said Iris. 'One can never be too vigilant.'

She climbed down the canal side of the *Cecilia* to a rowing boat tied next to it, then held it steady against the ladder as the boys joined her. They sat side by side on the bench across the stern, chattering excitedly while Gwen handed down the picnic basket, then came down.

'Thank you for arranging this,' she said as she sat in the bow.

'These are two gentlemen I can never refuse,' said Iris. 'Right, everyone ready?'

She untied the dock line and coiled it, then picked up the oars and used one to push the boat away into the centre of the canal. She sat, settled the oars into the rowlocks, and began to row.

'What's in the picnic basket?' she asked.

'Sandwiches and fizzy lemonades for everyone,' said Gwen. 'The "delicate question" need not come up.'

'Let's hope not. But if I get too hungry, I know what I'm going to do,' Iris growled at the boys, who giggled in response.

At the same moment, in another part of town, Laurence Haight straightened his tie one last time, then walked up a small set of steps to a doorway and rang the bell.

A moment later, a blonde woman in her mid-thirties wearing a nurse's uniform opened it and smiled.

'Mr Haight, is it?' she asked. 'I'm Claire Williston.'

'Laurence Haight,' he said, handing a bouquet of flowers to her. 'I'm very pleased to make your acquaintance, Miss Williston. These are for you.'

'Oh, lovely,' she exclaimed. 'Thank you. Come and sit down while I find something to put them in.'

He sat in a small parlour while she fetched a vase and put some water in it.

'There,' she said after she had placed the flowers in it and set it on the windowsill. 'They do brighten up the place. I must say, I've never been on a breakfast first date before, but when the ladies at The Right Sort suggested it, I thought it was brilliant. I don't have to start my shift until one, so we have the entire morning. Shall we . . . Mr Haight, are you with us?'

He had closed his eyes for a moment while she was talking. Then he opened them and looked at her.

'I am very much with you, Miss Williston,' he said, smiling at her. 'I was just thinking how much I liked your voice.'

'Well,' she said, returning his smile. 'That's a good start, isn't it?'

'Yes,' he said as he helped her on with her coat and offered his arm. 'A very good start indeed. Shall we?'

Acknowledgements

In addition to books and articles previously cited, the author wishes to acknowledge the following with gratitude:

W.J. Baker, *A History of the Marconi Company*
David Hendy, *The BBC: A Century on Air*
Joe Moran, *Armchair Nation: An intimate history of Britain in front of the TV*
John Swift, *Adventure in Vision: The First Twenty-Five Years of Television*
'London's Nightworld,' British Pathé, 1947

The characters for the most part are fictional. However, Ernest Trevor Spashett was the actual architect assigned to the restoration of Alexandra Palace after the war. While the details of his life are accurate, the depiction of his character is wholly speculative. His redesign of the Rose Window stands to this day, and is rather glorious.

www.ingramcontent.com/pod-product-compliance
Lightning Source LLC
Jackson TN
JSHW020323130325
79793JS00001BA/1/J